NEXT YEAR IN JERUSALEM

NEXT YEAR IN JERUSALEM

JOHN KOLCHAK

Published by
Ward Six Press
PO Box 852
Pasadena, CA 91102 USA

Cover Image: The Apotheosis of War
by Vasily Vereshchagin, 1871

Design by Geraldine Baum

Next Year in Jerusalem
Second revised printing, 2016
ISBN: 978-0984013036
wardsixpress.com

CONTENTS

In the name of God, Sir, do not speak to me any more about that man, and let me die in peace.

—Voltaire on his deathbed

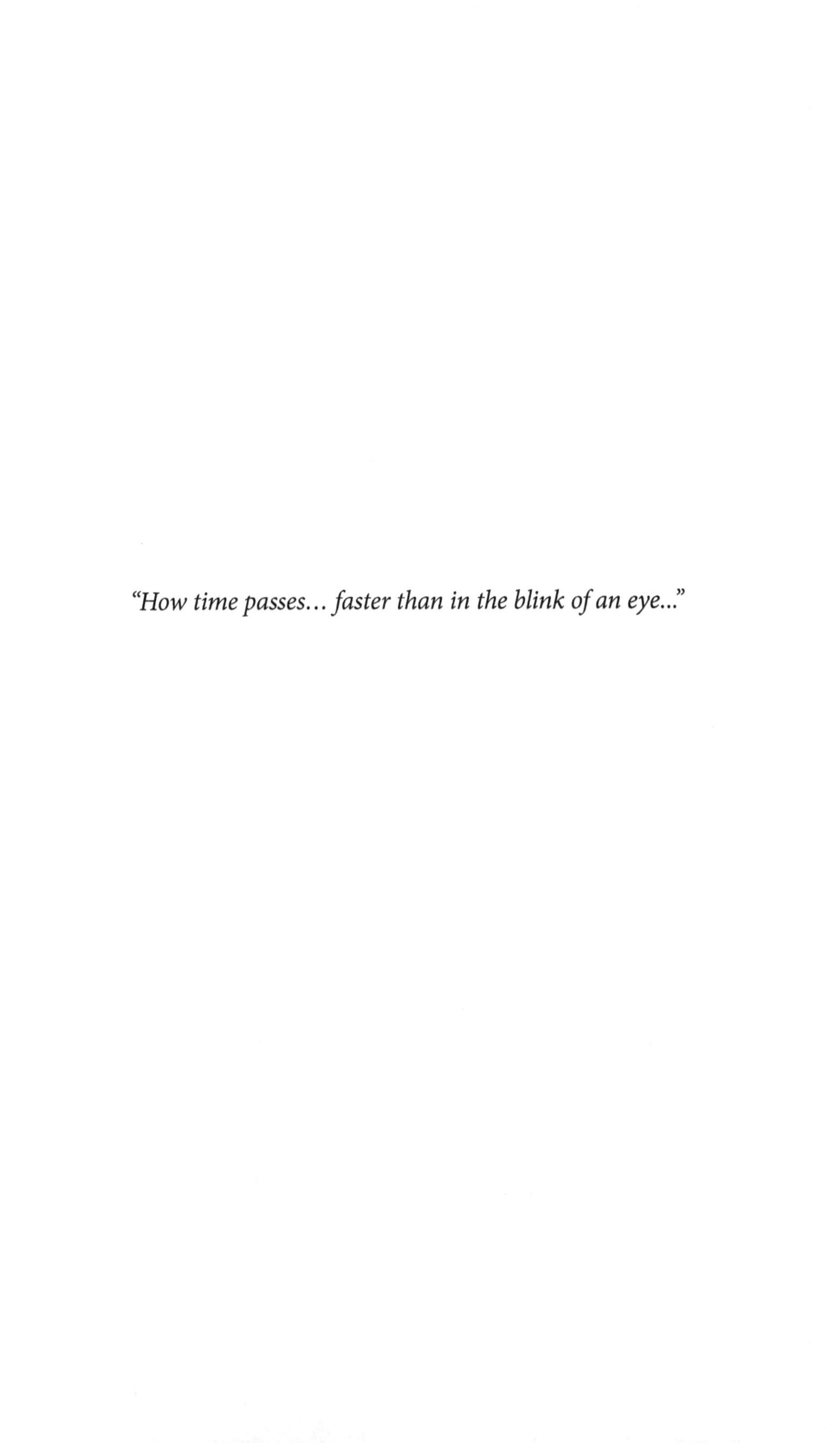

"How time passes… faster than in the blink of an eye…"

FOR MY MOTHER

THE BIRTH

HAMSIN

"It's all coming from God and whatever comes from God is good!" Eliyahu shouted to the merchant who waved him into his tent, offering shelter from the hailstorm. The drumroll of celestial ice pounded the ears and rendered both men deaf-mute. As much as Eliyahu strained his vocal cords, the merchant could not hear a word and was almost resigned to futility until finally, with the aid of wordless grins and gestures, fingers pointed to the sky, they exchanged understanding smiles and nodded in agreement that the hail was a blessing indeed.

For weeks, Judea had been plagued by violent storms of dust and sand. The Hamsin, whipped up from the barren plains of the Arabian desert had made its way north and attacked mercilessly. At dawn, the atmosphere grew orange like the embers of a fire. Objects yards away disappeared as if a curtain had been drawn in front of them. Nazarenes would rise with a sour taste in their mouths and a film of dust formed under furniture and over beddings. For days, Eliyahu would wake struggling to breathe.

Townspeople remained in the safety and darkness of their houses, windows sealed shut, burning valuable oil only when needed, singing and praying to Yahweh for the storm to pass. In Eliyahu's home, the desperate pleas for God's mercy were sometimes happily interrupted by passages from the Song of Solomon. Eliyahu's daughter, Maryam, was soon to be married, and the gloom of nature turned less fatal by thoughts of future joy.

And now the Hamsin broke. Dust and sand settled, a cold wind came first, and now, finally, rain and hail. Wild rumors began to spread that the storm was so powerful and the hail so thick that a neighbor's donkey was felled by a chunk of ice and killed on the spot. Eliyahu chuckled at this rumor as he knew how much Judeans (and that included all: Jews, Greeks, and Romans), like to exaggerate. He looked at the sky and saw sunlight as the hail storm subsided and presently lost all its teeth. All that was left was a gentle rain and soon enough the sun started peeking out. Eliyahu smiled. He did not remember the exact first time he saw sun and rain together but he had a vague memory of one instance from childhood. There was a horse in a pasture peacefully drinking from a stream. He remembered watching the horse and its reaction when the rain clouds started to break. Observing from afar, the young Eliyahu was afraid. The beast was large and frightening, peaceful as it was. His family was poor and couldn't afford horses, it were only the Romans and the wealthy Greek settlers who had the means to keep such animals. And then he saw, or maybe imagined, how the horse lifted its head up at the sky as if to praise God when the clouds started to depart. He saw the sun pushing its way through and there it was—sun and rain together, seemingly irreconcilable foes, lion and lamb. Eliyahu actually cried when the horse gently raised itself from indifference as the remaining little clouds rained and melted, and the sun shined… There may even have been a rainbow.

Then came work, labor, struggling to earn his crust—there were more sun showers that he missed in adulthood but it didn't matter for they never reproduced the original magic. The memory was flimsy but Eliyahu always mused over that moment with fondness and drank in whatever remained. All he could really remember was "horse," "rain," "sunshine," and there was a stabbing feeling of regret that the flashback was so threadbare. *"Horse… rain… sunshine…*

rainbow..." and then he returned to the present. *"I'm old," "I can't remember much"* and *"But I can remember how beautiful it all once was..."*

No rainbow appeared for Eliyahu as he exited the tent and bid goodbye to the kind hawker who sheltered him from the hail. He looked up at the sky and smiled. The heavens looked open. The storm had passed. And sadly, the future seemed gone. Even if another sun shower or rainbow appeared now for Eliyahu, it would not be the same as that first glimpse of mystery and he bit his lip and wondered again: *"Where did it all go?"* In quiet melancholy, with the Hamsin gone, he started his walk home. His daughter was getting married soon and he needed to be there for her. He shuffled quickly, watchful of shadows, for now that the hail stopped, there were certain folk crawling outside who most Judeans wished to avoid.

Throughout the land, bitter fruit borne of anger and indignation fell to the ground and sprouted from fertile soil. Young shoots and medium sized stalks, nurtured by the blood that soaked the earth, grew tall and strong, fierce and proud, and had only one thing on their minds—the glory of death through murder and self-sacrifice. So it came that the sand shovel in the child's hand was soon replaced by a sword for beheadings. The saplings gained strength and from their seed more poisonous weeds took root. Names came to define them—the Kanaim, the Zealots, but most often as the Sicarii, named for the Roman dagger, the one they stuck into the guts of Roman policeman, petty officials, Jews they considered sellouts and collaborators, and sometimes even random strangers.

They carried out their assassinations with ingenious efficacy. It was done so that a crowd would form around the stabbing, usually in an open market or outside a place of worship. The assassin would then drop his weapon and in the few moments he had before the police pounced on him, would scream and burn out his lungs, exhorting the townsfolk to revolt against the Roman occupation. His time, of course, was limited, for when the police ran to the scene, their first priority was to silence him, beat him to a pulp, smash his mouth against the cobblestones and drag the wretch into the dungeon where he would inevitably expire. The commanding officer would then order the shopkeepers to wash away the blood and sweep away the teeth.

Just recently, before the sandstorm forced everyone inside, a merchant was murdered for selling melons on the Sabbath and the high priest was stabbed just as he exited the temple, accused of collaborating with the Romans.

Judea was a backwater, a dusty and nearly forgotten piece of the Empire. But these homicidal attacks were increasing with such fervor and frequency that they had come to the attention of the Emperor himself. After some deliberation, Caesar sought to replace the current weak and incompetent governor with a stronger man.

"They want their freedom? Their land? I'll give them enough land to cover an average Jew and shovel some extra soil on top!" the Emperor decided, and summoned his officials to begin a search for the right man for the job.

THE KING OF THE WORLD

Groggy from heat, Pilate watched in lazy detachment as a fly landed in his glass of beer. It made a valiant attempt to free itself but the tiny little wings were waterlogged and the insect quickly drowned. There was no disgust in Pilate's mind or throat. The beer had turned too warm anyway, and the few cups he had already drank were making him sleepy. In fact he almost felt grateful to the fly. It had distracted him from his boozy haze and made him wax philosophical, thinking to himself, reflecting on the brevity of life. He smiled as he pondered what an odd place to die an ocean of beer was and how it's not such a bad one when one thinks about it, but that little bit of wit left as quickly as it came. Melancholy was the order of the day and Pilate did not wish to fight against it. *"Strange how it comes even on perfect days,"* he thought. *"Yes, it's too hot but, sun, sea…"* He winced when he remembered his days working in the German provinces and how repulsive he found snow and darkness concluding in a self-admonition that he should be thankful for his lot.

The fly made him think of his mother and how she told him once, when he was a boy, that a moth's lifespan was one human day. *"What a rubbish joke! One is born and then dies almost immediately?"* The story stayed with him for years. He pitied the moth and found it the saddest creature in the world. He recalled fighting, teary-eyed against believing his mother about the cruelty of such a short life. Even after praising the gods and trusting in their wondrous munificence which they bestowed upon the world, and Rome in particular, he refused to believe the story about the moth. It was too cruel. What is a day? For weeks, if not months, he tried to catch a moth and hold it captive to disprove his mother. Eventually he captured one and it died within hours. The theory was confirmed. Life is a flicker. Later, after being appointed governor, he often recalled the line from the Jewish holy books: "All is vanity."

The sea gently washed the shores and kept licking the sand—motherly, like a cat washing her kittens, while the sun's eyes grew wearier and so did Pilate's. And the water looked warm, warm…

Pilate certainly did not miss Germania where he had spent most of his military career, but Judea's heat was sometimes too much even for him, despite being a full-blooded Roman. He often found himself in need of sleep, overheating. This made him wonder if it was just the temperature or if there was something wrong with his liver or perhaps that problem with melancholy that he struggled with, and if so, which humour was at fault. (*'Bile, perhaps?'*) He rarely took naps—they would guarantee a foul disposition upon waking—so he avoided them as much as possible. Mostly he felt that he could never get enough sleep or rather get one decent night's rest. It seemed as if almost every night, after a few minutes of forcing himself to dream he would have to get up again, whether to piss, drink water, or sometimes just to sit and think.

He was not alone. He had his wife Claudia and her plump flesh and sweet breath always made his heart feel warm, squeezing her meaty ass in the morning, tasting her sweat when they woke in the heat of the Israeli summer. Yet for weeks now, Claudia did not even exist for him. She tended to household chores, bossing around the slaves and the gardeners. She had her own life and he was scraped by loneliness.

When Pilate would rise in the morning, his heart racing, wide awake and exhausted, he would slowly lift himself off the bed, sit for a few minutes and then realize how tired he truly was. Presently, he would lie down again and force himself to close his eyes but the eyelids would pop open almost automatically. Thoughts of his mother would weigh heavily on his ability to sleep. What bothered him most were certain phrases she would utter to him as a child, then as a teenager, and even as a young soldier in the Roman army years later. "You will be famous one day… world famous…" And so he was, at close to fifty years of age, a hated, mediocre bureaucrat presiding as governor over the toilet of the empire.

"I've seen Jews who have lived to a very long age but maybe they're lucky or maybe their blood can handle this place. Not me… I could die any minute and my accomplishments will mean nothing. What accomplishments? Ha! Another cold beer would be good… " He looked over at the fly cemetery in his cup. For a brief moment shame set in. Who was he to complain? He lived in what was essentially a palace by Judean standards and managed to rise to the position of governor at a relatively young age. And then Claudia, busy with her own chores... He did not dare to interrupt her or tell her how he felt. It would be unseemly for a man who supposedly possessed the power that he had. Shame gave way to self-pity once again and Pilate felt weak and old.

"I will be fifty this year and I've accomplished nothing. And perhaps… No, not 'perhaps' but most likely, this has been my own fault. I have suckled on the armored nipple of the Emperor. I should be grateful to him and to Claudia too, I suppose, but the truth is I will never amount to much. I shall never be famous. I have amounted to some things in my own right but…" He smashed his fist down against the oak table in self-loathing rage. *"I will still be forgotten as quickly, just as quickly as I have been remembered. I am nothing. All is vanity… emptiness."*

The emptiness of the universe perversely gave Pilate periodic hope. Gazing up into the meaningless space above during twilight hours and seeing the stars flicker, he would sometimes look forward to death just to see what it would feel like, to finally experience living on the other side.

At forty-nine years of age he was either too young or too unprepared to face death. He knew he could still do something. He could quit his post, leave Claudia, perhaps find another wife, retire, perhaps move back to Italy, or even stay in Judea and buy a farm or a vineyard. What was fifty anyway? The emperors had lived into their eighties. But he was no emperor and never would be. Self-doubt and self-hatred flowed through his veins simultaneously like wine and water, the way the Greeks mixed it.

"I'll be fifty this year. Half a century... the worlds, the world, it spins. My time. I should love every day that I possess, every day which is given to me, yet all I feel is sand in my mouth, a pain in my gut and a stranger in my heart. I should be grateful but I want to spit. It's too brief. It's a mockery. This can't be real."

"One day you'll be famous." His mother's words continued to taunt him. *"Famous for what? For following orders? I've had nothing to contribute. A stinking province. A land burnt by the sun that produces nothing but garbage and criminals. Let me go back to Italy and die in Rome and let my mother die before me so she will never have to suffer the shame of the fact that her son who she claimed would be famous disappointed her so hideously."*

He looked over at the cup of beer again. Another fly had committed suicide by diving. It too struggled to leave but perished even faster than the first few victims. Another angry living thing felled. At this point, Pilate became repulsed by all the little corpses. He picked up the cup and poured it and its casualties out over the balcony and went indoors.

Tomorrow was another day of life.

The palace was cool and dark and while it offered relief from the heat, he could not stay inside for long. It reminded him of a tomb and though romantic ideas of death had often lulled him to sleep in the past, now he felt he could not breathe and went back out onto his balcony.

Looking out onto the beach, he saw a peculiar sight. A woman was struggling with the birth of a child right on the sand, screaming, holding her enormous belly. "Oh God! Oh God!" she screamed, followed by a string of obscenities. Pilate had never fully learned Aramaic, but he knew enough to understand her cries, particularly the choice bits with which he was familiar and it made him chuckle. Suddenly, as if out of nowhere, a young Jew, a fisherman perhaps, rushed to the woman's aid. The young man must have known what he was doing, for soon enough the baby appeared, covered in slime, screaming for dear life while the warm water of the sea splashed its gentle waves.

The sea was warm and appeared endless. It would be there forever and there would be countless more children born on its shores. Plus ultra, non plus ultra, quid est differentia?

This odd episode, witnessing the birth of a human, briefly snapped Pilate out of his melancholy. He had a fondness for children. In a roundabout turn inside his brain, it made him think of happier times. He wondered what this child's lot in life would be and considered that perhaps his own life was not all that dreadfully pointless as he imagined. His appointment as Governor of Judea by the Emperor himself was a huge honor. He tilted his head and closed his eyes, thinking back on that sunny spring day in Rome, so many years ago…

When Pilate first learned that he was nominated for the gubernatorial position, he had a fear, which seemed insane to him now when he'd reflect on it, that the Emperor's palace was probably made of marble and there would be no dirt around for him to dig a hole to bury his face when he came into the presence of the divine light of Imperial Majesty. Luckily, his military training and discipline (he had recently finished twenty years of service in Germania) proved that in this situation he was able to stand tall, asshole clenched tight and to remain humble with military professionalism—but never groveling.

He remembered that day with perfect clarity and what he remembered most were the colors. Standing in the Emperor's palace he felt as if the entire universe were composed of only gold and white. Even the sky, which would normally appear blue, seemed parched by Sol Invictus, the yolk of an egg, a drop of honey in a glass of milk. It was overwhelming.

As he stood in that blinding whiteness, the thought darting through the cranial labyrinth made yet another detour and he drifted off to other scenes. He remembered how in Germania, sometimes in the green, green groves, a fire flickered in the distance. A pagan ritual in progress, he pushed through the branches quietly and watched the orgy from afar in wonder. The grove and the gold of the fire still vaguely remained in the muddy ocean of memory and in the cesspool of time. The standing pool was forced to part its green mantle when Pilate recalled where he was.

What surprised Pilate most when he entered the reception hall in the Emperor's palace was the Emperor himself. A slight old man, gray-haired, affable and pleasant, avuncular one could say, and yet the ruler of the known world, from Scythian lands to the east and Germans to the north and everything south and west of there until the Pillars of Hercules. So much might in such a small frame and yet he was just another man and hardly a god, unless it was one of those instances where God hides himself in the frame of a butterfly or a hummingbird, but the stories told of greater incarnations, a bull or a swan for example. In fact, Pilate felt a bit of a disappointment at first but when they began talking he immediately forgot about the Emperor's physique and demeanor that was in such contrast to the vastness of his possessions. The Emperor was old but he wasn't senile. His mind was sharp as a blade. He recalled how His Majesty explained the tasks to him, taking his time, feeling out if the man was right for the job.

"Come, soldier," the Emperor smiled and took Pilate gently by the bicep and let him out onto the balcony that overlooked the miraculous city of Rome, truly a modern marvel and a wonder of the world. In between instructions and palaver, the Emperor would need to take breaks. "Excuse me..." he would say. "Come this way and wait for me. I will return in a moment". The Emperor's guts were rotten and he had to interrupt his conversation with the gubernatorial appointee several times to make visits to the latrine. Pilate felt embarrassed listening to the sounds of excrement of the Emperor God splashing against the walls of the imperial toilet. He would remind himself that there was no need to be embarrassed until he realized that it was meant to embarrass him. The Emperor's shit was the shit of God and he should be grateful to be in the presence of such divine sounds. His business done, the Emperor took Pilate by the arm again and they returned to the balustrade to attend to a business more important than evacuation.

"How well do you know the Jews, soldier?"

"I know them...but not very well. I'm sorry, your Majesty, my service was in Germania."

Pilate stammered, his heart raced, he did not expect to be quizzed on the Jews. He had never seen one before and did not know anything about them. The Emperor smiled kindly. He wasn't testing Pilate, he was just curious for he had never seen a Jew before either but as the holder of the divine throne it was his duty to hold the empire together down to its most sorry bits and those sorry bits were the Jews. There was too much trouble in Judea right now and if this plague went on and Judea went, then so could richer more prosperous lands. *What would be next? Syria? Asia? Then what?*

"They are an interesting lot," the Emperor continued, as Pilate clenched his jaw and sweated, wondering, *"Will I get the job?"* It seemed stupid to him now, so many years later, how he toadied up to this man, Emperor or not, he was a man after all. And this man continued to lead him, Pilate walking a few spaces behind to show his respect.

"What I am telling you now is useful information. I do not expect you to know them as we have very few Jews here in Rome. They are an interesting folk by all accounts. Unique, one could say. You know, they think they are an entity unto themselves, a chosen people. They have one god and they are his beloved. Everyone else can go to hell. Have you ever heard of such rubbish?" the Emperor chuckled.

"I have heard of it."

"And that they entered into a special covenant with their god who they considered to be the one true god? Have you heard of that?"

"I have..."

"And hence you know the origin of this insurrection."

"I do, Sir."

The Emperor stopped and looked directly in his eyes. Pilate felt as if he had woken up from a peaceful sleep to find a mongoose sitting on his chest staring him squarely in the face as if he were a snake, but the soldier in him came through and this was his time to shine. He did it as a soldier and a civil servant, not as a lackey and he did it well, without a hint of a stammer.

"Your Imperial Majesty, I believe that the people who do have a covenant with God are us Romans. Look around Imperium Romanum. We rule the world. Jupiter smiles upon us and our lands... all our lands. Your wise rule which brings us prosperity, happiness, and glory is a living testament to it, and it is obvious to all but fools. And fools these Jews are and they need to be taught a lesson."

"How odd of God to choose the Jews," the Emperor chuckled. "Have you ever heard that line? One of our poets made it up. I think it's quite droll."

"It is, Sir." Pilate wished to hasten and return to his speech, to prove his worthiness but the Emperor cut him off.

"What is not droll, Pilate, is the 'insurrection', as they call it. These fanatics will not stop, do you understand? They do not value life for they believe they are already assured a spot in their heaven and hence they will stop at nothing! Which is why they need to be exterminated!" The Emperor's voice rose to a volume and intensity which Pilate didn't think possible coming from this old man, and he understood that the old man wasn't Emperor for naught.

"Crush the insurrection! Crush them like flies! Destroy them completely! Show no mercy! We are facing an enemy that is ruthless and cold-blooded. They kill their own, you know, and they don't care if they themselves die. They hate our way of life. The most dangerous are the Sicarii, those who attack in broad daylight and know they will be killed but not before they take innocent people with them. I will give you plenty of reinforcements and will ask Flavius Augustus to organize an army for you. I do not wish to move any troops from Syria just now. Your reinforcements will have to be moved from other places in Asia and Thrace and it will take weeks. When they are ready you will land by night. Do it in daytime and it will cost you much trouble. I want them to wake up and see our ensigns everywhere. It will infuriate the insurgents. These insects will crawl out of the woodwork hotheaded and brazen. They will increase their attacks and that is when I want you to move in swiftly and capture every insurgent on sight. Those you can't capture, kill, and the ones you do capture, crucify! I want this insurrection stopped especially as it threatens to spill over the borders. Syria is much more valuable to us in the long run, but for right now Judea is the centrum of this malice and we cannot threaten the security of all our lands. Syria is filled with people of many faiths. What if each of those peoples got the bright idea that they too are the chosen ones? Romans are the chosen people, you are correct, Pilate. You will be on the forefront of this war, which is nothing less than a war on terror."

Pilate saluted the Emperor.

"I will not disappoint you, Sir!"

"I have a feeling that you won't. I have faith in you. Excuse me once again for a moment… Governor…"

The Emperor smiled and went indoors. His rotten intestines beckoned him to his gold-plated shit bowl as he left Pilate standing on the balustrade. The new appointee's brow broke out in a bucket of sweat with the relief that the job was his. His heart beamed with the tingling delight of success. The Emperor was the king of the world. It was no small honor or privilege to serve as governor even if Judea was the armpit of the empire. Armpit or not, it was the Emperor's armpit, and it was far, far better to live like a louse in Tiberius' underarm then to continue to buzz around like a fly around his toilet. At least he was inside his tunic, inside his flesh, a commander, a governor, and someone who may even make history one day.

CONCEPTION

Eliyahu returned to the house safely without incident. *"Say what you will about the pagans and the occupiers"* he thought. *"But they do keep the peace. It's in their interest and in ours…God will provide, God will save… there are big days ahead…"*

The sun set and the last candles in town were extinguished. Eliyahu nodded off to sleep with a peaceful smile on his lips. The challenges of the dowry were outweighed by the rewards of having a grandchild.

It was just the first hint of a sunrise that peered in through the window of another part of the house but Maryam awoke too excited to stay in bed any longer. Though it was still much too early, she could not sleep. She wasn't hot—the sun was just starting to toast the land. She wanted to get her prayers over with as quickly as possible and jumping out of bed, she kneeled and recited the morning blessings.

"Blessed are you, Lord God, King of the Universe, who gave our hearts the understanding to distinguish between night and day. Blessed are you, Lord our God, King of the Universe, who made me an Israelite who did not make me a slave. Who made me in His image. Who formed mankind in His wisdom…"

And then she stopped.

Everyone recited the Birkhot Hashachar but she wanted to talk to God directly, and smiling in shame for her boldness, wishing to cover her head as one does when biting into an ortolan, she implored Him.

"Oh Lord God, soon I will belong to Yosif and be his wife. Lord, you know my cousin Elisheba could not conceive until you intervened and blessed her with a child. Lord, I pray that when Yosif takes me to his house that I am not barren and that I too will conceive and give birth to a child." And perhaps to make up for such an impetuous personal message to God Almighty, she quickly added the formulaic plea for the coming of the Messiah, the one who will deliver Israel from the enemy. Lord, you have promised to redeem us, so hasten the period of our redemption. The enemy wounds our heart, throws stones at us, afflicts us, steps on us, and laughs at us and our hope of redemption. But Israel will rejoice, for our Messiah is coming. Amen."

She threw herself back down on the bed and thought of Yosif. *"He is a good man..."* Though she hardly knew him, this was a mantra she repeated to herself ever since the marriage was arranged some time ago. All she had to do now was wait. Wait for that day when Yosif would be finished with fixing their future house, so he could perform the wedding ritual and steal her away from her parents. *"How fun will it be to be kidnapped!"* she laughed.

She heard some movement on the ground floor, *"My sisters must be awake by now. I should help them"*, she thought and went downstairs.

Maryam was the youngest. Reuth and Salome were older but spinsters—neither one had married and it was unlikely that they ever would. They were not unattractive girls; the only obstacle to finding a husband was that they were a bit feisty and possessed "character." Maryam was more obedient but the spirited qualities of the other two sisters aside, all three clung to their father with utmost devotion. Maryam knew her days with their father would not last forever and it was time for her to make a new start as a wife and mother in the home that Yosif was building for her.

The sound of gentle singing came from below. Maryam smiled

as she recognized Elisheba's voice in the choir. *"I will go down there now and join them in the happy melody and help them make bread for breakfast."* But when she went downstairs and saw them singing together she got a lump in her throat. She loved them, loved them dearly, and yet just now she felt a wave of repulsion against them. Singing, baking, mending their father's shirts… Why did they not wish to find a man in their own right? Why did they refuse all the offers of marriage that came to them? And with them was her cousin, Elisheba! The one who couldn't conceive for years and years and now finally, doting on her son and raving about him… She had become insufferable to Maryam. *"Why does she always come over so early every day?"* And then, as if the Almighty had tapped her on the shoulder and waved a reproachful finger, the resentment left.

Her frown turned into a smile. *"They are my sisters, my family. May God bless them. But today I will not stay in the house and bake bread and mend my father's shirts. The Hamsin has ended. I will go into town today."*

"Come Maryam, have you forgotten the words?" Elisheba smirked.

"I'm going out!"

"Now? But whatever for?"

"I want to go out. The Hamsin has ended and the hail has stopped. I'll go to the market. We need eggs for baking."

"You shouldn't go to the market alone. Don't you remember Gedaliah the melon vendor? How they killed him for selling on the Sabbath? How awful that was! It is not safe now, not on any day, and especially not for a young girl like you!"

"I'll be fine. And I'll be back soon."

"Cover yourself. Don't leave the house without your veil."

"I won't…" she answered, stifling resentment. The sun was up and it was already too hot and uncomfortable to cover herself, and while she had gone out unveiled many times before, she realized her sisters were right. Their insistence wasn't prudish—they only wished for her to be safe. She wanted to tell them she would quickly return unharmed and there was no need to worry. Yet she also knew they were right—in these times of troubles it was better to err on the side of caution. She did not wish to quarrel, and dropping her gaze to diffuse the rising tension within her, proudly announced: "I dreamt I gave birth to a boy!" and smiled nervously.

Elisheba rushed to embrace her cousin. "My sweet girl. You will be so happy. Happier than you can even imagine!"

Maryam walked down the dusty street in the direction of the market. The streets were empty—it was still early morning, though the stalls were slowly opening, the merchants preparing for another routine day of back-and-forth haggling. The entire region had a Hamsin hangover, especially after the hailstorm. First sand, then ice, then hail, everyone was too lazy to start work so soon again. One day of rest, one morning of sleep, that's all they begged for, all they wished for.

The streets were mostly empty. The Hamsin was over but the temporary relief from the ice storm was already gone in less than a day. This was a land of dust and sand and relentless scorching sun.

Maryam would heed the precautions about leaving the house without her veil. She never argued with it, it was the right thing to do but on the inside she felt that when it was a hot day, keeping the veil on was cruel and pointless. She undid the cloth and tried to inhale as much of what remained of the cool, the last chance to breathe in bits of moisture. As she inhaled, for a second it tasted like what she remembered the sea to taste like. When Maryam was a little girl, the family went to visit some relatives in Caesarea. That was the only time she had seen the sea. She still retained the olfactory memory to some extent, though now, just like her father's vision of the horse, to her it was just random words like beach or sea… Not everyone in Nazareth was so lucky to have visited the

Mediterranean even once in their lifetime, though it was only a few dozen kilometers away, but one Madeline moment that everyone in Judea shared was the odor of piss, stale Italian wine and vomit. While the Jews and the Greeks were still setting up shop in the marketplace, the Roman wine stands were already open. The sound of boozy laughter and retching and then stomach contents hitting the ground followed by laughter and applause, and the gibberish of a foreign tongue was what greeted Maryam on her walk. Quickly she put her veil back on, not so much for propriety but to cover her mouth from the stench, at least at first. Recognizing that propriety was more important, she wrapped herself further and mummified her face deeper away from the glances and the stares. But the stares were catching up with her and so were the sandals. She picked up her pace, darted into an alley, but the footsteps were right behind her as she came to a dead end. A hulking brute of man, a soldier just done emptying his stomach on the street, was wiping drool and disgorged bile off his lips.

Maryam stopped and turned around. She could still hear from far away, raucous laughter erupting from the tavern. The soldier wiped the sweat from his forehead and continued to leer, muttering something in Latin, and after spitting out the last of the vomit and drool mixture onto the Roman road, which the authorities prided themselves on, made his intentions known. Maryam darted past him and rushed back quickly in the direction of her house. As her heart began to race, the streets began to look the same, pounding faster and faster, she felt was she was in the labyrinth with the Minotaur just around the bend just as in that Greek fairy tale her father told her when she was a child. She could hear the sandals kicking up dust behind her, the Doppler Effect closing in and the last thing she remembered was how painful it was to have your forehead smashed against a wooden door. What came next was laid to rest in the mercy of oblivion.

Maryam was discovered much later, when darkness had already covered the town. Her brothers, Amran and Aaron, when scouring through the streets for hours had probably missed the spot where she lay unconscious and walked right past it several times. They eventually found her in a stable, bloody and semi-conscious. It was when she came to and started first to weep, then wonder and then realize what occurred, that she began screaming. The beasts who shared her temporary dwelling, perhaps aware of her pain or perhaps simply braying in anger and frustration that God made them walk on all fours, and if that wasn't punishment enough, denied them the gift of language as well, formed a ghastly chorus of woman and cow, woman and ass, a sickening orchestra of pain and blind stupidity and a wail against the shackles of the world. That was the music that led Aaron to Maryam. He kicked open the door of the stable and saw his sister bleeding and cowering in the corner.

INVASION

The galleys landed by night while Judea was asleep, upon Pilate's command and the Emperor's suggestion. Emperors don't make suggestions, they issue orders, but for his own dignity Pilate still considered it a "suggestion", with the actual execution remaining all his own.

He stepped off the boat and waded through the shallow waters toward the beach. *"It is the same sea, it is our sea, Mare Mediterranea. It is the same clear water that washes these shores as well as ours. It is just as warm and just as clear."* He bent down and splashed some of the water of the sea on his face and when he opened his eyes he saw that the country he landed in was actually quite different from his homeland.

The locals huddled together, wretches dragged out by his own soldiers, families, women and children, fathers and sons, grandmothers and infants—they huddled together. Kneeling, they implored, "Please don't kill us!" but in their eyes he saw deceit. He read it as *"Don't kill us so we can kill you later."* The new governor, the new ruler of this land, was being tested immediately. "These wretches that cling together will not bring us or themselves any good fortune. There is no good that can come out of this. We should not be here. Let them kill each other and leave us be."

He was sickened at the sight of grown men fully fit for army service kneeling on all fours or crouching. They wept. The Germans never did this, so does this mean these Israelis are making kind, was that it? He felt there was a specter looming. Something very, very different than he had ever seen. Behind every man's back he imagined a dagger.

In an opening gesture to the Emperor, Pilate ordered all the men beheaded, the women to be sent to Jerusalem as slaves or whores, and for the port village to be burnt to the ground.

Even the Greek settlers who hurriedly wrote on the walls of their meager dwellings *"Domus Graecus,"* so that their houses and lives would be spared, met the same fate.

Pilate loathed fulfilling this "suggestion", or so he told himself. In fact, the Eichmann "only following orders" mentality aside, he did believe that these people—all of them—were enemies of the Empire, and as enemies they had to be liquidated. Like a certain SS doctor who, when questioned in Nuremberg as to how he could obey the Hippocratic oath and still send innocents to the gas, said he found the Jews to be a cancer on the Reich and his mission was to remove it, so Pilate clinically instructed his brain to consider his mission in similar terms. Deep down somewhere he felt shame and guilt but after decades of military service and obedience to the state, that crinkle in the brain was ironed out utterly straight with no deviation from instructions possible.

He told his soldiers to begin the process of completely "cleansing" the town only when his chariot was out of their sight, when he was on his way to his new residence in his new duty as the louse in the armpit of the King of the World. Pilate liked the self-loathing moniker he chose for himself and smiled. He felt that he respected the louse. A noble insect. It was loyal and it always had a home, and even an imperial one at that.

ANNUNCIATION

Months had passed but no one ever dared to speak of what happened to Maryam, despite that Yosif, polite as he was, was becoming frustrated—for the date of the marriage was nearly set and now had to be postponed again, without explanation. What happened to Maryam was committed to memory, open to none.

Yosif waited and waited but was politely and firmly told to wait more. In the evenings, after his work in the carpentry shop where he apprenticed, Yosif would be tempted to pay a visit to Maryam's family but he would always decide against it, thinking it would be best for them to come to him. "If they find fault with me then let them say so and I will go my own way."

And so he would end his day, close up shop, put away the adze and lock up the lathe and walk through the marketplace on his way home, thinking of Maryam. He would pick up a loaf of bread for dinner, enter his lonely house and dream of his wife as he lay wrapped in scratchy rags instead of her golden arms.

Taciturn, strong, but prone to melancholy, Yosif was a hard worker who was not much for words, and though the marriage was arranged, he knew somehow that Maryam was the one for him. So the days passed and in the weeks and months he waited for a response looking at the sliver of moon from his window.

From the roof Maryam watched as the soldiers marched into Nazareth. It had been two months now since she knew for certain that she was pregnant. Yosif was kept in the dark as the family still tried to find the cleanest way out after Maryam had refused potions. Periodically though, they would still bring up abortion as a potential fix to the problem.

Salome watched her sister deep in thought and struggled for a way to break the ice and get to the matters at hand. The best she could finally come up with was "Then you're sure?"

Maryam turned, indignant at the question which rang of insincerity.

"Salome! It's been two months!"

"Maryam, I told you I can get you some herbs..." Elisheba spoke quietly—for everyone to hear but not hear it too loud.

"No, no, and no!" Maryam screamed.

Concerned about propriety and family values, the sisters huddled around her making pronouncements like, *Yosif will kill himself from the shame! What will we say to him?"* and proceeded to ad lib as needed to create the right tone, to let the girl know her position was precarious but Maryam would only reply, "I will not kill the child. I can feel him inside of me. He. Him. I know it's a boy, I can feel him." And she would weep as she wept now.

"Don't make me kill him! Don't make me do that! Don't make me kill him!"

Elisheba and Reuth tried to comfort her and put their hands over her and yet Maryam screamed again, "No potions!"

"We only wanted to help..."

"There is a life inside of me. And I am going to let it live. I am no murderess. I feel it growing inside of me! I know it is growing."

Elisheba broke down as well.

"Oh, Maryam, Maryam! What are we going to do..."

Such is how their conversation would go and they would repeat the same thing. Until, on this day of Maryam's despair, Reuth blurted something out to stop her fit of bawling.

"Maryam, I have a solution!"

Drenched in fear and snot, Maryam could only lift her eyes up a tiny bit to mouth "What solution?"

A conspiracy of smiles formed around the sisters and cousins. Reuth smiled and spoke first.

"A miracle! A miracle occurred!"

"When?"

"Now!" she laughed. "Or over a month ago or two months ago. Do miracles not occur, Elisheba?"

Elisheba nodded but Maryam was confused though intrigued.

"I suppose they do, but I've never seen one. Have you? I suppose if you believe, they are easier to see, but I have never seen one."

"Oh Maryam, listen to me! Were not others barren and then gave birth?"

"I was not barren."

"It doesn't matter! "

"Reuth is right," said Elisheba. "You remember, I couldn't conceive. Why, I thought I was too old and then, that was a miracle indeed…"

Maryam considered the outrageous idea.

"What do I say?"

Reuth seemed to have prepared the alibi in advance.

"Tell them that the Archangel Gabriel came to you and said that you would bear a son and he would be of divine birth. Conceived by a virgin. A miracle. Do you get it? It's…"

"It's preposterous!" Maryam was disgusted by this proposal.

"It's preposterous but it could work! The Angels blessed your union and gave you a child before Yosif even… did anything. Do it. Do it or die. Do it or die from shame. It is your only way out."

Elisheba kissed her cousin, envious that despite the circumstance she conceived so easily. She placed her hand on her stomach and kissed her forehead and said in a half whisper, a half prayer.

"Blessed are you among women, and blessed is the fruit of your womb."

Maryam promised to sleep on it, to think about this idea but that night, she couldn't sleep at all.

The next morning, Maryam again went to the rooftop to watch the soldiers while she pondered. And then it was time.

She did not need Elisheba to remind her but she went to her anyway. When the cousins stood face to face, Elisheba knew and spoke first. "Go see him now," and Maryam answered, "I will."

So she went.

In silence she walked with Yosif to the outskirts of town, away from the maddening crowd, away from everyone. "I don't want anyone to hear us" she told him. "It's too dangerous and too important." Yosif, obedient and steady followed her up the path without saying a word. Maryam was the most beautiful woman he had ever seen and by all accounts she was indeed startling in her beauty. Yosif almost enjoyed the walk at times, despite his trepidation, they would hold hands once in a while until she would slip her fingers out of his paw; not sure how to behave, not sure how to act, and when they reached a place outside of town that was far enough from people to hear, Yosif knew. He knew that there was something dreadful that she was going to reveal to him. Yosif was more of an ass than an ox, for donkeys have a self-preservation instinct absent in other equine breeds. He followed her and he knew that whatever it was he would have to accept it, for the alternative was none.

Maryam started with the fantasy, her voice shaking…

"An angel came to me, Yosif… It was the angel Gabriel… I had never seen anyone so beautiful…" Her mind began to race for fear that Yosif would become enraged with jealousy when she said *'He was so beautiful'* and that tears would come too soon. She did not have to speak so much for in a minute she was gurgling snot as she tried to keep the breakdown going for as long as possible in order to elicit compassion, even going so far as to fall on the ground and choke on dust while wailing. When she finally managed to mouth to him that she was with child, Yosif fell to his knees and kissed her feet when most of all he wished to punch her square in the jaw and break her face. The thought was senseless and mean and he couldn't have hated himself more for even thinking such a thing and though he knew she was dishonest, he kept repeating the mantra *"I will believe her, I will believe my Maryam..."* She in her own turn, kept reminding herself that this was the right thing to do, the only white lie that would save lives, the only way out of the situation. She tried lifting him up but the ass brushed off her tiny hands and raised himself up from his knees by himself.

She swooned from the force she exerted in order to lie, but the loyal ass picked her up and wiped the tears, mucus and dust off her face, and kissed her. And when he kissed her, he kissed her passionately and he felt the deepest love for this woman. *"I will never find someone more beautiful..."* he swallowed all of his resentment, though that resentment was stopped by a gag reflex, the heartache's rising stopped; a jugful of vomit rising up in his esophagus was dammed when the time was important. He looked her straight in the eye but found himself absolutely speechless.

"Believe me, Yosif!" she pleaded.

It was exactly that particular choice of words that told him she was lying and while he tried to ignore it and be strong, he could not help himself and averted his eyes. He looked into the distance, away from her, away from the physical evidence of the lie, and spoke almost as a Roman soldier, so professional, almost rehearsed.

"I will believe you Maryam, my wife. I will believe," and then quickly realizing what he said added quickly, "I believe!"

Maryam smiled and whispered, "I know you believe...my husband..."

"My husband" helped him calm down just as he feared he would be heartbroken forever. He pounced on that dog biscuit of a word and was satiated enough to prevent him from ripping into any flesh that was in sight. It did not save him completely but on their walk back to town he kept thinking and repeating his new formula: *"I will believe, I will believe, I will believe..."* And he promised to himself never to ask what really happened.

Walking in silence and mutual understanding periodically holding hands, the one thing that bonded them was that they both knew. One accepting the lie, the other pretending to believe it was what made it easier for both of them.

Upon re-entering Nazareth, the bittersweet silence was interrupted at once. No sooner had the cuckold couple entered the city gates—she, head in the clouds talking about angelic visitations, he, cock between the legs taking any crumbs from the table—reality came in like a blitzkrieg with requisite screams and blood.

An insurgent was being dragged by police but still resisting, he managed to shout in defiance.

"Go ahead and beat me, you unclean beasts! You unclean filth! Get out of Judea you swine! Yes, I forfeit my life now but I do it for my people and my land and for my faith, and the occupiers must leave this land for it is holy! And only then can we-"

The aspirant martyr's pleas were crushed by a Roman foot.

"Shut up, damn you!"

He tried to keep going, in between gulps of air and gulps of blood.

"People, listen to me! Stand up! Raise yourselves up and smash the Romans, smash the occupiers and the infidels! What does it matter if you lose your life when the glory you shall receive is a thousandfold greater? I sacrificed my own life for you! Oh people of Moses and Abraham, rise if you want the Messiah to come!"

"I said shut up!"

The guard picked up a rock and smashed the Sicari in his face, and the wretch fell to the ground screaming in agony as blood flowed and broken teeth fell out of his mouth.

Maryam screamed in horror and Yosif quickly covered her eyes. "Don't look!"

She whimpered but the ass was strong.

"You who have been touched by a divine spirit should never see such horror! And the life inside you should never witness it either!"

Her tears burst forth so strong as to seep through his fingers.

And in his brain, the recurring promise: *"I will believe, I will believe, I believe…."*

THE IMP

Years passed oh so quickly—that's what they like to do, and they love to pull more jokes on you the older you get. Yosif and Maryam lived together in a banal peace, ignoring most things that went on outside of their house and yard.

Yosif proved to be a kind and loving husband and when he became paterfamilias after their first child, Yeshua, was born, he proved himself even further and established himself as a fair and decent father to their son. Though at times dour and stolid, his devotion to his family was unquestionable. He had finished his apprenticeship and had set up a shop of his own and he was proud to be a provider for his family and took pride in his trade.

And yet his nights were filled with pain. An imp nuzzled itself into his breast and would take little bites of his heart each day and each night, not enough for the heart to break and stop ticking but enough to make it ache. "Cuckold! Cuckold!" the imp would whisper into his ear and break out in hysterical laughter, clutching his stomach, his little tail between his legs going into spasms. "You fool! You stupid fool! I'm the angel your wife told you about! Now I get to live inside your heart where it's nice and warm and bloody until you croak! You've given me a home, Yosif! You invited me in!"

Yosif would toss and turn while the imp laughed. Sometimes the little creature would tickle him too or even take out a toolbox of special needles intended to prick the heart in just the right places without making too much of a puncture. The holes would add up after the years and eventually make the heart fail, but for now, the needles were intended to prolong the heartache as long as possible. Yosif would bite his lip, bite his wrist, soak the pillow with tears but he would never tell Maryam about the tiny stranger he invited into his heart who made the center of his body his permanent abode.

With heavy eyelids, eyes bloodshot, weak from lack of sleep, he would chew his bread in silence in the morning. Maryam knew something was bothering him and the lie was naturally the first thing she thought of. Just like Yosif, she in her own turn would avoid talking about it but "it" would never go away. "It" was what she called the rape and conception. She couldn't call it anything else. And she would look at him with love, pity and resentment all at once and would force herself to think *"Yosif is tired"* or *"Yosif has been working too much"* or *"Yosif isn't doing well under this heat"* and so on. And though she tried not to admit it to herself, she often resented Yosif for believing her ridiculous alibi.

"Their" boy, Yeshua, was healthy and grew well, seemingly without any physical issues. The years passed without event. Judea was quiet for the moment. The insurgency continued; it was neither quelled nor crushed, but some pockets of Judea were able to avoid much of the conflict and Maryam and Yosif had the luck of living in just such an enclave of relative stability. One morning, while Yosif toiled and Yeshua, still too young to work, was lingering in the yard playing with makeshift toys, a group of neighborhood children ran past.

"Yeshua! Aren't you going to see the crucifixion?

"The what?" He lifted his eyes up from some patterns he was drawing in the sand with a stick.

"The crucifixion! It's when Romans kill a bandit by nailing him to a tree!"

Yosif overheard and dropped his tools but it was too late. Yeshua had run off and joined the neighborhood kids. He yelled after them, "Yeshua come back! Don't go there!" and stumbling over some wood, tripped and fell. Quickly, he picked himself up and started after them again but the children were much faster.

The execution site, on the outskirts of town, was pitiful rather than spectacular, a far cry from the spectacle of bread, circuses and corpses—that was for the colosseums—and the crowd too was small. Nazareth's residents, mostly Jews and Greeks, did not care much for these things. Still, there was enough of a gathering. The children got there just in time for the jeers and laughter as the soldiers were nailing the man to the cross. One would have had a hard time to ascertain who laughed more and with more enthusiasm, the children or the adults. The children, perhaps unaware of the cruelty, thinking this just a game; the adults used to cruelty and aware that this cruelty too is just a game to God. It was only Yeshua who did not laugh. He shook and felt dizzy, and when the cross was elevated and its shadow fell on him, he collapsed in a fit of spasms and hysterics.

"What's wrong with him?" one of the children asked derisively. It was just then that Yosif pushed his way through the crowd, saw his son on the ground and rushed to pick him up. As they covered some distance away from the place of misery, he repeated to the child that he needed to calm down. Yeshua was rocked by the walk and in the safety of his father's arms, began to gently weep.

"I told you not to go, Yeshua…"

"I'm sorry Papa. Why did they… Why did they…."

"Shush, my child… You will understand much later. We live in a very sad land."

After Yosif had put the child to bed, he told Maryam what happened.

"Don't let this be known to our neighbors…" Maryam whispered. "They will blame it on demons, possession, but from what you described, I have seen this before. The Greeks say that you are seized by someone, they also call it a divine disease that perhaps the gods are taking hold of the person. What the pagans believe is none of our business but maybe it is indeed the Lord clutching him. In any case, let's not allow the rumors to spread."

"We won't."

And they didn't. Yeshua did have more fits but they became less frequent and his childhood was, for the most part, not unlike that of the other boys in Nazareth. Soon enough, he grew strong and able-bodied and helped his father in the shop, breathing in sawdust along with the sand. But at night he often lay awake in his corner of the house, looking out the tiny window, marveling at the night sky, breathing in the cool night air, especially in spring when everything smelled and tasted differently. He felt the universe spin around him and he would lay awake all night in such a state. Never having learned to read and write, poetry was out of the question. The fear and wonder was kept to himself. The kind of fear and wonder that only occurs when you're young, when you can still feel things and smell spring.

Thus life went on until something strange and unexpected happened. The imp decided to leave.

For a week or so, things had turned quiter in the tiny abode under Yosif's breast where the imp lived and poked his little tools into the ventricles. The jabbing had stopped. The imp began packing his bags.

"Where are you going?" Yosif would ask him. But the imp would say nothing and continued to diligently fold his clothes and close up shop. Yosif began to panic. He knew it was silly to miss this demon who had lived with him for so many years. Why should he miss his tormentor? Because one gets used to the constant companionship, odious though it is, as much as the constant pain. In the evening the imp was gone for good.

Yosif collapsed at just around noon, when the sun was strongest.

He was carried back into the dark of the house. Maryam hoped it was the heat, for Yosif continued to still breathe fitfully, but by dusk all the years of the imp's pinpricks had done their job and the heart collapsed.

REVELATION

Yosif was respected in town for his skills as a carpenter who always did a fine and timely job but the family was far from well off. A prolonged drought, as well as the disruptions in trade due to continued clashes between the insurgents and the Romans across the province, meant less money and less work and he was contracted for only the basics in his trade. A new door perhaps, or if lucky, an oxbow or yoke and even those only sporadically. They had no savings, they could not even pay for school for the children—the couple had two other boys since, this time without the aid of angels or miracles—and now they had to bury Yosif. What to do? God will provide, but how, exactly? In order to give Yosif a proper parting from this world and send him off on his journey the family had to sell two donkey jennies, valuable beasts, but that was what livestock was for in case of an emergency or tragedy. And the Rabbi wasn't cheap, but it was the right thing to do.

Standing above the resting place of Yosif's earthly shell, the priest spoke.

"Oh God full of mercy, who dwells on high, grant proper rest on the wings of the divine presence, and on the lofty levels of the holy and the pure ones who shine like the heavens for the soul of Yosif, who has gone on to His world. May his resting place be in the Garden of Eden and may the master of mercy shelter him in His wings for eternity..."

The family walked back home in silence. The younger brothers were put to bed and mother and son remained alone.

In the kitchen, lit by candles, Maryam and Yeshua sat on the floor drinking wine and eating boiled eggs. After wiping the tears off her face and mumbling some prayer chants, Maryam stopped and looked over at her eldest son.

"You don't have to sit on the floor with me."

Yeshua's mourning was shattered.

"Why? It is the Shivah."

"Yeshua, how shall I tell it to you? How should I tell you my sorrow?"

"It is my sorrow too, mother."

"But there is something that you do not know."

"Have I done something wrong? What have I done?"

"No, my boy, you have done nothing wrong. You did nothing, it's just that… I love you, you are my son. And your father loved you very much too. But he was not your father."

Yeshua jumped up.

"*Of all times, of all times to say something like this. What is she talking about?*" Blood shot up into the temples.

"What are you saying? What are you telling me?"

"Yeshua, you are indeed my son. And Yosif, may his soul find rest, he loved you too. He loved you as much I love you, as your brothers love you. He loved you as his own son, but he was not your father…"

"What are you saying?!"

"I have to come clean. To come clean before you. I had wanted to tell you for some time, to rest my conscience that I had lied, and lied to Yosif." And she even smiled, bittersweet as in how life throws you treats and tricks indeed. "I told him that an angel came from the Lord, and passed a shining light over my belly and that was how you came to be. That you were divine. I don't know if he ever really believed it. I doubt it. What a fantasy. But for the sake of decency…"

"What decency?"

"So no one would know."

"Know *what*, Mother?"

"Your father was a Roman."

"Who is he? Where is he? Where is my father?"

"Gone somewhere. You will never know him. He's probably dead. And may the Lord forgive me but I hope he is dead indeed."

Pacing, fuming and unable to process these words, Yeshua could not stop. "Why did you have to tell me this now? Why now?!"

Maryam continued, confessionally. She needed to atone in some way for lying to Yosif and she knew that this way of atonement was wrong because she was torturing her son despite herself.

"Your grandfather, my father, was a religious man. He knew the holy books quite well. And it is indeed stated in the Second Book that no one born of a forbidden union may enter the Kingdom of the Lord, not even until the tenth generation. It is said that you will be lost to the faith and serve other gods and the Lord's anger will destroy you. I am already destroyed… I lied to your father but what else could I do? If anyone found out I would have never married and lived in shame, and you too, we would have lived out our lives like the most wretched in the dust…I don't know what to think but it is in the laws and I wanted to tell you now."

She was still reticent about revealing what actually happened—that she was violated—but Yeshua spared her from divulging further. His rage liberated her from admitting her shame and sorrow.

"To hell with your laws! Damn your laws!" he screamed. It was enough for him to know that Yosif was not his father to madden him. He did not care about the details at that moment and with an indignant hand, right off the sideboard came crashing down the crockery.

Maryam burst into tears. The broken vessels now only added to the maudlin scene and Maryam almost wallowed in how pathetic it all was.

"Oh Yeshua, look what you did, son! We were never rich people but with your father gone now we will be poor. Don't break the pots, come on, pick them up, pick up the shards. We can mend them."

Yeshua's brain screamed. *"But he is not your father... but he is not your father... but he is not your father... he is not your father... but he is not your father but he is not your father... but he is not your father... but he is not your father... but he is not your father father father not your father!!!"*

Somewhere, an imp chuckled.

It rang like a bell inside his brain, a pendulum in his skull hitting the inside of his head, a bell that rang with rage and death and deafened him. *"But he is not your father... but he is not your father... the man I loved the man who held me, who wept, who held me tight, but he is not your father... who protected me, but he is not your father, from evil, but he is not your father... not your father not your father not your father oh God not your father not your father not your father... then who was he who was he who was he who was my father who is my father... he was not your father, he was not your father not your father, not your father, not your father, who the fuck was my father, then?"*

All that Yeshua felt at that point was rage. Nothing but rage and hatred. He wanted to know more but anger trumped curiosity and the awful words exploded from his mouth.

"You whore!"

As quickly as the shameful insult was shouted, he collapsed in a seizure, sweet foam spewing out of his mouth and Maryam, still his mother, hurried to stick a rag between his teeth so he wouldn't bite his tongue off just as she had been doing since he was young.

"Where did he learn these words?" she wondered. *"Did he mean it when he said them? My God, he is my own, my own child. I will love him forever, this vomit and drool, this shit he's spewing at me, I'd drink it if it made him well, I would do anything for my child!"*

"My child, my child... What a selfish child you are..." she chastised him silently as she wiped the froth from his mouth as the convulsions subsided.

Devastated by the foul words he vomited before collapsing in his fit, instead of helping her son up and putting him to bed, she threw a blanket over him, left him on the floor, and walked upstairs to her now solitary bedroom to weep alone.

She thought of a bird, the name of which she had forgotten, that someone told her about. There were few of them in Israel, if any. A simple little bird like a canary, this bird would take in other nestlings or maybe she would steal them, but raise them as her own. Maryam couldn't remember the name of the bird or what exactly it did. She was exhausted. Her husband was dead.

EYELESS IN CAESARIA

When the man in the moon (Cain, son of Adam) set the wheels in motion and let go of those levers, destiny took over. In this case, destiny consisted of two interstellar orbits of fate hurtling towards collision.

Pilate had seen a strange occurrence every day at sunset. Crows, a murder of them, had been sweeping over his palace each evening at dusk, flying in one mysterious direction. He briefly recalled that in Aesop's fable, the thirsty crow's persistence allowed him to finally drink from the pitcher. He fancied the birds good omens, who flattered him by their appearance as a testament to Roman ingenuity and assiduousness. *"Just like our aqueducts, we bring water to quench men's thirsts"* but just as soon the humor left and he recalled that other tale about the crow—the one who, goaded into singing by the fox, fell victim to his own vanity and dropped a piece of cheese right on the ground which was immediately snatched up by the clever and hungry canine. He recalled his modus operandus. *"We must never let go of our grip on this land. Never!"*

Despite his training as a soldier and subsequent work as a civil servant, Pilate was unable to emotionally disconnect himself from the more odious aspects of his job. He was not so cold as to come back from a hard day's work overseeing the crematoria in Birkenau or Belzec to dig heartily into his pork intestine stew washed down with some echt Deutsche Lagerbier, put the kids to bed, maybe fuck his obese wife—porcine as the meal they had eaten—and retire onto the balcony for a final smoke, observing vegetation and giving thanks for the good life while a sweet almond and peach smell emerged from the chimneys of the camp "bakery."

Pilate was consumed by a struggle to understand his place in the universe. Academically there was nothing he could find that would offer even a hint of solace. There were no solutions and nothing had any source of meaning except one: I must exist. *"It is obvious that I exist unless I am in someone's dream. Someone else's dream. Some of the Jews have told me that we are all living in a dream, that we are actually players in the dreams of Moses. How terrifying. It means that we only exist in someone else's brain and what will happen once Moses wakes up? And what is most terrifying is the fact that I am still wondering, who is the one who's dreaming, me or Moses?"*

And with such convoluted thoughts he'd dive into even bleaker musings. *"We are all dog meat on the bones of ashes,"* he would say to himself and quickly return to comforting thoughts of familiar pain.

The other night, he dreamt that he was covering his mother with a shawl, as she was cold and shivering. The old woman said nothing and continued to shake from cold despite all his efforts. He found it disturbing and the rest of his day was subsequently wretched.

Again, suicide and the consolation to be found in Mother Death were two of the primary comforting ideas. To slit one's wrists in a warm tub and slowly lose consciousness was a blanket of the softest, warmest wool, or in Judean heat, lightest, coolest gauze. Another thought which brought him great self-pitying pleasure was how he missed and lacked the human touch, and not just kindness but the actual, physical touch of another person's flesh.

Claudia had stopped sharing the bed with him recently.

"I miss her body close to me, or even just her hand rubbing through my hair. Even a dog gets petted."

This was a case of some exaggeration, although it held some

truth, but the sentiment seemed so poignant and basic to him that he kept repeating it, even when he knew he was doing it solely for effect. With no audience around, Pilate would become the player and the public, a hermaphrodite making lugubrious, morbid love to himself. It was part true, yes, but as far as the human touch there was also an army of Italian whores in Caesaria who were readily available to provide comfort for any man, and certainly for high paying clients like the Governor of Judea himself. He did not partake of those pleasures. The mercantile nature of the oldest profession repulsed him. He needed more than just to taste a stranger's skin. He *could* have hired someone to pet or fellate him but mostly he pined for intimacy with Claudia and she had become out of reach.

To Pilate's credit, he never took out his dejection on the prisoners. Each one of his decisions came from the calculated brain of a soldier and flunky. Never did he let his amateur philosopher persona interfere with his duty. If the subject was sentenced to death, it came from the one coil in that organ which was made of steel, the one which permitted no emotion when executing official functions. He was a civil servant after all.

Government service however, did nothing to assuage the burning feelings.

Sometimes Pilate couldn't believe the bizarre visions that popped into his head. Sitting in his chair, overlooking the beach he would at times wonder whether he had turned to marble. Each day seemed like eternity and he was wondering if he had become just another statue. *"What shall remain? The marble too, will shatter..."*

Some days were different, and the origin of this statuesque emotion originated in dread. It was almost when a man loses some of his faculties after a stroke but it wasn't quite that. Pilate was in relative health—he was solely overcome with fear that memory, so vital for him, had lost its importance. Time passed and certain remembrances had been completely drained of what once was a pungent, lachrymose bag of goods. In the background somewhere, emanating from the town below, he heard a kithara being plucked and a Greek singing a tune he recognized from way back in his youth. Oddly, these songs didn't conjure up the emotions that came with these memories. He remembered being brought to tears by that melody, thinking already in his twenties that he was getting old and that time was passing him by. But the response and reaction were different now, notable in their sterility.

"Why does it no longer feel the same?"

He cried himself to sleep humming that melody, pretending that when stationed in Germania, he heard a similar tune, which would have been impossible. The Germans had their own boring music but he'd try to associate the Greek melody with his youth and tried to fit the scattered puzzle pieces to form an imaginary past. The past when his love for a local girl in the Northern Territories of the Empire made him want to dig out his heart but that was lost as well. That girl's importance faded also. And when philosophical sobriety "reared its ugly head" is when Pilate became as cold as a sicarius.

When numbness was firmly in place, Pilate was particularly efficient in sentencing prisoners for execution. On an active day, he was able to carry on his duties with utmost bureaucratic skill. *"These two dozen shall be hanged, these three crucify, the rest of the lot send to Rome for the Colosseum."* Yet despite his skill as the executioner manqué, it offered him no satisfaction whatsoever. His brain was split in two, one following orders, the other drowning in the mire of his own guilt. He knew his men were committing atrocities but duty and loyalty to the Emperor were priority. He did his job quickly and professionally, but it did nothing to help him with the emptiness he found in brutality and he always searched for something to fill that void.

Several times Pilate tried to write in a diary. Part of it was due to the fact that he couldn't remember as well as he did before, once he started growing long in the tooth, and his fondness for wine often made things blurry. At first he would try to share his feelings, read something to Claudia or to one of the slaves, but they would only either nod or praise. Then he would give up and would give up even further with each new feeble effort. Whenever he would pick up the stylus, the first thought was *"Who will read it?"* and after struggling with a sentence or two he would drop the pen and pour himself another cup of wine. He knew he was being frank with himself. He knew that whoever would read his writing at a later date would find him silly, though he was wrong not to consider that others might find his notes different or even unique. Sometimes he would acknowledge that each man's thoughts may be of interest to at least one other person, but with each new day his emotion would change and the brain, too, would get older and wearier, and the desire to write would ebb.

Then he tried to simply write down the day's events, which made things even odder. He would write things like "First day of Sextilis, woke up, ate an egg, executed so-and-so, drank wine and looked out onto the sunset and started writing a letter to mother in Rome. Had burdensome dreams. Ordered a slave to be whipped…" and so on. He wondered how these lists of events not only sounded repetitive, they also sounded so familiar, as if life had already been lived, as if he had already lived this experience before it even happened and that made him track the date and stop. Thus the diary would again be abandoned. He tried to resurrect the idea a few times but would drop it again each time. In the past few years he tried to do it just to remember what happened a few weeks ago, just to keep track of time but that did not work either. The days blended into weeks and into months, and the days would last for more than a hundred years…

For the Hindus, time is an ocean of milk, for Pilate it was a lake of wine. He never read what the philosophers brought back from India. He preferred to philosophize on his own, looking out onto the sea and drinking.

"What will happen to me after I am gone?" He would be tortured by the question which would keep him awake throughout the night, only to wake up in sweat-soaked sheets with the dumb servant standing mutely before him, waiting for instructions. Pilate would see the inbred stupidity on the servant's face and it would infuriate him so much to see this creature he considered only partly human as such a complete cow. He would reach for the nearest object he could find, a candlestick, a brass cup, the contents of his chamber pot, and throw it into the direction of his servant. The lackey would scurry out. "Typical. Just like a rat..." he would snicker, and then immediately regret the damage he caused to an object he may have liked, a favoured goblet or inkwell perhaps.

When he learned that his mother died, it had already been close to a month by the time the news reached him from the continent. The first reaction was a strange numbness. The second was a clinical observation that, in time, he would indeed miss her. Though he had not seen his mother in years, they did exchange letters on occasion and he at least knew that she was there, somewhere. Now he felt further unmoored.

The sea was always his consolation, and he was lucky in that respect—to have the mystery of the sea at his daily disposal to further aid in contemplation. A lay philosopher, he was like every other amateur who wished to fathom the mysteries. *"Pity the one who lives inland. Of course they can also build fires and many a civilization has done well with the desert, but those desert dwellers always focused on devils, for it is true that evil thrives in the heat. It is the sea that is truly the source of philosophy."*

And so, Pilate would look out onto the water and think about the mystery of death. He had seen many corpses in the course of his life but it never ceased to amaze him just how odd a dead person looks—like a dummy, a mannequin, a gaudy statue in the palaces that he always found were too overdone and kitschy. It was unseemly to him the way they painted in the eyes and the lips.

What he remembered most of all about his extensive experience with death, was how the mortal shell comes to appear so devoid of spirit; inanimate, a corpse gives no hint that it was ever a living being, and this always made him ponder: *"Where does the spirit go? For surely there are fires of some sort, something to make the heart tick, the brain think, the lungs to inhale, the limbs to move, something unique and unusual, something that cannot be explained and something that must be eternal."*

He drank himself to sleep that night and woke up weeping yet again. The sheepish, dumb servant came around as usual, but Pilate was kind to him that morning and simply asked to be left alone and instructed him to announce to any visitors that the governor will be indisposed for the rest of the day. He managed to make his way to the balcony and sat, simply looking at the sea and drinking wine for breakfast. Soon enough, the drink and heat went to his head again. He returned to his dark, curtained chambers and slept for sixteen hours.

"Tomorrow, I must return to work..." he kept repeating as his mind battled Morpheus. His attempts to stifle emotions only met with more resistance from the body, for the nagging question of what resides in flesh and bone and what makes it all animate, live, love, enjoy and suffer, aggrieved him throughout both sleeping and waking hours. The most burning and persistent question was: how could he leave some type of legacy? Pilate and Claudia were childless, but even children aren't an insurance against oblivion and eternal disappearance, against being forever forgotten, against being nary but a soap bubble that pops and sighs out in the vastness of the universe. How can a man become immortal? How can one leave something for people to forever remember him by? That was the beast scratching at his soul, the monster under his bed, his flightless bird on a string.

THE LIFE

QUO VADIS?

Yeshua left at dawn in order to avoid his mother. He knew it was cruel but he couldn't help himself. He felt he had nothing left in Nazareth after what he perceived to be the revelation of a great betrayal. Yeshua's heart told him it was cold and unnecessary to part in such a way but his brain told him there was no other choice. He also knew his departure was a betrayal on its own and was arguably more unforgiveable to him than his mother's confession. If he was to come to terms with it all, he needed the time to be alone and reflect on it soberly. Rage and guilt competed until he exited the town gates.

The excitement of going off to see the world got the better of him. At thirty years of age, he had never before left a radius of more than just a few kilometers extending from his father's shop. First impressions were positive. He admired the quiet and the beauty of nature and inhaled freedom. In some cynical way he embraced freedom from his parents as much as he delighted in the physical freedom of movement. Unlike Prince Gautama, he had already seen disease, decaying corpses and the occasional ascetic who happened to wander into town. While he did see plenty of cruelty and even managed to learn from it, he was far from having had his fill.

And so he walked, under the godless sun, across the sinful earth. At the entrance to the first town he stumbled upon, after the obligatory frisking by the soldiers, Yeshua witnessed a great commotion. The guards and soldiers stood by, watched and did nothing. Clearly there was no rebellion or other pesky business for them to quash. Townsfolk, dozens upon dozens of them, all hurried in one direction, laughing and beaming with excitement. Occasionally one would trip on a rock and fall, causing a pileup and just as the shouts began and it looked like a fight was about to break out, the soldiers lazily intervened to break up the melee and the villagers continued rushing to their destination.

Yeshua had never seen such a sight before. Most gatherings were banned in Nazareth, but then a dim memory from childhood darted into his brain. He grabbed the sleeve of a passerby, an older man who walked slower than the others.

"Hey! What's going on here?"

The man stopped and indignantly tried to pull his rags back from Yeshua's grip.

"What do you want? Come on man, I'm in a hurry!"

"In a hurry for what?"

"What are you, blind? What do you think we have here for sport? Football?" He motioned over to the Roman soldiers. "That's for those pigs over there. We don't waste time on football. We pray and wait and study, and we'll see the Messiah come to exterminate those lice. Now let me go, damn you!"

Yeshua began to understand what was occurring but could only stare in disbelief as the childhood horror had been all but erased from his memory and his parents had spared him from witnessing other ones.

"But please tell me! Where is everyone going?" Yeshua pulled on the man's tattered coverings again.

"God damn it you're dense! It's a crucifixion, man! You going or not?"

The man continued on his way and Yeshua followed. The stranger kept scrutinizing Yeshua, darting glances at him, until a shadow of a slow smile appeared on his lips and his eyes turned oriental.

"You won't want to miss this one. They're about to execute a Sicarii!"

"The Sicarii are a bad lot..." Yeshua sighed. "But who has the right to decide who lives or dies if not for..."

The man cut him off.

"Bad lot? They are our heroes! True freedom fighters! I thought you were a Jew!" The man turned indignant again but they continued walking. "You're new here aren't you? Where from?"

"Nazareth."

The yellow eyes stayed fixed. They were the only parts of the face that were static while the rest, every inch of skin folded and morphed into a head sized smirk.

"Nazarenes have always been soft. Come on, keep pace!" The man wheezed but kept soldiering on. Yeshua was genuinely perplexed.

"If you like the Sicarii so much, why do you not mourn his death instead?" At that question the man had to stop.

"You don't get it do you? He will be martyred! No greater glory exists!" He paused to catch his breath for a minute and then picked up again. "Here's a shortcut to Skull Mountain. Not the big one of course, that one's down in Jerusalem, but we got our own here. Now we'll see the glorious sacrifice and the Lord will look down and be pleased."

"Pleased with what? Murder?" Yeshua found the whole ordeal hard to comprehend. He had heard of the great martyrs from Abel to Zechariah, but they were innocents.

The man was resolute. "He wanted to help his people and he did it as a true son of Judea! He could not bear to stand it any longer."

"And just what did he do?" Yeshua asked, though inside, he was afraid to find out.

"Set a Roman house on fire! The whole family burned alive, glory be to him! May his sacrifice bring us closer to the coming of the Messiah! All heathen occupiers shall burn in the fires of hell and he only hastened their fate. Come on, move faster!"

Yeshua was afraid to ask more. When they came to the top, the crowd was cheering and chanting, interrupted by one lone voice who repeated the necessary reinforcement of belief.

"Holy martyr! In death you have brought life to our will! God is great!"

The police stood by and did not nothing to interrupt the chants. On guard to protect should violence break out, they let the ridiculous prayers to the soon-to-be dead continue.

"Where is the logic?" Yeshua wondered. Never much for matters of logic—that was the Greeks' pastime—and barely schooled in general, he still couldn't fit the gruesome pieces together.

"Don't the Romans know why you're here?" he begged his companion. The stranger was exasperated from the walk and annoyed by Yeshua's questions but like any fanatic it was his duty to explain his faith to anyone who asked, for repeating the mangled thinking over and over eventually made it not only quite reasonable but made it easier to settle into the mold of law and into the ironclad canon of God's will.

"They think we're glad he will be killed, but we're glad for the opposite reason, you see. We cheer his deeds and his martyrdom, not his death. For his rewards in heaven are great. There's a huge difference, you need to understand. They're not very smart, the Romans. Once they figure out the truth it will be too late for them. God bless the martyr, for he dies so that our people may live free and in dignity."

"Dignity? What dignity? The man will be put to death! Where is the dignity in that?"

"Oh, be quiet already!"

Yeshua glanced over at the Sicari writhing on the cross which was laid out on the ground. The poor bastard bit his lips, his eyes bulging, his body filthy and dehydrated. With the first blow of the hammer and the first puncture of flesh and bone he did not scream, biting his lip further. The din of the crowd came almost to a hush with anticipation. It was during the second hammer blow when the hand was actually penetrated straight through and nailed to wood, that the 'martyr' bit off part of his tongue and with excruciating pain coming from both mouth and hand he spit that chunk of muscle out of his bloody mouth and screamed in bestial agony. Now the howls would continue uninterrupted. As another soldier started with the other hand, a swell of cheers ("God is great!") rose up, with another group quickly picking up to recite prayers, a sinister choir and war cry in dissonant unison. Yeshua could not watch anymore. He began to walk away and weep, but then swiftly turned around. He needed to ask the stranger one last thing.

"What is the name of this town?"

The stranger, enthralled by the crucifixion, was beaming. He barked back a quick reply without looking at Yeshua.

"Bethsaida."

"Woe unto you, Bethsaida," said Yeshua, and walked away.

"What?" The stranger darted around with a quick glance and saw Yeshua disappear away from the crowd. "Idiot..." he mumbled and returned to drooling and watching the bloody spectacle.

So Yeshua continued on his tour of the world. Behind him the townspeople cheered yet again. The spectacle had now become a massive opera of filth, a grand chorus of screams from the executed, the chorus bleating "God is great!" and among them, some barbershop quartets drumming out ancient prayers over a bloody planet.

Yeshua had not seen hell on earth yet, though that was to come. This was just the start of his travels and the start of his troubles. There were plenty more ahead, many more circles to descend. When he left Bethsaida, his repulsion and sadness over the crucifixion was suddenly offset by the pain he felt in the back of his skull. Suddenly a dizzy spell came on that forced him to sit down, but sitting didn't make it go away. Lying down on the ground didn't help either, so he walked until he found shelter from the sun under a sorrowful family of desert palms, and embraced one of trees.

"Please Lord, don't let it be another fit..." he prayed, but nothing helped. If he looked down or sideways or made too rapid a movement he feared he would collapse right on the ground and accidentally crack his skull open over a rock. Eventually the vertigo left him but he still felt ill and weak. He knew it was the stress but at least it wasn't a fit. Walking back out into the sun he thought *"I am strong. I can't allow myself to be weak. It was the heat, those people. There is cruelty all around. My heart is not stone but I will keep walking until I find water and more shade and it is only then that I will think about Bethsaida, not now."*

He brought hardly any provisions with him and was almost out of water. Presently he began to panic and ask himself, *"What am I doing? I will die here in this desert!"* It was too late to turn back and he would never reach Nazareth before nightfall when the curfew began. To return to cruel, repulsive Bethsaida was out of the question. Soon enough he saw greenery up ahead and praised God silently for looking after him. He wasn't sure if God looked after anyone anymore after today's events but it was something he felt was proper to think, perhaps hoping that God would somehow hear what he was thinking. He pushed closer to the grove, a small oasis with a watering hole, a patch of green among yellow, a jade ornament on a dress of ochre.

In the deep of the growth he saw a settlement, and through the trees, in fear for his own safety he crouched as he saw a group of men assembled in a circle reciting prayers, the same prayers he had heard all his life. It took him a few minutes to see that in the middle of this circle was a human head. He squinted a bit and then understood but still could not believe what he was seeing. Buried up to her neck in the ground was a woman accused of adultery, about to be executed by stoning. Here were priests, villagers, and from what he gathered, even some relatives. The woman was allowed to give birth to her child who, as a male offspring, was valuable to the family despite his origins in sin. She was even allowed to breast-feed the child until it could be weaned. Now that the child was able to take solid food, Yahweh's laws had to be upheld. The rocks were in her husband's pockets.

Unlike the Sicarii whose executions Yeshua had witnessed, the ones who screamed and raged until the end, this head was unable to speak. Her teeth had all been bashed in prior to putting her in the hole, for the expressed purpose that she would not be able to shout anything coherent before she was killed. It was her husband that threw the first stone, and the sticky egg of a cracked eyeball slid down her face, slithering into the dust. Yeshua had arrived too late to see the ritual gang rape of the accused which the villagers had to take part in, not that there would have been a shortage of volunteers if there was no draft.

It was when the eye slid into the dust that Yeshua lost consciousness.

THE KNIFE

When Yeshua woke, it was not in the grove but in the scorching sun in a barren, sandy stretch of desert. His eyes were gunked with mucus and when he rubbed the eye snot out from the lids, his eyeballs burned, the skull felt dry, and the brain was on fire. As he looked around, on the ground he noticed a knife.

"How odd." he thought. *"I had no knife. I did not even think of bringing one, though I probably should have. Why is it here?"* With the confusion, the pain in the back of his head came in again and he kept thinking, *"Why is it here? Why here? I suppose I need a knife. Someone must have lost it."*

It was a blade not unlike a sicarius, the Sicarii's namesake, that lay next to him. A dagger. Except this was no ordinary dagger. Just as he looked down at the blade and reached to pick it up, it jumped up, the metal bending and wiggling. It made a few jumps back when Yeshua tried to grab the handle, but then giggled and jumped closer and closer and rippled up and down as if it was laughing. And then the blade spoke.

"Why don't you kill yourself, Yeshua?" the blade whispered to him gently, patronizing but with sincerity. "You aren't of any use to anyone. Once the blood starts pouring from the neck, it's just a few minutes of pain. And then, when shock sets in, why, you won't feel a thing. Your hands will go numb, then your arms, your legs, and then you will lose consciousness and soon you'll be in paradise. There you can work as a street sweeper but have eternal life.

Everyone in paradise has a nice job, each according to his talent. You'll get set up nicely, with a pension and a pleasant retirement after a hundred million years or two, or ten. A garbage sweeper is what you are, Yeshua! That is your calling on earth, and if you don't watch out, you'll end up on a rubbish heap yourself!" And the blade giggled again, not unlike Yosif's imp.

"Get away from me, Satan!" Yeshua kicked the knife out of sight and over some rocks, but the resonating cackle echoed from the crevasse, and then the Doppler Effect set in and the blade immediately reappeared.

Now the knife decided to switch its tone and began to speak as if it was weeping.

"You didn't save that woman, Yeshua, you weakling. You didn't stop them. You could've said they were doing wrong to that poor woman. She's dead now, beaten to death by stones. You knew they were wrong. You knew that only God has the right to give and take life. Why didn't you say anything?"

Then the blade's voice turned deeper and more grave...

"Where are you going, Yeshua? Quo vadis? Where are you going? You hate yourself because you left your mother, don't you? Why don't you pick me up now and slice your throat? You can greet her in heaven when her time comes. Show some hospitality. She'll have someone to welcome her to the next world."

Yeshua kicked the blade away again and started walking but he kept hearing the sinister laugh chortling behind his back. He glanced over his shoulder and thought he saw fire in the background but kept moving. Still, a voice kept popping up. He was not sure if it was the blade or not but he knew that someone or some *thing* was sadistically mocking him. In rhythm, in monotony, went the catechism as they marched.

"Who are you?" Yeshua finally asked out loud.

"Your brother" came the immediate response but Yeshua kept on.

"Who are you?"

"Your mother!"

"Who are you?"

"Your father. Your real father."

"Who are you?"

"The woman you didn't save. My name is Maryam. Your mother's name is Maryam. They beat me to death with rocks and bashed my brains in. Would you like to look at my pretty brains? Look how they did me nice!"

"Who are you?"

"I am a blade…"

"Who are you?"

"I am a preacher whose name is death."

"Who are you?"

"And with my sickle keen, I reap the bearded grain at breath, and the flowers that grow in between."

"Who are you?"

"I am your brother."

"Who are you?"

"I am you!"

Yeshua stopped. He was back in the grove and the blade seemed to have left him. There were no more responses to *Who are you?*

"Perhaps Satan lives in the desert." he wondered. *"If that's so, I need to get to water quickly."*

Yeshua approached another grove. He saw no villagers but he was still careful to avoid the sight of any man. Or the sight of any clearing with a hole in the ground or worse, to see the remains of such a horrid ritual. *"I wonder if they buried her…"* he thought, and within a nanosecond the cackling returned. "Coward! Coward!"

"Get away from me Satan!" he would utter under his breath like a mantra and eventually the cackling would dissipate into an echo and fade away. He passed a stream, filled up his goatskin flask, washed his face and continued. And as he left the oasis he was back in the desert, back to the barren times before and when he saw the lifeless rocks he cringed and wondered if the blade was right after all. Why did he not speak up against those who were stoning the poor woman?

It was late and the skies turned dark. Yeshua had no idea how long he walked or for how long he talked to the knife or what time of day it actually was but it appeared that dusk was setting in. The sky was turning purple. The rock and sand stayed constant.

In the distance he saw lights that seemed to come from fires lit inside a complex of caves. A troglodyte city. Instinctively he started walking toward the caves, despite his less than joyous introduction to the outside world, he couldn't tell if he was strong or weak, exhausted or foolhardy. All he knew was that he had to keep on walking to avoid another night or morning in the sand, face to face with the knife. The total silence of the desert started to break when Yeshua first heard the faint sounds of human voices coming from the complex.

"Whoever they are, they can't be worse than the blade..." he decided, and headed toward the rock dwellings.

DREAMER OF THE DAY

"This, therefore, is a faded dream of the time when I went down into the dust and noise of the Eastern marketplace, and with my brain and muscles, with sweat and constant thinking, made others see my visions coming true. All men dream, but not equally. Those who dream by night in the dusty recesses of their minds wake in the day to find that all was vanity; but the dreamers of the day are dangerous men, for they may act their dream with open eyes, and make it possible."
    T.E. Lawrence

Decades ago, around the time that Maryam, wife of Yosif, was pushed into a stable and raped by the Roman, a certain child was born in dust and hate, in a cave not unlike the one that Yeshua now stumbled toward. That cave was the fortress of Jews who refused Roman rule and rebelled against it by any means possible. These were the Zealots, the Kanaim, the Sicarii. The terrorists. These were the people and this was the human dawn for we who live in the year of our Lord.

As they scrounged around for morsels on the floor, beaten into absolute submission by their husbands, their daughters smothered and thrown into the rubbish, the women of this pitiful settlement also begged for morsels of love and affection, but the men's priorities were different. Their priority, above all else, was murder.

Certainly, the women's loneliness would sometimes be assuaged by the scimitars between their husbands' legs, erect not with passion but hoisted to cleave the vulvas they so feared. Still, the far apart and rare orgasm the women would experience even during what was nothing less than a standard rape, despite the tears they stifled, would make sleep easier.

Abbas sat in the corner, planning the next murder, the next suicidal attack. He was inured to the women's cries and the birth was nothing more nor less than a simple nuisance, no reflection even on the biological and political aspects of his own reproduction. The "donkey" as he called his wife "affectionately" was giving birth to his son. He vaguely hoped it would be a son, who as a man would better serve the cause, *"A son would be fine,"* he thought, but the romantic musings about creating a dynasty left as quickly as they appeared.

Finally, the midwife screamed with joy. "Abbas! A boy! It's a boy! You have a son!" With his cultivated stoicism he was unmovable and only mumbled "Good…" He was pleased that it wasn't a female that entered the world but that was the limit of his satisfaction. *"A boy will become a man, and a man's duty is to kill, for killing is to man what maternity is to woman."*

When the woman's bleeding did not cease and the midwife began shouting in fear and warning her dear leader that his wife may die, Abbas only barked to tell her to shut her trap. "We all die," he followed up by muttering in a rare contemplative moment.

"We all die… all die…" It was time to dispatch more souls into the next world and Abbas stood up and spoke out loud, addressing no one but himself, though the followers heeded his words like the words of Yahweh and knelt and praised him even as Abbas spoke to the cave's wall.

"I only help push these souls towards paradise… And whatever holds for them there is out of my hands… We build a paradise on

earth, and we lay our trust in the Almighty..." he murmured to himself before delivering a pithy call to arms.

Abbas was dead the next week. The new governor had done a fine job with the security of the province and intercepted Abbas' caravan of death just as they were about to claim more innocent lives, but the son, Bar-Abbas, cached in his cave, was never found by the police. Under the guise of night, the infant was quickly smuggled out of Judea and into Egypt, where, as the rightful heir to his father's legacy, he was groomed for murder and took to it like a cow to cud.

Bar-Abbas grew up nourished on hate. He had no mother's tit to suckle on, but he could breathe air and knew Aramaic, and he inherited his father's bloody talent from a very early age. Remarkably, the young man, nature and nurture both be damned, found little pleasure in killing and torturing birds, lizards or small mammals—the staple youthful pleasure of the budding sociopath. He set his standards higher. From the very beginning his targets were men. And so it was in Egypt, the land of slavery from where his people had escaped, that he found the perfect place to install himself as the Pharaoh *"Dauphin"*, and found no irony in his pharaonic stature. And as the Dauphin, he was admired, venerated and obeyed.

Seeing so many humans reduced to a slab of meat, observing that the body of a decapitated dissenter, when looking at the torso resembled a block of head cheese or Greek "kokoretsi", Bar-Abbas' initial absence of conscience only magnified. He would even go so far as to joke that when he "grew up" he would like to apprentice with a butcher, which drew loud laughs and applause from his adult followers, men and women alike. Sand ran through his veins, not plasma, and in the heat of the desert sun, the silica melted and became glass—though not before the brittle grains emptying out of the vena cava ground his heart to dust.

Bar-Abbas grew fast and smart, and as a "cute" boy, was a "dear" leader indeed.

And as he grew and as the bones solidified, the heart stayed in place and ticked away, a stolid, solitary task that just meant clocking in and clocking out, overseeing the head cheese, the quotidian depravity and bloodlust. Sometimes Bar-Abbas, the godling come to earth, would be asked to separate the prisoners, be it by age, by race—he did it with calm and authority, never allowing himself to appear as a psychopath. Everything was done with cold precision.

The prisoners would be dragged into the camps in dozens, and it was the godling's job to separate ones from certain death from the ones who would face torture, stoning, interrogation which would also lead to stoning, and other miserable and painful ways to leave the world. Two thousand years from then, Bar-Abbas would be reborn as Josef Mengele, giving a lollipop to a child whose organs he was about to dissect without anaesthesia.

Poor Dr. Josef. What fun he would have had living in the world of those same Jews he operated on. With no fitting subjects and on the run for decades, drowning off the coast of a Brazilian beach, perverse scalpel and garbage can for a brain. Bar-Abbas lived two thousand years too early to see the apotheosis he drooled over each night during his adolescence.

When it was time for him to come into the world, he was ready. A natural leader. And a natural born killer. With clean hands. Each one of Bar-Abbas' waking hours was preoccupied with an obsession "I will be king!" and "I'll show them all!" But he cloaked his perversion under a mantra and a mantle—"To rid Judea of the Occupiers" and "By any means necessary" and "The enemy of my enemy is my friend" by which he acquired friends and fellow nationalists. By the time he reached the age of thirty, his following was enormous. From the time of his infancy, Bar-Abbas lived in darkness. The blazing sun of the desert did not illuminate his mind or his heart. It set it ablaze with anger.

The Sicarii traversed the land, always staying one step above the law. They existed on the perimeters of the known world, on the outskirts of life... But their revolts continued.

At night they would rush in and destroy temples of Apollo, Isis, Jupiter and Hecate, and ruthlessly drive the Greeks and Roman settlers from their homes.

As the towns became depopulated, the Romans authorities tried to encourage immigration to resettle the colonies but found few takers brave enough to be placed in an unfamiliar land surrounded by eyes that glowed in the darkness, watching and waiting to raid the settlements.

The Sicarii atrocities were relentless. Sometimes the hacked up bodies of the victims were left in the town center, with a sign reading "Fresh Meat." Depending on how impoverished and starved the town was—for there were isolated towns that suffered from hunger—sometimes the villagers would say to themselves, "No one will know" and indulged in their sinful feast, proceeding afterwards to pray to Yahweh or Jupiter for forgiveness.

Oftentimes the Sicarii would pile the bodies up and burn them so that no trace of the Greek village remained and no dead left to bury. The ash from the burning corpses would be picked up by the wind and thrown up into the atmosphere.

As time went on, and their success in murder continued, the Sicarii added another trick to their list of terror techniques. The village cleansed, they would dump the bodies in the stream, and the river first became awash with red, and upon reaching its course would bring disease and putrefaction, poisoning the water supply of some hapless elements downstream. Bar-Abbas watched as the bodies floated down the course of the waterway decomposing, and this image was to stay with him for a long time as a symbol of efficiency.

If it was suspected that police would arrive or new settlers come to the village they cleansed, they would throw dead bodies in the well. Shouting out "God is great!" fists raised in the air, the victims' corpses would be thrown into the water to produce yet more corpses out of the next settlers.

Honor killings were common in the backwaters—and they were encouraged by the Sicarii to maintain purity of Jewish blood and maintain a family's reputation—but their prime directive was terror—to unleash the wrath of God through his most devoted servants. Often they worked in an uneasy but powerful collaboration with the Romans themselves—both striving for different goals but using the same techniques of fear and barbarity. Indiscriminate slaughter helped both parties even though they were technically at war with one another. When the Sicarii would decide to ambush a town, often a settlement of fellow Jews, the Roman cops would do nothing for the purpose of using the atrocity for propaganda, while the Sicarii, through their process of bloody intimidation would secure the village firmly under their control through the bloodiest and most monstrous of excesses. On one occasion, to expedite the killing machine, they recruited a three foot tall butcher's apprentice named "Moses the Dwarf" who during one of the night raids managed to decapitate forty eight men, women and children in just under a few hours. For his productivity, the Dwarf was rewarded by a trip to Jerusalem to pay his tribute at the Great Temple.

Bar-Abbas would walk around like a God-King among the men, and he was indeed revered as almost such a being, like a tiny child Buddha in the Himalayas, an infant emperor. At first it took him a while to understand the reason for the cruelty, though growing up with it his entire life, it soon became second nature to him, and sooner than later, it kindled a bloodlust of his own and he began to be more assertive. By his early teens he was already planning some of the massacres on his own. He had learned the scriptures and knew the story of the coming of the Messiah. The fawning he had received as the symbolic leader, the endless recitation of the old holy books, the vampirism he developed and nurtured with each raid and the sweet taste of power that he had always enjoyed, mushroomed. By age fifteen he was the Sicarii-in-Egypt's undisputed leader and it was time for him to command real power. He was the Messiah. He would return heroically to Judea and drive the Romans into the sea and take his place as the King of the Jews.

It was time for his triumphant return and after careful deliberation and communication with the Judean rebels it was decided that Bar-Abbas would return home. They set out at night on horses and camels, crossing through the harshness of the Negev and into the safety of the caves that were there waiting for them. Egypt was nothing to them. It was Judea that was the prize—their home, their land, not the Romans' land—and with the Boy-King securely protected by an army of butchers, the Sicarii established their base of operations and proceeded to wait, and plan, and plan how to reap.

There is a Reaper, whose name is Death...

"I have always been here and I will also be here, forever... This is my life. This is my mission... This land is ours!" Bar-Abbas would proclaim. His heart raced at times, but he knew that patience would win. And so they waited.

In short time, the son was worshipped as much as the father, the rightful heir to the throne of blood. Even in adolescence, he would oversee in monarchic pose, the executions of heretics and Romans, Jews and Egyptians, idol-worshipping Blacks and pagan Arabs and Parthians. But when one of his soldiers, a Sicarii would offer Bar-Abbas the dagger to ritually finish off the victim, a gurgling bloody mess that spewed hate and sputum on his executioners, he would say no. A man whose throat had been cut, his chest coated in sticky blood would pierce his heart with what Bar-Abbas himself used to call "righteous anger" when referring to himself and the terrifying look of hate from a man suffering the greatest injustice, the injustice that would deprive him of any future time in this world forever, the piercing shot of the dying eyes would make Bar-Abbas give the knife back to his underling with a quick nod that meant "finish the job." He would go back into royal repose and even turn away from watching the man's spirit leave the body. It was not for him to do the dirty work. A born leader, he was preparing for the role planned for him: leadership. *Let the others follow my orders. My hands are clean.*

Yeshua, isolated in Nazareth until just a few days ago, and protected from the atrocities, would have had no way of knowing who Bar-Abbas was. Nor would he have even guessed whose lair he entered when seeking shelter was his only objective. Lit by fires, with no brash sounds or troubling signs apparent, the troglodytes seemed harmless, and so he approached the cave.

THE SNOT BLUE SEA

Pilate kept looking at the sea, wondering why it smelled differently than it did in Rome. The same body of water, what was so different about it?

"If I go up to it and kneel, I would most likely still smell the salt, the rotting fish and all the pleasures that the sea provides... I drink too much. But what will it matter when I'm gone? What will it matter if I have not left something behind? What could that something be? I am not a writer. They will have one thing, only one thing in the history books to remember me by. My name, Pontius Pilate. Nothing more, nothing less. There lived a man, and now he's gone. What is in a name if the name means nothing? Too much, too much... How shall I solve this puzzle? For what shall I be remembered by other than my name chipped in a small slate of marble?"

He recalled what happened yesterday with disgust—he was obliged to fire a guard whose duty was to escort the prisoners to Golgotha. The man would have to get drunk before taking the prisoners up, and he would often fall and make mistakes. Pilate questioned the guard who confessed that he found the work repulsive. Pilate nodded and had the man transferred to Syria. He understood the repulsion, but duty and logic had to be maintained—he tried to maintain belief in the necessity and value of punishment. Of course, never having actually nailed a man to a piece of wood, he only understood it as an idea and not from any personal experience. In the evening he pondered what went through the mind of an executioner, the one who was only doing his job, only following orders, and how he could come home for supper with his family after flaying a fellow man, a human being. A dreadful itch appeared in whatever lobe was in charge of guilt or responsibility which was shooed away with the fly whisk of a conviction. *"I only give orders, I do not torture, I follow orders, and I uphold the law."*

It did not help much, these apologies to self and state. He drifted back to geopolitics and the depressing notion of the fruit falling to rot in order to produce another tree.

"This civilization too will fall..." he thought. *"Just like the Persians, the Greeks, we are in our twilight years, we Romans, and we don't even realize it...."*

Unlike most of his compatriots, Pilate did not hate the Jews as a nation in itself. In fact, he tried to study their scriptures and laws and knew a decent bit of their history, enough to be actually quite conversant with even the higher ranking priests or historians; he found their plight and culture somewhat fascinating and he admired their tenacity. What he feared most was what he saw as a wily mercantile nature which he maintained needed to be kept in check at all times and there was a prophetic, apocalyptic fear that would often surface. At present there was no concern for Jews infiltrating Rome, for few were allowed to settle there and many of the ones given permits were only there temporarily. *"But what if some Jew is able to pull a trick, become the fifth column and settle in Italy by stealth, assimilate or pretend to assimilate and then from inside our own intestines spawn like maggots inside our rotting corpse? It would have to be some type of new Judaism...."* And then back to reverie *"Just as we will never be young again, never know the joy of youth and health again, so we will never regain our civilization from collapse.... There's a worm in the apple....more than one worm... Why the whole damn apple tree is lousy! Who are these maggots?"* Pilate lived among the Jews but Judea was not homogenous and if he wished, could have surrounded himself only with Romans. Gradually, though, the Jews began to obsess him more and more. While he often felt that their perceived threat to Rome was precisely that—perceived—he knew that as Governor he was obligated to make the Emperor's fears his own.

The mutual distrust and fear saddened him. A place like Judea did not deserve it. He recognized that it was a wondrous, bountiful land, and not all that much oppressively hotter than Italy. Deep in his heart he genuinely wished for all this rotten business to be over, and gentle daydreams of retirement came running back. *"This is a fine land, a gentle land."* He waxed sentimentally. *"The weather is mild, the sea, the sea, the sea, it's right here… Yes, it is hot and dry, but I complain too much…"*

His lips formed a half-smile, half from happiness, half from regret. *"This could be Jupiter's land were it not for the killings. Yet we, who pride ourselves on civilization, also pride ourselves on murder… We, who bring language and culture, we who create the most magnificent architecture and works of art, we who build cities and states, we are also the ones who throw living slaves to be eaten alive by lampreys, we nail people to wood, we flay men, we put them against beasts for horrid, cheap spectacles, and in the meantime we create…"*

They were dark thoughts—thoughts wherein Pilate desperately struggled to find reconciliation but it was impossible. *"These are the people."* He was resigned. *"This is the human world."* And then a queer afterthought darted in. *"Yes, perhaps we are cruel, and yet, we create art. The Jews do nothing of the sort."*

THE CAVE

As the lights from the fires of the cave city flickered ahead, Yeshua looked up and saw in counterpoint the flickering of the stars in the night sky. *"What a starry night!"* he marveled *"And how much more powerful those starry eyes of God are which illuminate us straight from the heavens. Our feeble human fires only lead me to a miserable spider's house where we seek shelter from the cold and from the hungry beasts who come out at night."* And he thought how beautiful and how wondrous both human and heavenly fires were and remembered hearing how some Persian tribes still worship fire as a deity, and understood their fascination.

When our story took place, the stars were objects of much debate. The Greeks and the Persians certainly had much interest in them. Desperate for striking meaning into chaos, both people tried to imbue them with specific characteristics, trying to grasp what they couldn't grasp, as we do to this day. The Greeks, in desperation, associated the orbs with gods and spirits. Instead of floating objects or spheres, they became "planets." They had done this for hundreds of years. Their epigones, the Romans, consumed them in their boozy and worldly Weltanschauung. They were romantic but also prime for scientific examination. "What's that bright light up there?" a functionary would ask. And the scientist, no more than a lackey under these circumstances, would answer impromptu, "That is the chariot of Helios, drawn by solar bulls, the one you call Apollo now..."

"Is that so?" would come the sleepy response and the porcine body of the official would chew some nuts and olives and appear to think. Drooling, he would reach for another goblet—the feigned interest would disgust the philosophers and scientists who did their work in earnest—and in a brief moment before the drunk sleep set in, the servant of the state would look in vain for Apollo's chariot and nod off with the astronomer left standing and feeling like a fool for sharing his most intimate poetry with the true fool in the room.

Much like Pilate and the Jews, Yeshua knew little about the Romans, despite living next door to them all his life like most Jews in Judea. It was only a few days ago he even learned that he was half Roman, but now his *a priori* quest was to find shelter. He was weak from hunger and from walking and as he reached the entrance to the caves in utter exhaustion, he felt warmed enough by the fires that emanated from inside that he lay down on the ground and fell promptly to sleep before even asking for hospitality. He did not know how long he slept but it could not have been much. Dreams that seem like hours, days, and months actually only happen in a few seconds. And it was only a few minutes later that he felt a spear prodding cautiously into the nape of his neck. Yeshua swallowed dust and didn't speak. At first he feared the blade had followed him, but the spear's touch eventually turned gentler and he began to recognize that this was not a hallucination, not a temptation, not Satan, that it was wielded by a man. And then he heard the first words. "Are you a Jew?"

Without hesitation, Yeshua answered "Yes", though an instant later, the memory of his half Roman blood flashed inside him.

"Then come... Get up!" said the man whose face he had not yet seen, and Yeshua obeyed and was brought into what he hoped would be safety. Thus he entered the cave.

The warmth enveloped him, the silence made him queasy. A cauldron of lamb soup boiled in the center. Bread and wine and fruit were laid out in abundance. At first, it looked like a simple, albeit unusually large, Bedouin family, but Bedouins do not settle in caves. The men and the women were separated into two sides. In the center sat who Yeshua understood to be the leader of this group. The man was young, around his same age, and his very presence, *just his very presence,* seemed to be enough to maintain total devotion and obedience among the dozens of men and women and children who were assembled around him.

Yeshua's captor addressed the leader.

"He is harmless, no weapons. Looks like a beggar looking for food."

The leader inspected Yeshua in silence until finally...

"There are no settlements here for miles other than this, our cave. A traveler?"

"Yes. I was seeking a place to sleep where beasts wouldn't harm me. I heard sounds and I saw the lights. I did not want to disturb and I was very tired, so I laid down outside."

"You must be a weary traveler. There is much in the world these days that can make a man weary."

"There is. You speak the truth. I saw awful things today, awful..."

"You should rest with us brother, and eat. We have wine and bread, we are making soup, there are some dried fish. Even melons. And you can tell us all about your travels. Are you hungry?"

"Yes, I am. Thank you!" Yeshua was starved but the peculiar troglodytes made him cautious and apprehensive.

"Come on then, sit down and rest, weary traveler." And motioning to the henchmen, servants, and women, the man said "He's all right, let him stay with us. Come. Feed him. Then he can watch."

Yeshua had considered that there was something odd about the whole setting but his hunger had the better of him and he greedily slurped down the lamb soup, biting off huge chunks of bread, washing it down with gulps of wine, but this only lasted for a few minutes. The gorging abruptly stopped as he saw that there were too many eyes focused on him. He slowed down. On this apparent leader's face was an interrogative look—pensive, his eyes followed and scrutinized this new guest's every move.

Yeshua had not yet learned much about people but he had a survival instinct and the gene of self-preservation, at least at this stage of his journey. And now he could sense, much more than sense, he was certain that something did not seem right, especially since this leader was staring intently at Yeshua, observing just how he chewed his lamb, drank his wine, how he bit off chunks of the bread, and so on.

Soon enough, just as Yeshua had expected, a provocation came up but not without the preliminary "throwing off guard" techniques. Yeshua was naïve and wise, both. He took it in stride as best as he could.

"What is your name, traveler?"

"Yeshua…"

"Yeshua? Funny… My name too is Yeshua. And your father's name was, I mean is, I hope…"

"Yosif. Was. My father is dead. Yeshua Bar-Yosif…"

"And I am Yeshua Bar-Abbas," the host replied with enigmatic smile. "I will provide you all the hospitality that you wish for."

With the facade of ice broken, our Yeshua felt safer but still remained wary, for the other Yeshua persisted in looking at him intently and intensely. In between slurps, when the sound of the gristle and the crunch of the grain wasn't there to provide a white noise, the quiet was deafening. Yeshua understood that something was not quite right. Bar-Abbas broke the silence.

"Have you ever seen a crucifixion, Yeshua?" he asked.

It was then that the lamb stuck in his throat. He knew that he needed to maintain composure, surrounded as he was by people he not only did not know but who he was starting to fear. And he knew he needed to reply as calmly as possible, while still unsure of the motives of his hosts.

"I first saw one when I was a child. I felt ill and I almost forgot what it was like... But yesterday I saw one again in Bethsaida. It was a dreadful thing. Horrible."

"Horrible? Yes. That's what the Romans are like. They are that horrible thing you speak of."

"You can't blame them all. You can't blame an entire nation." Yeshua knew that he was flirting with his own safety. Perhaps fortified by the lamb and the wine he believed he could get away with it, or would be given the opportunity to speak. Or perhaps that even by engaging Bar-Abbas and stating his own opinion he would gain some respect, retain safety and would eventually be allowed to go his own way.

"Oh yes I can, Yeshua! Oh yes I can blame them all! I can say with confidence that we need to fight back and that even one beetle is still part of the swarm and needs to be crushed and burnt. Perhaps it's an omen that we have the same name, eh? As if our paths were destined to cross. Don't you find it queer?"

"I don't know."

"Oh come on! We finding you outside our cave sleeping? And you just happening to wander over here, in which case maybe I am wrong but… Perhaps you are a spy? Do you work for the Romans?"

"I am not a spy."

"But then you are on the run from something?"

"From what?"

"Not from the Romans. I can tell you're too soft to be a fighter. You're on the run. From who? Your family? What did you do to them?"

"I did nothing."

"I can sense things. My family is the family of faith. Faith brings us together. We can be your family, Yeshua, your real family. You know that my name means 'son of the father', but I am a father as well. These children that come at the enemy with knives, these are my children, this is my flock, and I am the good shepherd. And their father. Don't you need a father, Yeshua? Doesn't everyone?"

Yeshua struggled to say it out loud for he still grieved, but he managed to say the words again without tearing up. "My father is dead…"

"And you must miss him." Bar-Abbas put on compassion. "I knew there was something missing in your life. And now, God be praised, you have found us! Join us, Yeshua. Join us in our belief and in our struggle! Join our family and join us in our fight!"

"Well, what is it you fight for?"

"A free Judea! An independent Judea. An independent, mighty kingdom for Jews. And we fight for the expulsion and the destruction of the Romans."

"And once the Romans are gone? What then?"

"The kingdom of God on earth! For I am destined to reign as the King of the Jews!"

"You are saying that you are the…"

"Messiah?" Bar-Abbas laughed. "In order for the Messiah to come and reign over Judea, we first need to liquidate the unbelievers. By any means necessary."

"And how do you propose to do this?"

"Through terror! And by not fearing death! You know who we are, Yeshua. No man who lives in these occupied lands has not heard of us without seeing our noble work which we carry out in the name of our struggle and our faith!"

"Does your faith instruct you to kill?"

Bar-Abbas smiled sardonically. "When necessary. Faith is everything. Faith in our land, faith in our struggle. Faith in our divine mission. For the holy land of Judea. Come with us, Yeshua, we will fish for men together!"

Yeshua still tried to maintain a balance between sincerity and caution. "I struggle with my faith in God, Yeshua… I do not see how He permits the things I see. And I'm sure I haven't seen even enough of the horrors, but the past several days…"

Bar-Abbas hissed.

"And what do you do for God? Better yet what do you ask of God? God lives in next world, the one we wish to reach, and he expects more of us while we are here. When the unbelievers occupy us then it is truly a holy war. And we will struggle and fight and kill to win. We do everything for God, and for God only. But I am a man, a son of man. While I am here we need to save the holy land. And the Romans are sons of neither God nor Man. Sons of dogs. Sons of swine. Apes and pigs. They are not human."

Whereas Yeshua had overheard such statements around him, he gave them no heed, but now, though he disagreed with every hateful thing Bar-Abbas spewed, he felt that the gesture of hospitality gave him immunity to engage in dialogue.

"Yeshua! How can you say such a thing, that they are not human? Are we not all human? Jews, Greeks, Armenians, and yes even Romans too, are we not all people created by God?"

Bar-Abbas could only wince at Yeshua's naiveté.

"Oh they are very far from human, my dear child. Very far… and killing them is the same as killing a beast, a sheep. Only we are human, us Jews."

Yeshua again dared to be sincere and spoke, but this time, *sotto voce*.

"I know your group has butchered Jews as well."

"Then you know precisely who we are." Bar-Abbas laughed, self-satisfied, pleased with the recognition of his notoriety. "Good. Yes, we kill Jews. Unbelievers. Collaborators. Killing unbelievers is a small matter to us. There is no shame in killing them and there is no shame in death."

"You shall not kill. It is the law of God."

"Innocents!" Bar-Abbas interrupted. "You shall not kill *innocents* but they are *not innocent!* So you accept Roman rule instead? Hmm… maybe I was wrong. You might be a spy after all. Not a very good one obviously."

Bar-Abbas stood up and Yeshua began to shake. He had never sought out conflict like this before. This was new. Nor had he ever hit a man but anger rose up inside and he imagined beating Bar-Abbas to a bloody pulp, but he restrained himself, grit his teeth, and stood up in turn.

"I'm not a spy but I would like to leave. I would like to thank you for the food and the wine but I cannot stay."

Bar-Abbas, front seat in the house to Yeshua's shaking, only smiled.

"Yeshua. Why are you trembling? Do you worry about death when you eat meat? Do you worry about animals that are butchered? Come! I have something to show you. An initiation, so to speak. Once you're done with this you'll see how similar it is. Nothing to be afraid of. I think it's time."

Bar-Abbas signaled to his henchmen, glanced at Yeshua, and ordered. "Bring him in! We have a prize pig waiting to be slaughtered. We don't *eat* pig of course…"

Yeshua was terrified of a fit occurring in the cave.

"Please! Just let me leave!"

"You want to leave?"

"That's what I said."

"You will leave. But you'll stay for this first, so that it will be imprinted on your weak brain forever. I know you're not a spy, just an idiot, but even idiots need to be educated in one way or another."

"I need to go!"

Yeshua started for the exit but was stopped by the guards.

"Hold him right there and keep him still!" Bar-Abbas barked.

"Maybe you can make yourself useful while you are here. Do you write well? Latin, I mean?"

In fear for his life and wishing nothing more than to be spared any further involvement with these people, it was the shameful reality of his illiteracy that he hoped would help save him and Yeshua promptly admitted. "I'm sorry, I don't really write or read at all."

Bar-Abbas chuckled.

"Not only a coward but illiterate too. What use are you? All right then, record it in your brain, that which you are about to see. Tell people all about it, wherever your travels take you, wherever you tread. That is how you can repay us for sparing your miserable life that you so desperately wish to hold on to. Oh, but the rewards for martyrs are so much greater."

They tied Yeshua with rope so he could stay and witness the next act.

"Idan!" Bar-Abbas yelled out to his henchman. "You will be the scribe, and you will record the dog's confession."

"Yes, my leader." Idan replied in a burst and scurried off into another part of the cave.

While Yeshua trembled, Bar-Abbas continued.

"Killing occupiers is like swatting flies. Oh, their doom is dreadful. And they will not escape the fire and will suffer forever. Bring in the pig!"

From the far corner of the cave, the others brought in the prisoner. Some boos, some cheers, some gasps, some laughs. The soldier was a young man in Roman livery, blindfolded and gagged. Judging from his rather ordinary uniform it was easy to guess that he was not a high-ranking officer. On the contrary, he may have even been a conscript, but he was still a fine enough trophy, a solid specimen to execute. Bar-Abbas released the gag. Idan approached with a writing implement and a blank scroll.

The interrogation began.

"Watch!" He smiled to Yeshua and then diverted his attention to the pathetic soldier.

"Now you. Speak. You know what to say and what we want to hear. Idan, write! What is your name?"

"My name is Silvanus Sextus."

"What is your nationality?"

"I am a Roman from Taormina."

"And your family?"

"My father is Roman and my mother is Roman, and I am a Roman."

"And what are you doing here?"

"I am a Roman and as a Roman I am an occupier."

"Good. Thank you. You have spoken the truth."

The Roman gasped for breath, gasping from fear, clinging to a vague hope for mercy.

"We have already reached our verdict"

"Oh help me, help me, someone help me!" the soldier panted but it only made Bar-Abbas angrier and yelling out *"Shut your trap!"* he kicked the kneeling prisoner in the gut.

"The verdict is death. Let this be a pronouncement to the rest of the occupiers, and a message to them, when your head is placed on a stick by the city gates of Chorazim. I will now state the proclamation."

A scribe approached with a scroll and stylus and Bar-Abbas spoke as if he were addressing the entire world.

"A statement to the people from Yeshua Bar-Abbas, King of the Jews. May God praise all true Jews and humiliate those who attempt to defeat Judea — the ones who attack and insult her. The Jewish nation! Does any excuse for waiting remain? Oh how you sleep, eyelids closed and do not see Judea slaughtered and bleeding her dignity! Where is the zeal and the anger at the violation of our sanctities? Where is the revenge for our brothers held captive and humiliated in Roman prisons? We are the zeal. We are the anger. We are the struggle. We will take revenge for the blood of our brothers in Judea and elsewhere! And as for you, you Roman dog, Pilate, we wait for you. With God's help, you and your soldiers who rape our land today will regret it tomorrow. And to the traitor Herod, we say that we wait for your meeting with our warriors! We offered the Roman administration this soldier in exchange for some of our prisoners in Jerusalem but they refused. Know then, that the corpses will arrive to you one after another as your people are slaughtered! We will kill the occupiers wherever we find them and place their bodies where they can be seen. Our God is the greatest, the most merciful. Glory to God and to his messengers! Glory to Judea! Glory to the heroes and martyrs! God is great!"

The Roman kept begging for mercy.

"Please people, let me live, please let me live!" but Bar-Abbas, with a curt dismissive of *"Shut the fuck up!"* only asked Idan if the scribe had caught everything on paper and when Idan nodded was when Bar-Abbas said simply "Then do it."

As quickly as it was ordered, a headsman came up behind the Roman and started his grisly task. The human proved more resilient than a lamb or kid, and when the first strokes were unable to separate the head from the body, he proceeded to saw through the bone and gristle as pitiful, gurgling sounds struggled out from the victim. What was no more than a minute of time seemed like eternity to Yeshua, who watched and listened in horror as the Roman's protracted groaning and the plashing of blood seemed to continue even after the job was complete. The executioner held up the trophy—the eyes and lips twitched and blinked rapidly for a few seconds until the contractions ceased and the whites of the eyeballs floated up as the spirit left the body for good. The Sicarii cheered.

Bar-Abbas was pleased. He looked upon his constituency, saw that his handiwork was good, and said simply, "Well done. Long live Judea!"

A chorus chimed in, "Glory to Judea! God is great! God is great…"

Yeshua tried very hard to keep from fainting or from having another seizure. He quaked and shivered but Bar-Abbas turned to him and smiled.

"You!" he smiled "I hope you understood me well."

"Avram!" He called out to another of his henchmen but kept his eyes focused on Yeshua.

"Remember, Yeshua, remember only one thing, if there's only one thing I wish for you to remember is that I am the King of the Jews. It is only a matter of time, when you will see that prophecy fulfilled!"

Yeshua cowered and shook while Bar-Abbas was still.

"You are blind to the truth now, but perhaps one day your eyes will be opened. You will be free to go if you wish… in a minute."

The henchman approached and Bar-Abbas turned to him.

"Avram, is the head in the bag?"

Avram gave a silent nod.

Yeshua wished to simply walk away. He never imagined that the price of a bowl of soup was to be witness to murder.

"Yeshua you can leave but not so fast. You have to do something for us. Avram brought you this bag. We know you now, Yeshua. All you need to do is take this garbage to the next town and leave it at the city gates. Nail this scroll up too. Here, take these. Nails are expensive. Don't forget, wanderer, we'll be watching you too."

Yeshua stood up and hesitantly picked up the scroll and nails, and the hideous bag. Despite—or maybe because of—the shock he was in, Yeshua's first thought as he felt the weight in his hand was surprise at how heavy a human head actually is and how much strength it must take for the rest of the body to support it.

"Understand?"

Yeshua trembled. "I understand."

Bar-Abbas was pleased.

"Then go. Go! Go, Yeshua! Run! We'll meet again! My friend, my namesake. Yeshua!"

Yeshua ran breakneck through the desert, panting and crying. The moon shone bright. Periodically he would look behind to make sure he was not being followed, that he was out of eyesight of the cave.

"Earth. Earth will cover earth... All rocks, barren, all barren, all barren, like their souls..."

Slowly, the desert changed to an environment slightly more conducive to life. The sand and rocks gave way to some vegetation. Yeshua fell on the ground in exhaustion. There were some shoots of life coming out of the soil. He dug furiously with his hands to make a hole, to put the awful sack in the ground and to bury it. His weeping escalated and turned almost hysterical, and through the gurgling snot, sounding bestial himself, he began to improvise a prayer.

"Oh God full of mercy, you who dwell on high, grant proper rest to this man, *Oh God Oh God Oh God...*"

He began to convulse and his body went into a fitful mass of spasms and jerks which went on and on until the seizure ended and he lost consciousness.

THE PROPHET

Yeshua was becoming accustomed to waking up on the cold and rocky ground. He opened his eyes as the sun began to lift the blanket of night but continued to lay on his bed of nails, remembering with a bitter taste the events of last night. He surveyed the landscape and was again surprised at how different the desert looks during the day. Running from the Sicarii last night, he was unaware of how much distance he had covered and only now saw that vermillion had turned to viridian. Ahead of him was a stream and though his bones felt ancient, he wearily managed to drag himself over to the water to wash his face and drink. Quite like a beast at the watering hole, Yeshua knew he was exposing himself to a predator's fangs and claws so when the sound of hooves and muddled voices approached, he darted into a cluster of olive trees and crouched.

Through the branches he watched the procession. The human cattle, on foot, as if on exhibition, were led by a mounted leader. These were not Sicarii, Yeshua understood that. They would never dare to display themselves as such, though he supposed that in the desert and away from authority it was conceivable. Yet something seemed queer and different about this particular group. Blindly, they followed the man on horseback, stumbling like specters, weary and exhausted. He noticed the banners and flags they carried, attached to a bar fixed crosswise against a spear. Some of the cloths bore a crude image meant to resemble the horseman at the head of this ragged army. There was no marching song, instead only some mumbling. How many were there? Dozens, perhaps hundreds? It was hard to tell when so many were lagging behind and the procession seemed to snake for quite a distance. What baffled Yeshua most was that as they reached the stream, the followers did not immediately dive into the water to quench their thirst and wash the dust off their bodies and faces. Any traveler or nomad would have rushed at the very first sight of a cool stream. The Horseman slowed down and some commotion followed, until a brazen one got on his knees in front of the horse, bowed and, supplicating, asked "Master! If we are stopping, may we please drink from this stream? Oh, dear leader, may we drink this water? Our thirst is immense!"

"Go ahead and drink," said the Horseman, calmly. It was then that the crowd turned into a herd of beasts, kicking and pushing each other to get to the water, pulling those who managed to get there first away, pushing others into the stream, bodies piling up, some almost drowning in a few inches of water when another body would land on top.

"Just don't all drown at once!" the Horseman followed up with a smirk.

Within the herd, Yeshua noticed a woman pushing herself through to get to the drink with as much ferocity as the men, yet to no avail. All access to the water was covered in knees and buttocks raised skywards. She still tried to push through, eye darting around in search of an alternate opening, and then she noticed Yeshua. Their eyes met. She did not yell *Intruder!* and when she turned her head back to her objective and noticed a spot that had freed up was when after a nanosecond of shame she dove her head into the stream unabashedly and began to drink with greed.

What mesmerized Yeshua most was not her behavior but her beauty, despite her eager participation in the fascinating, miserable spectacle. He decided to step forth to find out just who these people were. Surely if they were indeed such a maddened crowd with such obedience and devotion to the mysterious rider they would not hesitate to rip him to bloody bits at the lift of the Horseman's finger. Yet for whatever reason, Yeshua felt he was safe enough to approach, and so he exited the makeshift camouflage and approached the centaur.

"Who are you?"

"And a good day to you, too," the Horseman laughed.

"Good day…" Yeshua was polite but had to ask, "Who are you?"

"My name is Legion, for as you can see, I am many…" The Horseman laughed and spread his hand over the throng.

"And who are they? What are you-"

"I am Theudas. I am the one who will be king. The one who comes after Eliyahu. I have come to fulfill the prophecy and free the land. And the whole world will worship the One God of Israel!"

And so Yeshua's indignation gene made itself known again. His own audacity surprised himself more than that of this "prophet" and when it got the better of him he was unable to back down. Just like the time anger grabbed him after his mother's revelation— something he thought about daily with guilt and shame—so too now, he ignored fear of consequence and spoke with reckless courage.

"You're a liar!" Yeshua came up around the side of Theudas' steed and continued, indignantly, "What trash you talk! Why I just met some murderous scum who claimed the same thing you did! King of the Jews, my foot! Where are you taking these people?"

"They are following me to the river Jordan. Why don't you join us as well? You're more than welcome." Theudas looked away toward the horizon as if surveying his future conquests.

"Like hell I will! You charlatans seem to be a dime a dozen around here lately! How on earth… How did you get these people to-"

"People follow the truth. Do you not wish for our land, our

great land to be free? Look around you! The splendor of our Judea! I, and only I, can and will restore its greatness, and all of it will be ours again. We do not need to massacre the Romans, we do not preach 'for every settler, one dagger' the way the Sicarii do. All that is needed is for you to do just like the others. To bow down and worship me! In unity is strength and with my swarm we will set the land free!"

"Then get on your merry way and take your pigs with you." Yeshua yelled, now fully confident with the knowledge that the man spoke utter nonsense.

The horse whinnied. Theudas tightened the reins.

"Listen, you can come with us! You're feisty but I'll take you. But know, this river will part for us for I have come and once it is accomplished, then the rest will follow, smooth as butter."

"Get away from me, Satan!" Yeshua frothed. "You won't part any rivers and you damn well know it! What are you doing to these people?"

As he raised his voice, Yeshua knew he wasn't being completely honest for it was the sight of that woman reduced to something less than human that made him furious.

Theudas only laughed. "Do what you must..." he said to Yeshua and then in a completely changed voice, commanding, yelled out "We're going! Now!"

The wretches, clinging together, picked themselves up and kept walking, following the leader as he led the way on his steed. Yeshua managed to again make eye contact with the woman, though there were no smiles exchanged, no mutual understandings or secret signs. The herd kept going.

Just as they began to disappear, Doppler returned and Yeshua bounded for a hiding place again. Darting low into the ground he heard Theudas' clip-clops drowned out by the sound of dozens of better shod horses and faintly he heard the Latin shout of

"Imperium!" which was followed by sickening screams as the cattle were culled by the Roman legion that had been waiting in preparation for the idiotic advance.

Yeshua crouched further down and found shelter under some brush, putting his trust in the Almighty, hoping that the Romans would only swiftly dispatch Theudas and his core followers and that the woman would somehow find a way to escape.

THE AQUEDUCT

"Where the Jews live, Pilate!"

"I'm sorry? Yes, yes, of course. Where the Jews live…"

Pilate was battling a terrific hangover and was having a devil of a time paying attention to what his guest, Lucius Aelius, the Governor of Syria, was saying. He knew this was an important meeting but the cats were scratching the inside of his skull and they refused to go away. Excerpts, just fragments from the earlier conversation, darted back.

"The Emperor is very pleased with your work…. But you must stop calling on my army reserves to deal with your problems…"

"I am so sorry, Lucius, I didn't think you had the same problem in Syria as we do here. I did not know you had a large group of suicidal madmen threatening not only to establish an 'independent' Jewish state but who also call for the annihilation of the Roman Empire itself. My power to call in the troops has been granted to me personally by the Emperor himself, and I have used that power to-"

"You have used it but the attacks continue. Now they are spreading to Syria where the Jews are not even a significant part of the population, and our Jews are nowhere near as pesky as the ones in your province. I spoke about it with the Emperor."

"And?"

"And he feels you may be well advised to modify your approach"

"Hogwash!" he thought. *"How dare this cocksure upstart challenge my relationship with the Emperor! Another one whose*

ambition will get the better of him!" Pilate became further irked.

"Modify how, exactly? Appeasement? Dialogue with the murderers? I'd rather fell all the pine trees of Phoenicia for crosses and plant my own forest of Jews than engage in any talks with the insurgent scum! I protect the state, I protect the Roman citizenry, the sovereignty-"

"Calm down, Governor." Lucius smiled in utter confidence. "You see, the problem is that these insurgents are becoming more and more popular. The people are with them—the Pharisees, the Sadducees, even the moderate Jews. They all give a silent nod of approval to the terrorists. "

"They do not. Not all of them. By the way, what the hell is a moderate Jew?"

"Yes they do, Pilate. Yes they do. Sure, they often find themselves victims of the Sicarii as well, victims of their cowardly attacks, but can you blame their attitude? They want us out of their land."

"This land is ours!"

"Of course it is, but in order to hold on to it, we have to-"

"What do you propose, Lucius?"

"More carrots. Fewer sticks. Throw them a crust."

"I'll throw them a crust and they'll claw us to death for the whole loaf! Speak, man! What type of 'crust' exactly will satiate the hunger of a venomous serpent?"

"You could try and improve their lot…"

At this point Pilate was positively outraged.

"Does not our very presence here improve their lot?! They have become degenerate! You know that! Everything they learned from the Greeks has dissolved in the salt of the Dead Sea!"

He spit in disgust, disgorging a big ball of sputum, but Lucius continued calmly and even more resolute.

"Pilate, I say this only for your sake…"

"You don't need to worry about 'my sake', I am governor here. I will be governor for life, and if I am removed, I will be senator for life. Now tell me, damn it, what is it that you wish to propose. To 'improve their lot' or whatever other rubbish proposal you have in mind. Go on..."

After a calculated pause, a smile formed on Lucius' lips and he answered quite gently.

"An aqueduct."

"Aqueduct?" Pilate snapped out of his anger but was perplexed, and though he did not wish to admit it, moderately intrigued. "We have an aqueduct here in Caesaria and plenty of clean water. Why do we need another aqueduct?"

"Here in Caesaria, sure, Pilate, sure, but what about Jerusalem?"

"Jerusalem?"

"Where the Jews live, Pilate!"

"Where the Jews live, Pilate!" was the phrase he remembered and which helped to snap him back into this conversation. The indignation over how the Syrian governor was addressing him was ameliorated only by ennui. Lucius bored Pilate dreadfully, a fatuous lackey who he felt no need to waste valuable boozing time on. The man was a bore.

He wondered if a glassy stare made it look as if he was thinking. Lucius kept looking straight at Pilate, waiting for a response. *"Stupid. He is a stupid man,"* Pilate thought. *"I'll let him wait and let him believe that I'm thinking..."*

"Where the Jews live..."

"It's true, that is their city. This one, Caesaria, is ours. My policy was plain and simple. They can keep Jerusalem, we do not want it."

Pilate despised Jerusalem and dreaded going there when he was forced to hold court for the Jews. He had seen Italian slums before, in Rome and other cities, so he did not consider it a Jewish trait to maintain filth. As far as the neighbors went, Lucius himself was complaining about the sanitation problems in Damascus. The

Germans, savages as they are, preferred to live in forests, so Pilate's time in the Saxon lands, when not in battle, was mostly spent in tents deep within the woods, or sometimes even outdoors with nary but a bed of grass and a blanket of stars and so he couldn't comment on the hygiene of the northern tribes. He enjoyed the warm German summers and preferred to sleep outdoors. He hated the snow and the winters spent in drafty, flea ridden tents but the spring and summer made up for it. Those mild seasons in the north, the smell of the pine trees, the fond Madeleine moments of his memories were interrupted by the matter at hand. Jerusalem made him retch. The fleas and mosquitoes of Germania and the north, that was nothing. Nothing could have prepared him for the impenetrable squalor of the Middle East.

Jerusalem stank. The lack of adequate plumbing, an achievement that was praised in other lands as one of Rome's finest inventions, was almost completely absent and the city smelled like an open sewer. The wretches and beggars huddled on the grimy streets were even filthier than the ones Pilate had seen in the worst slums of Rome.

Worst of all was the Valley of Hinnom, outside the south wall of the city. Pilate learned later from an old Jew that in ancient times the Hebrews would sacrifice their children to their old god Moloch, the one who was now displaced by Yahweh. This old Jew, one of the Sanhedrin, was invited to Pilate's Jerusalem palace to discuss the state of the province and all the issues he was supposed to stay on top of, but just as with Lucius, Pilate was bored to tears each time the man came to visit him. Another day, another murder, another massacre. At this point it no longer sickened him. It wearied him. And when the opportunity arose to change the subject matter but still be the polite diplomat, he would ask the Jew about his peoples' history, their religion, their faith… and the Jew would gladly oblige. Pilate would listen, but only up to a point. Sometimes the flicker of the candle would capture his attention more, and he would meditate instead on the magic of fire while the Jew's recital of his nation's history would go in one ear and out the other.

"Then did Solomon build a high place for Chemosh, the abomination of Moab, in the hell that is before Jerusalem, the abomination of the sons of Ammon." Such were the things that the old learned man recited to Pilate as the governor dozed off. The old man disregarded Pilate's lack of interest or even his snoring or his position as protector of minority rule, and he would continue, and even speak with bitterness about those Jews still revering Solomon for his wisdom but ignoring his abominations. It was politically wise for him to ingratiate himself with the head authority in order to protect his people.

Claudia would sometimes pass Pilate and the Jew during these exchanges on her way from the gardens to her quarters and wince. *What a fool. What a fool I have for a husband. Why does he bother with these people?* But Pilate was engaged and listened closely.

"Tophet held Moloch, which was made of brass, and they heated him from his lower parts, and his hands being stretched out and made hot, they put the child between his hands and it was burnt. When it vehemently cried out, the priests beat a drum, that the father might not hear the voice of his son and that his heart might not be moved."

The Jew stifled tears and told Pilate that his people had erred in their ways, that they took the abominations from their neighbors, the Canaanites, who worshiped an idol which was hollow and was divided into seven compartments. In the first one they put flour, in the second turtledoves, in the third a ewe, in the fourth a ram, in the fifth a calf, in the sixth an ox, and in the seventh a child, which were all burnt together by heating the statue inside.

Piqued by the sadism, just out of curiosity, as the Jew wept and repented for the sins of his fathers, Pilate would ask questions.

"But if God is one, is not Moloch also Yahweh?" He struggled to understand the religion of the Jews. The Jew would protest and say that Yahweh forbade the abominations and Pilate would again drift off while the Jew would continue to talk and defend Yahweh's omnipotence. The man was a scholar of the Hebrew scriptures, this man that Pilate befriended, one of the Sanhedrin. Pilate, in turn, would think of the Roman gods, gods of the hearth in particular, and of how much more sense they made and how much more beautiful was the Roman pantheon. But he did appreciate some of the Hebrew sayings. His favorite was "all is vanity."

Now solely a garbage dump but the most odious smelling one he had ever encountered, the Valley of Hinnom was harrowing at night when the flames of the pit, where dead criminals and diseased beasts burned, licked the sky. Looking over the trash heap on his return to Caesaria one evening, Pilate imagined the flames resembled the souls of the dead, begging for a helping hand to drag them out of their eternal punishment. Eternal, for the fires were never extinguished. On each journey back to Caesaria, Pilate praised Jupiter for the cleanliness of his palace and for the clean sea and sand, and he would sit for hours on the balustrade, looking at the Mediterranean, drinking cold wine, as if washing himself off from the filth and the horror of the city he had just come from.

"Where the Jews, live, Pilate!"

"Ah, yes. Where the Jews live." Pilate began to emerge from his dive into memory's murky waters.

It was time to reassert himself, or at least maintain his position. And so a boot stomped, at least in his head to make Lucius pay attention.

"Jews live everywhere!" He was still groggy and could not let go of the image of Hinnom's garbage pit, the one they later named Gehenna, but as a bit of bile rose up from the esophagus and into his mouth, the disgust increased and now the sole object of Pilate's disgust was Lucius. And the Jews. *"Why do I need to talk so politely about the Jews?"* he wondered. *"At the end of the day, most of them a filthy lot. Back to business."*

"Everywhere!" he continued. "I wouldn't be surprised if they start infiltrating Rome itself soon and bring their so-called struggle to Italia! First settling in as merchants, hawking their rags, their shit, and soon their cousins who talk about the struggle or the revolution will bring that revolution to the center of the universe, Rome, carried on plague ships, oared by rats!"

Lucius was unmoved and undeterred.

"How often do you go to Jerusalem, Pilate?" Lucius spoke softly but carried a big stick, a stick he carried with a poker face, one that was always hidden with one word behind another. "The place is overcrowded. It's hot, dusty. The plumbing is-"

"They have no plumbing. At least not any that works. Filth and sewage. If it was up to me I would say raze the town and rebuild it the Roman way. Of course they won't let us. Too many sacred garbage dumps. The place is a disaster waiting to unfold. There are too many people there to support life."

"Right on so many counts. Now think, Pilate. Think. Stop pretending you are in Europe. This is Asia Minor. Yes we built them things, we built them roads, we built-"

"We built this! Everything here that's worth its salt was built by us! White men! Europeans!"

"I don't disagree with you, my friend. I don't disagree with you one bit, but you must open your eyes!"

"My eyes are more open than you know!"

"A part of them is closed. We are a minority here. A minority. We must adapt or we will die."

Lucius had thoroughly exhausted Pilate by now. He only wished for one thing—that the conversation be over.

"You just said it yourself. Jerusalem is overcrowded. It can't sustain life. Then let us give them the gift of life, water, and win their hearts. We can rip out their hearts with impunity once loyalty is secured. Do you understand?"

"Speak…" Pilate pined for a pillow and nothing else in the world mattered.

"Think. Fresh clean water for the residents, built for the Jews by us, the Romans, their friends. Not the occupiers, but their friends. Get it?"

"I see your point but I am not sure if I agree. The goal may be noble or at least practical, but it is the method that I am confused about. Well, perhaps not confused, but… Are you done? Can we continue at another time?"

"Ah, but you see it nonetheless! Good! That is precisely what I wanted to achieve today!" Lucius stood up and smiled, self-satisfied, he had Pilate in check. "Dear Governor, you will be pleased to know that I have already presented your idea to the Emperor!"

"My idea?" Pilate stood up in turn and looked at Lucius directly in the eyes. Pilate was skilled at predicting treachery but this was a surprise. He had known Lucius for some time, never in a friendly way, just disingenuous politician-to-politician politeness. He remembered when Lucius had just first started his post. He knew the young man possessed ideas, projects, all for the sake of licking the Emperor's sandals in order to move up in life. A stark contrast to Pilate whose ambitions were no longer for any further promotions but for an honorable discharge and if not to leave the land, then at least to leave the army and the bureaucracy, retire, live somewhere in peace where he could look at creation with a smile, marvel at the beauty of a green leaf, witness the intricacy of a millipede, observe the mechanical genius of a grasshopper, weep along with the sad maternity of a cow, savor the sensory delights of a freshly baked piece of bread, enjoy the taste of a fried egg, accept the blessings of the water that came from heaven; to truly enjoy a glass of wine, to feel some type of connection with the heavens, to let the blood pressure rise with atmospheric changes and to brood with the brooding storm clouds, to feel immunity and impunity, flipping the finger to the gods of thunder and lightning, walking out into the fields during rain; to accept the kinder gift of water that drains from a gentler goddess. And here they were talking about the Emperor, public works projects, and appeasing this nation, these Jews, utterly foreign to him.

"These bastards… I could give fuck all about them right now."

Lucius was beaming, oozing with self-satisfaction. Pilate, the older and the sadder man, had very few words for this career lackey. And yet the lackey kept careering. *"When will you shut the fuck up?"* was all Pilate could think.

"His Imperial Majesty is looking forward to its completion."

"Completion?"

"The completion of the aqueduct, my colleague."

"Colleague? Very well, go on…" It was hard for Pilate to remain calm but he was a soldier by training and that training always came in handy.

It was difficult to pierce through Lucius's gaze, so giddy with the prospect of a bonus or promotion, but Pilate had experience, and his stare—when he was able to focus—would break down his opponents later or sooner. *"Just try to remain still… This smarmy bastard kid."* Today he was unable to focus.

He really wished for nothing more than the ability to simply punch Lucius, to smack that smirk right off his face. *"God dammit, how I wish he would just leave me alone, I want them all to leave me alone, alone! All I want is peace. If this aqueduct is… oh, blast the aqueduct. Why do I need to help these people, these people who would like nothing better than to parade my severed head on the streets of the garbage dump they call their spiritual home. And this smug bastard isn't stopping!"*

Lucius put his hand on Pilate's shoulder and squeezed it lightly. "Pilate, it is a wise thing to do…"

"*He just touched me, how dare he touch me! If the Emperor wasn't in this charade now I'd grab the arm he's trying to put around me and pull it out of its socket! I don't want to work for the Jews or the Emperor anymore. I don't want any of this anymore. I am finished!*"

Lucius guided the hung over Pilate properly, goading, with all the proper knowledge a bureaucratic apprentice learns during his first internship.

"*He's going to speak to me again as if he was who he thinks he is. Stupid bastard. I am older, I am much older and so much more experienced and wiser, yet he persists. I suppose that is how one becomes successful…*"

"Chin up, Pilate! Come, let's go outside…" Lucius lowered his arm from Pilate's shoulder and let it slide to his waist.

"*This is my palace, this is my villa, and this cunt is telling me where to go?*" Pilate was enraged, but knew he had to keep silent and walked along. Groggy and hung over, what else could he do but do what he had always done, follow orders. "*With his arm around me like this, we are a couple. We are husband and wife and I am the wife, the peasant barbarian wife, whose sole purpose is to be beaten and fucked. To be scolded and forced to launder shit stained clothes, and to open up my bloody, toothless mouth to receive a filthy cock. I am nothing.*"

Pilate did not offer Lucius a bloody smile, though he did picture that image. With the first breath of the Mare Mediterranea the hangover miraculously vanished and he became lucid. He understood the finality and recognized he had no choice in the matter. He merely wanted it to be over.

"An aqueduct… in Jerusalem… You know, come to think of it, Lucius, you are right. I think it is a brilliant idea…"

THE TRAVELS

What would madden Yeshua on his travels? Oh, many things, so many things. If it wasn't the pain of the barbarity it was the sadness of everyday life. The latter was often much stronger than the former, but another horrible concept would creep in ever so often: obliteration.

This he shared with Pilate, though it would still be some time before their meeting, where they recognized shared emotions, occurred. The two had much in common and were hurtling toward an encounter, two comets racing toward each other and defying the old gods. Then there was also garbage brained Bar-Abbas, coming in at third place, trying to keep pace, but he was way behind. Nonetheless, all three would meet soon enough.

As Yeshua stumbled wearily among the atrocities, he would often be overcome by a force of such heart rending compassion that it made it difficult for him to swallow, much less to be indignant. When he felt he couldn't go on anymore, still on he walked. He felt pity for everyone and he hated that feeling.

"Surely we all suffer, who is not immune from it? From the Emperor to the lowest ditch digger, from the majestic lion to the grey hen pecking around in the dust. And in our lives, doomed to oblivion, every day is a reminder of our death when it should remind us of something great and eternal instead." It wasn't merely mortality that weighed him down so much as a feeling of pity that felt physically painful to bear. It was for people, for animals... Every living

thing was for him bathed in pity; sometimes he felt as if even the vegetables screamed.

"Daddy, what kind of animal is that?" a boy would ask his father, a tanner.

"That's a kid. A young goat. See? There's the little tail..." and with the mention and look-see of the *"little tail"* the boy would burst into tears and run away sobbing.

And Yeshua would sob with him when the man mentioned the little tail even though Yeshua would refuse neither the cup of goat milk nor the sandwich of baby goat wrapped in a chunk of bread, the baby goat he had just wept over. *"I am an idiot..."* he would say to himself, and would thank the farmers for their kindness. They in turn, believed they were racking up points in heaven for giving a piece of bread and goat and a glass of milk to a man who looked like he couldn't take care of himself and probably never would. In the desert it was commerce—only what you could get in return mattered—and Yeshua felt out of place in the desert when he started to guess at the way it worked.

It weren't just the sentimental semantics that sent pinpricks into Yeshua's aorta as he walked among the people. An old woman shoving some beans and eggs into her mouth, drooling a bit, would smile a toothless grin and Yeshua would be heartbroken. Logically, though he hated to think in those terms, he acknowledged that he knew nothing about her. She could have been a murderess who committed infanticide or an abortionist or someone who betrayed her husband and sister in order to hold on to her meager crust, now reduced to near-blindness and powerless in her position, the bones brittle, the bowels shut, each movement an infliction of pain, each breath a gift of life, each measly spoon of beans a source of pleasure, each glimpse of the sun through the muslin covered lens of her fading eyes, dearer than any past ambition; and in these simple, basic delights of feeling the earth and its joy, however, stirred in was tremendous sorrow and Yeshua wished to scream and fall down on the ground and bury his face in the dust.

When Haile Selassie made a tour of his sad and absurdly prefaced "Empire" of Ethiopia in a sparkling Rolls Royce motor car, the most benighted of his subjects, upon his approach, would dig holes in the earth and stick their faces in the dirt so as not to be blinded by the solar aura of the living god.

The Ethiopians were too stupid to see that he was just a puny man lording over an African hellhole, but this is how Yeshua felt, although his desire to bury himself came from a different place. Not out of fear, but partly out of disgust, partly out of the intensity of his sadness and partly out of shame for the god who creates us and permits us the most dreadful transgressions who lets us be monsters but never lets go of our humanity.

"No human is a monster if he can still eat and shit and receive pleasure from it. No, that's wrong. That is all beasts do, but wait...." He tried to formulate his thoughts. *"Beast or no beast, no human is fully a beast because we still think. Even if we think about how good the beans and eggs taste, do we not praise God by thinking so?"*

Yeshua struggled, struggled, but his philosophical skills were never honed, and in frustration he would admit *"The camel can even eat a thorny twig without question. He can eat his owner's tent if he's hungry. But the camel is a good and honest man, he gives us milk, cheese and meat and he carries us throughout the world without complaints. He is a friend to people, but what does he think?"*

Seeing a hungry beggar thrown some scraps, gnawing on the stale bread with such ferocity that tears would well up in the unwashed wretch's eyes; watching the alcoholic who received a coin run with immense gratitude to buy the nearest cup of Roman wine and quench his thirst, eyes red and scratching, and then the cool, cool drink of the grapes. *"No, that was wrong,"* he thought. *"Or is it? Who am I to judge? One thing unites us all. We all love this world, no matter what pain it causes us. From the tragedy of death to the simple delight of a chicken leg and a piece of bread, there are so many pleasures from great to meek. But it is death that makes us cry while we suck on that chicken leg or look out onto the sun."*

And on he walked.

There is a Reaper, whose name is Death,
  And, with his sickle keen,
He reaps the bearded grain at a breath,
  And the flowers that grow between...

An angel or an imp sat on Yeshua's shoulders at all times. He could never tell whether the creature was a guiding light or a demonic piece of filth, showing him the way to the Valley of Death. Regardless, Yeshua walked along valiantly and made no attempt to swat away the little voice in his head, the one that was perched precariously close to his jugular, brandishing the same shiny blade that he encountered in the desert when he first left Nazareth.

The creature was just a gnat, and probably harmless but for the buzzing in the ears, and Yeshua castigated himself for carrying on, ox-like, chewing cud and waving off flies with his tail instead of swatting the bothersome insect. Waving off the ones that try to land on a cow's ass, where the good shit is, was the way Yeshua tried to wave away the demon from landing on the good part of his brain, the most sensitive one. Even flies themselves were unaware, just angry bits of life fighting for dominance, much how Yeshua was unaware who will be the smarter fly, who will bite whose neck, who will be the one that carries river blindness or another dreadful ailment that may prove deadly, or which one is just a nuisance. One of these flies was coming. One which combined nuisance, dread and death. That insect was preparing still for its grand finale. In the meantime, Yeshua often found himself ridiculously exhausted from sadder and sadder feelings. The two men had not yet met, but Yeshua did often think quite a bit like Pilate, a man twenty years older than Yeshua and twenty-fold more weary. They shared fears.

Yeshua's new imp, perhaps the progeny of Yosif's demon companion, found a place in Yeshua's heart, a place that few had really tapped into before. That place was shoddily boarded up, feeble resistance against attack and the little devil, upon discovering the secret compartment, easily pulled apart the nails and two-by-fours and made himself a nest. The nest was solely for the evening hours and for the night. When Yeshua walked around during the day, the imp sat on his shoulder enjoying the view, enjoying the rocking motions… sometimes these motions would make the imp sleepy, and he would doze off like a child rocked in its mother's arms, but it would also facilitate the rhythmical chants he would sing into Yeshua's brain via the ears. "Loser! Loser!" and chuckling before the cradle of the neck and shoulder, Yeshua would absorb the doubt and fear as he rocked the little devil to sleep.

The imp would sleep much of the day. It was too hot to do anything more than whisper into the ear, and even then it was hard work to stay awake. *"I can't imagine how he doesn't just croak!"* The imp would wonder out loud before wrapping tiny claws around Yeshua's neck in a perverse bloodsucking embrace. Adopting Yeshua as a surrogate mother, the imp would doze off under the heat of the sun.

Much like with Yosif, it was at night or in the evening when the torture began, when the imp would be refreshed by the cool of night. That's when the filth would climb down from the neck and enter the cellar and chisel his way into Yeshua's heart. He'd break out his toolbox like his father, the one who tortured Yosif and destroyed his heart, but it didn't work as well as it did with the old man. After a few attempts the imp would climb back out. He would prefer to sit on Yeshua's head instead, and he gradually learned that at the proper times, certain tools, particular ones, would prick Yeshua with the pain of memory and its weirdness with just the right precision. And just at the right time and with said precision, the desired effect would come. *"It was just a moment ago, that I was helping my mother peel potatoes"* or *"and then my father would say the prayers and we would have eggs for supper. I imagine a naked girl in front of me. Why do I feel so wretched? Why do I find sadness in a plate of eggs? Is it because the simple days are gone into oblivion, forever obliterated?"*

Pilate and Yeshua both fancied the concept that oblivion seems so merciful. To crawl into Yahweh's armpit, or into Jupiter's sandal, close one's eyes and go to sleep were the deepest and most secure comfort one could hope for.

The imp would laugh but it was hard working on his subject. The pinpricks didn't do much and after a while he went back into the veins and closed up the hole with the old, rotting, wood and sometimes even slept throughout the next day. This imp was lazy and even though he had a job to do, he felt a certain pity for Yeshua and perhaps that is why he did his job halfheartedly. *"I know where he's going. He'll end up following his destiny. My job is rather thankless all in all. And this one, he's a bore to torture. Or maybe I'm just bored... maybe I do not know my trade well enough"*... and so the imp spent most of his days sleeping in that condemned section of Yeshua's heart. He would only pop up when there was something worthwhile to latch onto, a particularly juicy thing like, say, a memory of a happy evening meal with his parents. Then the imp would begin his work, and summon black clouds to envelop Yeshua's mind. With the brain opaque, the little demon would burrow in the heart, the soul, and the armpit, and snuggled firmly in folds of flesh, he would pierce Yeshua with needles of heartache.

This was the way Yeshua traveled through Judea—with an unwelcome constant companion. Yeshua would not be felled by this little ball of filth the way his father was. For Yosif, it was a long and onerous process, one that sapped both torturer and victim. Yeshua's imp was still green, but despite his inexperience, was able to dole out a hearty helping of misery.

As he walked, Yeshua would sometimes notice an apparition—a pair of fellow travelers at the other side of the road who followed his every step. He would blink and they would be gone, but he knew who they were and he acknowledged their presence.

Two shadows, two blind old crones, dragged themselves across the desert, and what they sowed, they reaped.

There is a Reaper, whose name is Death,
* And, with his sickle keen,*
He reaps the bearded grain at a breath,
* And the flowers that grow between...*

Though skin and bones themselves, they marched on valiantly, sowing their seeds. The younger sister's name was Sorrow. She was the champion, the stronger one. She would support her sister Pain and mend her crutches, change her gauze as needed, but both sisters were dependent on one another. Pain was always spreading her handiwork through the earth, and as they walked she would hold her sister's hand and clutch it tight. And Sorrow, too, would respond in a silent gesture, smile a toothless grin, and hold her sister's bony, emaciated hand oh so tighter, implying reassuringly that at least they had each other. Thus they marched forth across the land.

When it was Pain's turn to gasp for air, Sorrow would stop walking and let the both of them catch breath. It was always a fine time to rest and pause, and look at their plentiful achievements. After some respite, they'd grin in agreement and pick up again.

These two ancient whores were immortal, and so the sisters

really cared nothing, not just for humanity but even for one another, since they both knew that neither one could ever die, but as familial obligation maintains, they did support one another. And despite their dreadful names, even Pain would sometimes feel pain, and even Sorrow would sometimes feel sorrow. So they would embrace each other during those times, change diapers, adjust walkers, switch gears on wheelchairs, drop in some drops of machine grease to make sure they could carry on.

Carry on they did, and when Pain was wheezing, and brittle sputum would form on her parched lips, Sorrow would squint to try and look at her many accomplishments, but the irony of it all was that she could not see her handiwork, for she was almost blind. And once her sister was done heaving, Sorrow would pick her up by her skeletal wrist, hold her up by the waist lest she shatter another bone, and tell her, "Let's keep going," and they would march on.

The sun would set slowly over the silhouettes of the two old hags whose destiny was to roam the earth and to visit as many humans as they had the strength, and shower them with gifts of misery.

Sorrow and Pain had another sister, a sister who they grew up with, but to whom they no longer spoke. Her name was Sadness. Sorrow and Sadness were closest, but they were completely different. Born of the same cloak, younger yet wiser for her age, she was no longer a sister to them. She was shunned, for she was the kindest one and the one with the most functioning eyes. Sadness was impetuous and bold, so bold as to comfort men who dreamed of death. Death was the mother of all three sisters, and she abandoned all three of them in the desert. When Sorrow showed her bony toothless face to a grieving husband, Sadness would come and wrap her arms and legs around him and hold the man tight. Pain would come in next and dig her claws into poor gentle Sadness's pale flesh and bite her neck. And soon enough, Pain would tell her sisters,

"It's time to go…" Thus they would leave the mortal alone, and let their cousin Despair take over—three sisters and a multitude of cousins all birthed by Mother Death.

It was the Mother who covered all in her dark comforting wings eventually—the comfort that is guaranteed to everyone in due time.

Everywhere Yeshua wandered he saw misery, and behind every unhappiness it was Sorrow, dragging herself across the land and with a broom fanning up the sand that blinded men to their own cruelty that he witnessed most often. It was not a reaper. It was a fly whisk stirring up disease and hate.

"Why does Satan live in the desert?" Yeshua could not let go of the question.

There is a Reaper, whose name is Death,
  And, with his sickle keen,
He reaps the bearded grain at a breath,
  And the flowers that grow between…

FISHERS OF MEN

Thus Yeshua continued, sleeping under the stars, avoiding soldiers, rebels, and hungry beasts. Peasant women would give him bread and onions to eat. The days blurred. He followed the road, unsure where he was heading to, letting his feet lead the way. One day on his random travels he reached an elevation and saw blue on the horizon. He felt it meant promise and he proceeded toward the water. Soon enough, he met the blue. This was the Sea of Galilee and the seaside town he entered was called Capernaum.

His hopes for a peaceful coastal village where he could beg for some scraps—perhaps some bits of fried fish that no one wanted, were immediately dashed. He entered just as half of the town was weeping for the "Prophet" Theudas who had many recruits from Capernaum. Yeshua's arrival coincided with the caravan of corpses of Theudas' victims' for their families to bury. They had dignity in death. The ones captured alive were paraded around town in shackles before they were sent to their holding cells in the dungeons, waiting to be transported to the colosseums.

Yeshua did not fear the soldiers. He committed no crimes. Just another hungry beggar to them. There were no laws against truancy. The cops eyed him suspiciously as he walked past them, trying to look as if he was solely attending to his own business, which he was, but his business was being engaged in observing and trying to fit the pieces together—how does one make sense of this earth? *"Apart from the fact that we do not even know if we are dreaming or not, let's take that on faith, but what about the now? Why do we behave with such cruelty, why do we seek out pain, why do we make it worse for the whole lot and the whole anthill? And what is so tempting about power?"* he wondered.

What was he going to do in this town? It was too dreary with the prisoners and corpses. Suddenly, as he walked through a narrow street, he saw someone dart past him, obviously avoiding the police. It was a woman. Though he did not see her face as she ducked into an even tighter passageway, perhaps it was the movement or just her form that told him he must know her, somehow. But who? He decided to follow. In between scurrying figures and darting glances, he followed her trail. And in a dead end alley, right behind her, he stopped, to make sure he did not seem like a stalker or rapist. The woman, her back against the wall, blurted out, "What do you want?!"

Yeshua quickly saw that it was foolish to follow her, what with the police everywhere. She could scream and if she screamed he would join the others to be shipped off as fodder for the "games."

"What do you *want?!*" she raised her voice enough to make herself sound firm but not loud enough to attract other listeners.

Yeshua said nothing, thinking of how to respond or what to say, and the woman now actually yelled out, despite the potential repercussions. "What do you want?!"

He recognized her immediately as the woman from the pitiful herd, from Theudas' procession, pushing her way through to get a drink of dirty water.

Before Yeshua was able to utter anything in his defense, the woman quickly produced a dagger and menacingly made her point known. "Stay away!" (If only his mother had the same option, a knife in self-defense.) Yeshua knew she wouldn't harm him, and that she was protecting herself, but he stepped back cautiously. The face was unmistakable. She was the one, the one he saw with that lunatic Theudas. Why was she in Capernaum? Was she hiding out? Perhaps she had somehow managed to escape after being herded into town with the rest of the believers.

"Don't come near me! Just stop right there!"

As a woman, she held the dagger like a butter knife. Race of Cain, race of Abel. He enjoyed having nothing to fear.

"Put the knife away. You won't dare do anything. The town is riddled with police. You will be caught and arrested at once and you know it."

"What do you want?"

"What happened?"

Silence and confusion.

"What do you mean what happened?" She suddenly turned sheepish.

"With you and Theudas and all his followers. I know who you are. That is, I don't know who you are, but I saw you, just a few days ago, drinking from the stream like a beast, begging for permission from your so-called leader just so you could have a sip of water. I saw you."

"And I saw you. We looked at one another. I remember. What do you want?"

"Tell me what happened!"

"They stopped us before we got to the river."

"And your leader?"

That was when her body crumbled. The weapon fell out of her hand and she broke down into stifled paroxysms. Yeshua stepped forward, kicked the dagger away, and held her head as she convulsed in sobs rapidly escalating in volume.

"Quiet, quiet…. You don't want them to hear you!"

"Oh my lord, my lord!"

"I said be quiet! Now come on. We have to go!"

He grabbed her by her tiny wrist, picked her up, and walked her down the street as she wept, but then came the sound of sandals, the sounds of stabbings. The Roman police continued to search for and weed out the last of the followers of Theudas and Yeshua dragged Maryam as they ran down the alleys.

"Let me go!" she would periodically protest but Yeshua kept dragging her, telling her to be quiet. The streets began to empty. All the locals scurried as fast as they could into anything that had a wall, be it their own house, a tavern, or even a stable. Yeshua found a tavern rather quickly. Still dragging Maryam by her arm, leaving blue bruises, despite her cries of "Let me go! Where are you taking me?" He managed to shove her inside a Greek tavern, away from the marauders.

Then he realized that he had no money, not a coin.

"Do you have anything?" Under other circumstances he would have been embarrassed but now was not the time for propriety. "Well, do you?"

She began to grasp that Yeshua was not out to hurt her but the contrary. "How much do you need?" she asked hesitantly.

"Talk to the man! We need bread, wine, and a place to sleep."

It turned out that Maryam had deep pockets. Hidden within her rags, there was a purseful of shekels she had managed to cache for emergencies even during her time spent with the cult. She had more than enough to pay and, hoping to secure safety, gave the proprietor more than he asked for the meal and the lodging. The proprietor gladly let Yeshua and Maryam stay overnight. It appeared he was not religious or political. Taking the hospitality trade quite earnestly, he showed Yeshua and Maryam his mangled hands. "This is what the Romans did to me, back in the days… I was too late with a dish, and a soldier lopped off two of my fingers! That's why they call me Three Fingers Yannis! But it is all good now. Come now, you are good people, a nice married couple, you can sleep upstairs. I will give you a special price. Shalom Alekem, as your people say. Come this way…"

They went upstairs.

"You have not even told me your name," she said when they were alone in the room.

"Nor you."

"My name is Yeshua. I was born in Nazareth."

"What are you doing here?"

"Walking. Stumbling. What about you? I know that you were with that Theudas character, but who are you?"

"Who am I?"

"At least tell me your name to start. I told you mine."

"My name is Maryam. I'm from Magdala."

"Well then, I suppose it is right to say that I am pleased to meet you, Maryam from Magdala."

"I did recognize you," she said as she lowered her eyes. "I was not lying. I do remember you peering out from the bushes, as we lay down to rest and drink."

"And don't you realize?"

"Realize what?"

"That you followed a fool!"

"I don't know."

"Why did you follow that fool, Maryam from Magdala?"

"I don't know. Leave all of that be. I believed in him. We had a community. He promised. He promised that…"

"He promised you paradise as long as you would bow to him. And so you, like all the others, ran hoping for an embrace but ended up licking heels instead! What was it, your parents?"

She turned confessional. "Actually, yes. They said I disobeyed the laws. They kicked me out onto the street!"

"And so you go around and latch onto any damn idiot who calls himself a prophet. With all the things in the world, with the whole world on fire, and you… damn… fools!"

"Don't preach to me! You are no prophet or sage!" she yelled.

"To hell with your prophets! These are no prophets! These are charlatans and madmen and you follow them into the abyss and when you're drowning you gasp for air and pray to your God of Israel. You people worship demons, just like the Sicarii!"

"He was not a Sicari. He was... I don't know what he was. But he was killed and that's the end and not just for him but for us as well. He was not the Messiah, no, but don't speak to me about him like that!"

"There is no Messiah!" Yeshua seethed. "I am sick of hearing that word! Don't you think that when the Messiah comes, if he comes, he would be quite a bit better than a pretender who led a wasteful life and suffered a sordid death and did nothing for the world? Or worse, a murderous scum? I spent a night with the Sicarii once!"

"My God, what did they do to you? Did they harm you?'

"My God? Yes, there is something you should take notice of and reflect on. Who is your god? The one who lets the horrors pass and lets them continue? That god? *Your* god?"

"Stop it!" She bit her lip. Although in her heart, she started to see that Yeshua was at least partly right, she couldn't bear to hear it or be talked to in such a way but Yeshua went on.

"Yes, the god who turns a blind eye to the killing, the one who destroys families, the one who beats them into bloody pulp, who lets women who sought love be banished or punished ignominiously, the one who allows and encourages for their brains to be bashed in by rocks wielded by rapists! The godling so insecure in his hierarchy among the planets, who always needs to be reaffirmed, the one who always cries out 'Worship me! Worship me!' That petty godling is the one you speak of? The one who looks upon the savagery and looks upon his creation, lousy with hate and rape and looks upon it and says 'This is my creation and it is good?' That demon? Is that the one you are referring to?"

"They did something to you!"

"They did nothing to me. I have been traveling and I have seen with my own eyes what these ideas about 'God' lead to."

"You are right, Yeshua." She was defeated. "We have all been deceived. All deceived. We are indeed all fools for trusting in men when we need God to guide us."

"You did not understand what I said!" Yeshua was irritated with her but relished the captive audience. "So then, tell me, woman! Who is god? Your god makes no sense to me! God? Who is god? These animals, vicious and vexed, they lash out and scream strange prayers to a blind sadistic idiot up in the sky whose main credit goes towards inventing death!"

"He is the Creator, we have no one else."

"Are we not supposed to follow at least two laws? The first to be decent and the second one, to love?"

"Come here…" Maryam embraced him. "Shush… Let's lie together…"

And at that moment, at the height of his first sermon, with her touch he crumbled. Everything changed and God revealed himself through ecstasy. Yeshua felt as if he found God when he tasted her sweat and the hair between her legs. He did not remember his dreams because he hardly slept—it was all a dream to him, a dream come true, the dream of intimacy and love.

When it was over, he looked at Maryam as she slept and touched her gently and inhaled the smell of her flesh, her being. He could not believe that she lay next to him. He drifted off in bliss, touching her white skin, inhaling her odors, marveling at the gentle curving anatomy as it went from her shoulders to her hips, the curve of her waist, silently laughing in admiration at the galaxy of freckles on her back. He fell asleep holding her as tight as he could without waking her up.

That night and that morning was how it came to be that Maryam became Yeshua's wife. There was no ceremony, no prayer, no blessing and no priest. It was the union of two humans as it always has been. The window had no shutters or curtains. Maryam awoke from the bright sun and dressed while Yeshua still slept, exhausted from his journey. She let him sleep a bit longer until it was time to go.

"Wake up, Yeshua. We have to leave."

At first touch, he was afraid to be awakened back into harsh reality; the images behind his eyelids in this half-waking state were flickering as miniature, sweet, often funny episodes. He grumbled but dragged himself out of the bed and lethargically put on his clothes.

"Yeshua… I have to leave Capernaum. And I want you to come with me. But where will we go?"

Reality returned and waking life was upon him again.

"I don't know. I left my home to see the world and all I have seen so far has been disgusting. We should try to find work on a Roman farm. There are more and more settlers moving into this land. I don't want to stay in a town and I've had enough of begging."

"A farm?" She was surprised and piqued but kept the rest of her thoughts to herself.

They exited onto the yellow morning, the town just starting to burn off the dew and mist. The glorious morning, the blue moisture of haze pushing in from the sea, it was as if life had just opened the skies for him and he hoped that Maryam felt at least slightly the same way. There was no way for him to know what she was thinking but he had a stirring sensation that these heartstrings aflutter were a vague premonition that somehow they would have a unique and dazzling future together. His heart bounced inside from the excitement that his life has forever changed now that he had been intimate with a woman for the first time. They moved slowly and in silence. Near the town's edge, they passed the fishermen's quarter and the adjacent market where the merchants were setting up their stalls.

Maryam clutched his hand tighter, which further increased his confidence and raised his excitement over this, his first romance.

"My stomach is growling. Can we get something to eat? I'm so hungry!" she pleaded gently.

The new couple approached a vendor and began to pick out some apples when suddenly, a squall of tears was heard coming from the direction of the shore. Maryam looked at Yeshua, surprised and frightened, but before she was able to say anything, he spoke to her and to no one in a voice resigned.

"I can tell what it is. Again, more horror…"

She quickly gave the fruit vendor a coin and tried to hurry to the epicenter of the tragedy.

"Come on, I want to see what happened!"

He tried to grab her dress to stop her from going but she was too quick and he had no choice but to follow along. He didn't dare risk losing her.

At first glance, on the shore lay what looked like a merman but on a closer look it became apparent that the scales of his fish tail were in fact the knots of a net. The hysterics came from two men who would alternate between holding each other for comfort and literally beating themselves to numb the pain of their loss.

A man standing next to Maryam spoke without turning his eyes to her, still fixated on the scene, as if he knew in advance what she was about to ask.

"One of their brothers. He kept the stall open on the Sabbath to sell fish to Romans. Looks like someone didn't like that too much. See what they carved into his forehead? 'Traitor.' And they weighed him down right where the other two usually cast their nets. They knew they'd fish him out. Sicarii maybe. Who knows."

"My God!" Maryam recently survived the massacre of her fellow followers of Theudas but she was still a relative stranger to violence. Before she could add anything, another observer joined in.

"He *did* disobey the Sabbath laws and for that he was justly punished! The Lord warns that for disobedience he will kindle the fires in the gates of Jerusalem that will consume the city! He was worse than a heathen, this man! An ape and a pig he was for working on the Sabbath!"

"They're Greeks!" protested the first man.

"Then they should go back to Greece! Heathens! We don't want them here! They're heathens just like the Roman scum!"

Yeshua knew that it would be wiser to avoid conflict, especially in light of the tension in town but at that point he could no longer contain himself, the blood boiled and threatened to spill out. And what came out was nothing more nor less than disgust.

"Apes and pigs?!" His voice cracked as he tried to control his rage and disgust.

"That's what they are! Like all heathens with their golden calves!"

"What are you, man? A murderer yourself?"

"How dare you! I'm a priest!"

"Some fucking priest!" Yeshua spit.

With that said, suddenly the attention of the crowd turned to Yeshua and the Pharisee and the people diverted their eyes and ears to them and away from the drowned victims. Even the brothers were startled out of their grief, and as the confrontation escalated, the crowd began to move towards the new focus of interest.

"Does the commandment not say 'you shall not kill'?"

"It also says obey the Sabbath! And for this he was punished. Apes and pigs. Apes and pigs, indeed!"

"Punished? Murdered for selling fish?!"

"On a Holy Day, yes. For there is only one God and his laws are..."

"Fuck your laws!" and turning to the crowd he erupted. "And you! You people! Where is your outrage?"

Maryam tried to pull him closer, frightened that the police would come to arrest any and all for disturbing the peace.

"Yeshua, calm down! Calm!"

He pulled himself away from her, barking. "I will *not* calm down!" And grabbing her by the shoulders, hurting her, his voice rising and cracking "I will not calm down! There comes a point in a man's life when he has to say 'enough!' When he has to stand up and speak the truth! I cannot hold silent any longer!"

Yeshua climbed atop an overturned fish barrel and began to shout. Where did the courage and the audacity come from? Even if asked now, were he alive, he would not be able to answer. This was it. Especially after last night's entry into manhood, there was no turning back, for someone had done a grave wrong and he himself was not quite sure which wrong that was: their sins, their cynicism, their sanctimony or perhaps even the rude awakening from the peaceful inner bliss he felt in the morning after the nuptial night. And his anger trumped self-preservation.

"You! You people! Come! Come closer! Did any of you hear what this bastard said? Did you hear it?"

Among the crowd came various grumblings and the din of confusion.

"Well, did you?"

Maryam tried to grab him but instead of yelling only implored "Yeshua, please!" which he ignored and kept shouting.

"Do you believe in idiocy? Do you believe a man can forfeit his life for selling fish?"

"On the wrong day..." someone mumbled to which Yeshua railed back, "I don't care what goddamn day it was. What harm did he bring? Well? What was the harm? He was trying to feed himself and his family. And when will you stop blaming the Romans and take

some blame yourself for the blood that is spilled in this land each day. Look at that bearded know-it-all!" he pointed at the Pharisee who in response only shook his head in self-satisfied disdain as Yeshua continued to rail.

"You think that sorry excuse for a man, nose in the books, who lacks any compassion, has the right to decide what God prescribed?!"

The Pharisee darted back and pointed his claw at Yeshua. "Heretic! He's a heretic as well! That's why he is defending these swine!"

The crowd swelled and it began to look as if violence was imminent but Yeshua's voice, loud and passionate, was enough to quell the surge when he continued.

"Who? Who among you will finally say that it's enough? That it's enough for us to keep on killing ourselves? That we need to be decent?"

"What is he doing?" came a voice from the crowd, anchored by shushes.

"What am I doing? What are you doing, you hypocrites! You damn blind hypocrites! Standing around like this, watching the spectacle, debating the Sabbath laws! Smug, all smug. Smug because you think you're safe, but it will be your hide that gets skinned next! Where is the comfort you give to these men who have lost their brother? Where is the outrage? I hear a deafening silence interrupted only by the words of fools and deceivers!"

The Pharisee chuckled. "Deceivers? Who are the deceivers?"

"You are! All of you! All of you who have come to gloat over the sufferings of men! All of you who came here to mock their sorrow and grief or even to enjoy a spectacle the way the Romans cheer when they execute men and beasts alike! They killed a man for selling fish. Open your bloody eyes!"

The Pharisee was unrelenting. "It was on the Sabbath!" and he even stifled a chuckle in his self-importance which was right when Yeshua took it to the next level, knowing full well he was provoking but at this point, he could not be stopped.

"To hell with your Sabbath!"

The crowd, previously enthralled, began to stir.

"You heard me! To hell with the Sabbath and to hell with the lot of you! You snakes! God gave you light but you prefer to slither in the darkness and choose to spew venom instead! And those who prefer the sky and sun, they are the ones you wish to blind!"

"It's against the laws!" The priests shouted and their adherents hummed in accord.

"What laws? Tell me! Tell me what laws?"

"What laws!" One of the priests screamed while feigning laughter. "He doesn't even know the scriptures and he talks as if he is the authority, not us. Insolence! The laws of Moses, you dolt!

"Tell me, which laws?" Yeshua had now assumed the full capacity of a prosecutor.

"There he goes again." The Pharisee smiled sanctimoniously. "How about Devarim, the fifth book? Greeks you say? Idolaters? It says in the book: 'You will smite the inhabitants of that city with the edge of the sword, destroying it utterly and everything that is in it!' That is what these righteous men tried to do! And as for you! It also says that if there arises among you a prophet, or a dreamer of dreams, and gives you a sign or a wonder then, that prophet or that dreamer of dreams shall be put to death! Because he has spoken to turn you away from the Lord our God, who brought you out of the land of Egypt and redeemed us out of the house of bondage, to thrust you out of the way which the Lord God commanded us to walk in. So you shall put this evil away from your midst! You are tempting fate, dreamer! Playing with fire!"

"I feel better not knowing the scriptures the way you know them!" Yeshua retorted. "For I do not twist these words in order to commit cruelty. And you are all still in bondage. All of you!"

More commotion began but Yeshua continued.

"Disgraceful! You so-called teachers of the law, you Pharisees, you hypocrites! You have neglected the main thing in your laws of justice: mercy and compassion! Your own kind kills you mercilessly and you condemn this man for disobeying the Sabbath? You strain your water so your lips won't touch a gnat, but then you turn around and swallow an entire camel! Don't you feel a little sick by now? With that camel rotting inside your intestines? Well let me tell you, that camel is your vengeful god, and his attendants are the Sicarii, whose diseased meat you chew and swallow and then ask for seconds. You vain, self-righteous bastards!"

"What do we twist? It is all in there!" The priest's laugh now turned menacing. "You will perish among the heathens! Faster than you know!"

Maryam grabbed Yeshua by his robe and tried to pull him away.

"Yeshua! Stop it now! We need to go. Come on, let these poor people be. Look at them! Look at their faces! They don't understand a word you're saying! We have to run before the police arrive."

"I can be quiet no longer!"

"Yeshua, we will get lynched, please, I beg you!"

Holding on to his leg and pulling on his pants made Yeshua lose his balance and he wobbled and slipped off the barrel landing on top of her on the ground. Maryam did not care that he bloodied her during his fall. They were both relatively unhurt but a few seconds after the initial blow of their heads hitting the cobblestones, Yeshua began to twitch and moan and froth appeared on his mouth and lips. Maryam became frightened and moved away just as one of the bereaved brothers rushed up, knelt by Yeshua, and held his head so that he would not injure himself as he began to jerk. As the crowd became both terrified and bloodthirsty, the Pharisee screamed. "He is possessed! That man is possessed and that is why he blasphemes!

There are demons inside of him! Beat him! Beat him and tie him up!"

When the crowd stirred further, the mob fangs protruding, was when the other brother ran up and brandished a large knife used for gutting fish. He circled around Yeshua and, flashing the knife, kept the crowd at bay.

"Just try it, scum! You step away! Don't you dare! Don't you dare move an inch closer! The Romans will protect a Greek much faster than they would protect you! I can stab you right now, and claim self-defense! You want to be one of these 'martyrs' who you adore so much? Then back away!"

The crowd moved back. The first brother, the one who kneeled next to Yeshua motioned for Maryam to come closer.

"Don't be afraid. He is all right. Come."

She knelt.

"Just hold him."

Yeshua's shaking slowed. She held his head, wept and embraced him. Soon the seizure passed and they held Yeshua up and moved away from the shocked and confused townspeople. The brother turned to Maryam.

"In Greek it's called 'epilepsies,' some say it happens when the gods are talking to you."

Maryam smiled bitterly.

"Here they say it's when you are possessed by demons."

Yeshua began to revive and asked "Did they beat me? I felt a thunderstorm come on… and the most serene peace…"

Struggling to get up, he spun around and said "We have to go, now. You are right. They think I'm possessed and want to lynch us." Turning to the brothers he could only say, "I am sorry for your loss."

Maryam held him up and they started to walk away but the fishermen brothers hurried after the pair and asked them to wait.

"Stranger! Before you go, tell us your name! I am Petras and Andreas is my brother. Yes, we are Greeks but we were born here and our parents were born here and all our lives we have listened to people preaching hate. We paid no attention to it, we kept to our own, we fished… Until today we would have stayed here until we died. All changed when we heard you speak. We had never seen courage like that before. Isn't that true, Andreas?"

Andreas nodded and Maryam smiled, turned to Yeshua and said. "They are right." And quickly added, "Where did you learn to speak like that?"

"I don't know. It just came out." And he smiled as well and turned to the brothers.

"My name is Yeshua. I am not a preacher. What happened just happened. I am no priest. I wander across the land and see the saddest things. Sometimes I say something about it and then I collapse."

"Yeshua!" Petras protested. "You don't do yourself justice! Those people there, the way you spoke, they listened, truly listened! Many may have disagreed but yet they followed each word. We have never heard such a thing in our lives! Where are you going now, Yeshua?"

Maryam smiled and admired her new lover. "You have a gift, a gift for speaking. You know what you are saying and you believe in it!"

Yeshua surveyed the crowd of admirers and took Maryam by the hand. "Let's go."

But where will you go, Yeshua? Where will you go? Quo Vadis?

"We will find work on a vineyard..." Maryam kept thinking of Yeshua's simple ambition, but she was so impressed with his oratory that she simply could not let go of the feeling that he should preach. After gaining experience in the art of the cult during her time with Theudas, Yeshua came as a natural replacement and so she whispered to him, "Come on, Yeshua. The brothers, they know

what is right, what is real, and *you* are real. I have never seen or heard anything like this, the way you spoke and stood up for what you believe is right that way, the way you did!"

As they walked away, down the dusty path, and just as they had left Capernaeum was when the Doppler came with the faint sound of Greek. They turned around sharply and saw Petras and Andreas, staring sheepishly. After a few seconds, once they caught their breath, Petras spoke.

"Yeshua, we want to come with you. We don't know where you are going but we need to leave Capernaeum. We may be next after they killed our brother Fotis. And it is not just that, we cannot live here anymore. This is no longer our home. They will hate us even more now. You seem a wise man. You spoke wisely and you are a great speaker. You should speak to the people, to all the people the way you did today. And we want to learn from you, and to help you and receive your help. We know nothing of your faith, but we have nothing left here."

Maryam was intrigued but frightened of the responsibility. "What about your boat, your nets?" and immediately regretted asking the question. She was only being practical, a dart of an idea but Andreas responded quickly.

"We rent them. We own nothing."

"Then come with us if you wish." Yeshua said. "Though we know not where we go, I cannot refuse you to come with us."

"We have to leave here, Yeshua. We will be murdered if we don't leave. Let us come with you!"

"Then, as I said, come."

"May we bury our brother first, Yeshua?"

Yeshua paused and thought for a few minutes before speaking, before proceeding, and then answered half-compassionately, half-clinically, and plainly.

"Your brother is dead, Petras and Andreas. And so are the souls of this town. Let the dead bury the dead. If you wish to come with us, then come with us now."

Stunned, Petras voiced one sentence even though he was committed to this trek. "Just let us get our clothes and money. Go on, we'll catch up!" Thus Maryam and Yeshua walked hand in hand down the dusty road for half of an hour only to be joined by a couple of ragtag Greek brothers running behind to join them in earnest. It almost felt as even their shoes smiled and laughed, and that in the middle of torment and misery, there was a bright chorus supplying a joyous soundtrack, celebrating their audacity.

THE PROBLEMS WITH ARCHITECTURE

Looking over the plans, Pilate found the entire structure grotesque. Everything was wrong with it. What made it all the more maddening was the absurdly slow progress on the aqueduct's completion. He was not skilled or qualified in geometry and math and was always more than eager to be humble and admit to it, asking for further elaboration, but this affair disgusted him. A stone Roman prick pushing mercilessly through sweaty Jewish thighs. The demolition of whole city neighborhoods. The displacement of residents. The ire of the displaced. He despised that city but he was keen on keeping the peace, and it was his duty. Apart from aesthetics and diplomacy, he loathed that he was under pressure to have the damn thing completed. It all jumbled together in his hung over brain and every little part of the equation was like a jigsaw puzzle made out of mosquitoes.

Professional, ministerial, he walked alongside Junius, his talentless lackey, observing the construction. It bored him to tears. And that drone, that droning voice of Junius…

"And with all due respect, sir, we really will have no idea if the Emperor will even come to Judea to see the aqueduct completed, but…"

Pilate was fed up. He wanted it out of the way but he was assigned this task and had to follow duty.

"It doesn't matter. It needs to be completed before the Emperor's birthday as we planned."

"We need more manpower, Governor. Without hired workers and only the slaves it will be months or years before we reach the city walls."

"And with hired help?"

"Then we can finish up construction much sooner. As it is right now, we are already behind in payment for the stone."

"What a dreadful bore..." thought Pilate and carried on without listening...

And with the reveries began a journey into the architecture of the cerebrum and the passage of time yet again.

Looking back on it now, Pilate wondered whether the Emperor too, had omnipresent thoughts like his own about the brevity of life. Thoughts that were driving Pilate mad with frustration—the feeling that something which happened a week ago was now buried deep in memory's cellar whereas something that occurred twenty years ago felt closer. The way the fortune tellers say they can tell your fate from the lines in your palm—the future is there, you open your hand and it's all there right in front of you, each microscopic fold in skin a future memory. A web, a spider's house of dreams. Many of them sweet and just as many bitter.

Pilate recalled that it really was not that long ago (What was long? Ten minutes or twenty years? It did not matter to him, and that was part of the problem), that when he was on guard duty, before being sent to Germania, his mother clandestinely brought him some food. He was malnourished from stress and meager rations. The guards were fed the bare minimum and Pilate never bartered for an extra plate. So desperate was he to succeed that he would neglect his health at times, be it through starving or staying up later for sentry duty while his legs were about to give out.

"Leave me alone!" he would shout inside and grind his teeth but never say out loud, when he would see his mother, veiled and cat-footed, walking at her peril through dark Roman alleys. She would see her son, come up quickly and drop off a kerchief tied

in a knot to make sure he ate. A boiled egg, an apple, a piece of bread, maybe a chicken leg… Pilate would yell at her at if she was a ruffian. "Leave! Leave now!" Partly from fear of embarrassment were he caught being a "mama's boy", partly to display valor and pride in his duties he would shoo her away. And as his mother scurried back, he would stifle tears and tear into the chicken. His stomach growled and practically screamed, and halfway into the meal he wept in shame for barking at her. He was being trained to be a guard dog and it wasn't in his nature.

When Pilate was appointed to Germania a few years later, he left his mother on the brink of lunacy. Whatever tethers had held her wits about her, the ones that were frayed and which frayed further when her husband was sent to Germania and was never heard from again, now almost disintegrated when she learned that her son too was to be sent to that same frightening land.

She stopped leaving her house and, attended by slaves, eventually lost the will to even leave her sofa. Pilate could not understand. He missed his father, who he did not really know, but his mother's affliction and descent into self-degradation bothered him and it became progressively worse. She became a millstone around his neck, for she was still alive, living in Rome, though she lived in a world entirely of her own. A dark and bizarre world, she became the queen of a tiny, black planet. Or better yet, an asteroid, dashing through space with blinders on, the ones they put on horses and mules, and she, laughing and rejoicing in misery and decrepitude, blissfully awaiting oblivion. She managed to live in this condition for years.

This pedestrian horror would not have, in itself, bothered Pilate all that much apart from the guilt. People get old, turn senile, or cultivate their eccentricities. If one could now call his mother's departure from the world an "eccentricity", the term would have done nothing to help his pain. It was the guilt that ravaged him.

The thing that stabbed him in the heart most was remembering eating the chicken leg she had brought him, and finally biting into the apple and realizing just how hungry he really was, and remembering how this woman who now lay delirious reigning over that dark little planet, was at one point sane and kind. And the memory felt just like yesterday. She gave him a clandestine dinner just yesterday… Just yesterday….

"Just yesterday…." he kept repeating. *"What an enchantress 'time' is. And how truly sad it all is."*

He recalled his conversation with the Emperor and how these flashbacks with his mother interrupted his thinking. He remembered the meal and the lump in his throat from recollections of both his mother's kindness (stuck like a chicken bone in his throat, stomach eating itself) and her fall into madness, these were the thoughts he could not let go of and never did, even when professionalism was the order of the day, even when talking to the Emperor. He compartmentalized these feelings and the guilt but they never left, even when alone and thinking of something else entirely. There was a chest of drawers in his brain overflowing with memories of his mother, one which he always tried to keep under lock and key.

There were times when Pilate wished for nothing more than to become a fetus again. As that was naturally an impossibility, then at least to crawl into a fetal position in plain reality, desperately clutch a pillow and go to sleep, was possible.

There was another episode that still haunted him from his stay in Germania. His commanding officer had ordered a raid on a town and demanded it be razed to the ground. It was something that as this "higher-up" said *needed to be done.*

Inspecting the handiwork his legion left behind, he walked through the destruction in horror. Amidst the devastation he found an infant in tatters, blinded in the attack, crawling and screaming with pants full of shit. The gut-wrenching guilt made it difficult for Pilate to breathe.

He searched around in a frenzy and quickly tried to improvise a toy for the child. He ripped a kerchief from one of the dead women and desperately stuffed it with dirt and sand, trying to shape it into a form of a child's toy, a primitive attempt at a doll shaped like a long eared rabbit. Hastily put together or not, the blind infant instinctively clutched at the pathetic shape. The warm and smooth cloth was something to hold, and it actually made the creature coo and stop its wails. Pilate, however, had to bite his fist in order not to bawl.

And then, presently, in another trick of time amid the fickle nature of memory, the sun blinded him out of his reminiscences and he dourly continued on with his business, nodding when necessary but mostly paying little attention. His presence was all that was required and if anything went in one ear and out the other, it was their problem, not his.

THE TEACHINGS OF YESHUA

Yeshua walked among the people. He would speak and sometimes the people would listen. What did he say?

The villagers and his own followers would ask him questions and he would answer, himself not knowing where the answers came from, not knowing whether what he said made sense. The seekers sought, but not within themselves. They sought meaning and they believed Yeshua knew a little truth which had always evaded them, and thus they followed him.

What did he know? And what did he preach? What did he tell these people who thirsted, other than tell them to be decent and to do no evil?

It was during his fits, or right before them, that he would see another world appear—an invisible world, a feeling of extreme calm and bliss, almost ecstasy. And he saw it in nature too. Just like Levi's horse in the sun shower he glimpsed that which he could not put into words, a transcendence. Like the flayed Chinaman Fou-Tchao-Li, tortured to death by the method known as "Lingchi" (that was yet to come), he would look up at the sky and around at nature and understand that God is unknown and unknowable but present in everything. Out of consciousness, out of body, and out of the world, a transfiguration out of the misery into an exaltation.

When he saw the blue and experienced the ecstasy, he saw God. The cynics, the scientists, the learned men of today would be keen on attributing Yeshua's experiences to neurons and brain chemistry, but speculative neurology aside, the point is, Yeshua did see other worlds, and saw that there was something beyond the present reality, something unknowable and unreachable but which he was able to feel somehow and it enraptured his entire being. These were not the "worlds" that today's college student and self-styled poet would speak of to the nearest pimply faced, knock kneed, drunk coed in the hopes of maybe getting laid. Yeshua felt something distinctly real. A haze of blue and white, a sheen of something so wonderful and so beyond the suffering of the world that it defied description. Much like Pilate's childhood song *"Vale Aeternum"*, Yeshua's blue was ethereal, longing yet present, especially on certain days when the haze was just right and the brain primed for the sensation. The blue of noon stood in direct opposition to the dusk and the curtain of the cypresses, the trees of death. How was he to express it in human language?

This feeling he started to call "the kingdom", and he would tell them that the kingdom resides in everything, that the spirit is present in all. Vague to the others, it was difficult to convey. "Seek it yourselves" he would tell them "and it will be revealed. The kingdom cannot be revealed through scriptures or prayers or discussions. It is revealed to those who seek it, to those who long for it with all their hearts!"

When the problem of good and evil were brought up, Yeshua would tell them, sadly. "You and I, we are all part of God. Like Him, we are eternal, and our spirit is part of Him. Whatever evil you do, God feels also." When asked why God allows evil to exist, he would answer that it is we who create evil, and since we are part of God, it brings him as much pain as it does to us. And when quizzed about the sorrow of the world, he would answer, "Happiness shows herself to men while wearing a crown of sadness. He who welcomes joy must also welcome sorrow. When we suffer, God too suffers!"

Inequality was another matter. This one was more difficult to explain because it was of the material world, the world that Yeshua could not and would not understand. He would tell them that the poor shall inherit the kingdom and get there first, and that the rich would have a very hard time doing so. Poverty affected them all greatly and when the stomach growled, all yearnings for the kingdom were unseated by the vision of a crust of bread.

Yeshua did not wish to lose them. He had formed a chosen family. He struggled to put into words his solitary experience, and it often spilled over into the very anger he preached against.

Even in self-doubt and longing he would speak and answer nonetheless. "It is love and love alone that I preach. Love never fails, today or tomorrow or years after. Truth will conquer. Love shall win the victory. Do you love your fellow men? Love them! What is the soul? It is part of God. Who is God? We are. We are the children of light and the children of God. Glory unto the kingdom, we will succeed. March on, God is our General!" he would tell them, and on they would march, scratching their heads over his obscurities but captivated nonetheless,while their leader stared at the brilliant ultramarine of the Levantine skies, seeing the heavens open and feeling infinite possibility, seeing the blue before it turns to brown as one gets older, and eventually fades away entirely, and then the curtain falls.

THE COW

Does the milk cow weep when she passes a veal calf's skin stretched out in the sun for tanning and wonder if it's her son? Or does she continue to chew cud in bovine disregard? In Judea it was the latter. Though their sons perished daily, crucified or disappeared, the people went on, lazily munching on scriptures, ruminating with even greater sloth.

There are no diminutives in Aramaic, but when Yeshua heard the sound of Greeks in their odd language making things small and sweet it sent pinpricks through his heart and made him weep for all of humanity. "A humble house, how we wish we could have a little *spitaki*…" And the house becomes a melancholic desire for something so basic as a dwelling of one's own which the housewife could care for and pretty up, and be proud of no matter how small or modest… Not a *spiti*, that was for rich people…

When the rare day came when a family could afford to eat a chicken, the *kotopoulo* became a darling *kotopoulaki*— endearing, a child's doll, love and respect for the dead bird destined for the gullet. And above all, the simple pleasure of food, a thanks to God.

What made him stifle tears thinking of the sound of ordinary things? He wondered about it himself. Was the diminutive a struggle against the cruelty of life, that one is born solely in order to wither and die? Was it a memory of childhood, when mother is still *manoula* before she becomes *metera*?

The words were those of people stuck in fear, feet planted firmly on the globe, terrified of the unknown that awaits everyone. The words spoke admiration for the little loves of temporal life that will inevitably be snatched away by a faceless man of marble, a puppet master whose cruelty one must find ways to deal with before they see his million faces and, in awe and trembling, shatter kneecaps, wash their faces in dirt and beg for forgiveness. How much more comforting is the *kotopoulaki*, a teddy bear in a hospital bed, a sucker candy… it also united humanity, or so Yeshua thought. Even the Emperor, if he spoke Greek would have called his mother *manoula*. *"All men bear the pain of living, and all deserve compassion,"* he decided.

"They all ask me what happens after you die." Yeshua would despair. *"How should I know? Have I been dead before? Even if I were, how would I know? If I had, how would I know how to describe it?"*

Breathing in the night wind of the desert, he looked up at the sky first and then down at the dust.

"Even if nothing happens, is that so bad? Go to sleep. No dreams, nothing. They want hope, though. Death is near but they clutch at a hand, clutch at this world that they know. The old mare sticks her tongue out for a final lick before her eyes are closed forever. They want a lifeline, they want angels. They want to still taste meat when sitting on a cloud. Didn't it say in one of the books 'all is vanity'? Ecclesiastes? I can't remember. Why do they want the same thing in the next world when they have it here now and should be enjoying it instead of worrying about what happens next. I can't blame them. Clutching at straws... And when you have a night of sleep without dreams, do you wake up dejected, as if you missed something? And when you sleep without dreams are you conscious that you miss them? Of course not. Even if there is indeed nothing afterwards, there is nothing to fear. But that is cruel. What is more cruel, then? What about the sadness on earth? If they choose sadness over nothing I

can't blame them either. Damn it all. No one can make sense of it." Thus he struggled.

"How I envy the tortoise!" he would say to himself. *"Kind beast whose home is always on his hump. Whose home will grow brittle as he grows brittle and withers but he, this kind, slimy beast has a shell on his back that is a stalwart nest and home, and as long as a hungry man or foolish child doesn't rip that home from his living flesh, he will always have that shell, always the security, always the ability to suckle on the nipple of God or his mother until whomever dies first."* And now Yeshua, for whom both the God that he was taught to worship and the woman who raised him were abandoned, he would think, *"My parents built a home for me. Now, for me, it is gone for I have abandoned it. And their house too was nothing in the end. All your life you work to build a home and then it's gone. And here I am a bastard son whose shell is missing and who still pines for the security and warmth of childhood."*

And it was at these times that Yeshua began to see that his house was not that of his mother's or his father's, but that of his true father, the God he sought.

Sometimes, while eating his meal, the food would disgust him. To think there he was stuffing his face when others picked through garbage or just simply starved seemed unbearable to him. The lump in his throat grew; he would sometimes spit out the contents of his mouth for he could barely chew as tears welled up. The act of spitting out precious food disgusted him further and made the case for further self-loathing.

How time passes, faster than in the blink of an eye...

Yeshua would often find himself having "Madeleine moments" but instead of going backward in time he would go forward and chills would run down his spine in fear—fear of the universe and he would even pine for a convulsion to experience that bliss before consciousness was lost.

It seemed to him it was just yesterday that he was sitting at dinner with his parents, gathered around the big oak table in the back, outside. He could remember gnawing on a goat chop, drinking wine, and feeling a unique calm as if he were at peace with everything... He could clearly remember the taste of the charred, gristly meat and the coolness of the wine they would purchase from a Roman settler. He recalled looking up at the sun and wondering about the Roman sun god, Sol Invictus... The taste of wine, wiping the sweat off his brow, the heat of the sun... His father was alive then... And then fear would grip his heart, as he raced to the future.

"Today will also seem like yesterday, years later, when I am old, and so my old age and death in turn seem like tomorrow." This made no sense to him, and he would ponder more about the nature of time and whether it exists at all. Maybe everything was occurring all at once, and if so, he was already dead. He tried his best to grasp it but it was not easy.

He looked up at the sun again and recalled the legend told to him when he was a child about Phaeton, the son of Sol Invictus, who bragged to his friends that his father was the sun-god, and who fell to a fiery death, and whose sisters mourned him so much that they were turned into poplar trees that wept golden amber.

"I am no son of a god," he thought. *"But who IS God? Who are you?"* He would look up at the sky and the dread of the unknown would continue to haunt him until nightfall. Gentle and mysterious night tenderly pushed his eyelids closed and oblivion would come and take him into another realm, which was just as unknown and fleeting as the daytime world.

One morning, Yeshua awoke with a sensation of tremendous pain as if he were an insect burning under a magnifying lens; and yet he was not experiencing any physical discomfort. It was as if he felt the pain of the world, the burden of mortality, the horror of decay, the loss of health and eventual loss of life—as if his guardian angel had taken him on a whirlwind tour of all the misery known to man in all its myriad varieties. The result was the unimaginable sensation of say, a cracked skull from a sledgehammer blow to the head. Yet the pain was not in his head, but in his heart, which beat in panic trying to forget what exists in the world. With the questioning and hopeful eyes of the followers upon him, there was no choice but to carry on, with the discreet charm of the paupers' empty stomachs and empty hearts which so yearned to be filled.

ALL THE PRETTY LITTLE CORPSES

Everyone dreams differently but every dream is interrupted the same way—by light breaking through the shutters of the worlds people inhabit when their eyes are closed. Yeshua dreamt of his father, though he was not his real father *(He is not your father, not your father...)* and a new follower, Mattityahu the taxman, dreamt of fantasies from the old scriptures, of Eliyahu ascending to the heavens in a golden chariot. The brothers both conjured images of catching a tremendous fish, one that could feed several families and which was purchased on the spot, yielding them plenty of silver. And Maryam dreamt she gave birth to a child who she nursed and held tight. *"He's right,"* she thought. *"We know nothing. One person dies, another one is born, replace, replace. We start from zero and stumble on, infinitely..."*

Every dream is interrupted as the baby exits the womb. What do we remember of our memories inside the warmth and comfort from which we are yanked? The travelers were pulled from reveries when they saw the lights, and the horror of the earth introduced itself again.

From afar, they looked like the same burning lights that Yeshua saw glowing from the cave during his encounter with Bar-Abbas and the rebels, but this time they were in a valley and it took them just a minute to realize that the village was on fire and the flames there were meant for death, not warmth. No one spoke as they walked toward the settlement. When they passed the necropolis and were within the town limits, Yeshua and the disciples stepped into a netherworld, a land of ghosts.

A young woman clutching her baby ran up to them, and pleading, begged, "Please, please save my son!" She quickly pushed the bundle into Maryam's arms and ran away in hysterics. Maryam opened the bundle of rags and saw an infant whose throat had been cut. The little boy, now no longer a little boy but a little corpse, was blue. The body was cold. Maryam gasped and immediately lost control of her hands, dropping the pretty little cadaver on the ground. She remained strong enough to wipe her tears and control her trembling. Yeshua held her hand firmly and they continued on the path. Andreas and Petras looked over at Yeshua in anticipation, waiting and hoping for their newfound preacher to say something but they sought guidance in vain as Yeshua said nothing and continued to walk silently, grasping Maryam's hand as she stifled tears. And then another apparition crossed their path.

Stumbling and mouthing inhuman sounds, the blind old man was reduced to animal emotion and despair.

"I want to talk to him." said Yeshua and motioned to his flock to stop.

The phantom-like figure had fallen and was creating bizarre geometric forms with his skeletal limbs as he groped around in the dirt in his newfound darkness.

Maryam shuddered. To her, there was nothing worse than blindness.

"You see?" Yeshua turned to the others. "The priests threaten us with hell but it's already here. We built it with our own hands."

"See? Can't see. I can't see anything, can't see anything..." the old man muttered as he tried to stand only to fall again.

Yeshua lifted the man up and sat him down on the gravel, restraining him from trying to walk again so that he would not crack his head.

"Thank you, thank you..." the man gasped for air.

"Sit. Don't move. Now tell me. What happened here?"

"Dead. All dead. Sicarii came at dusk…"

"Sicarii." Yeshua murmured. "Who but…"

The man went on, gasping but grateful for the chance to share his misery.

"They cut the throats of all my family. There were many. So many, I couldn't have counted them. They had knives, clubs… They asked me for money at first. I gave them everything and then, then they went for my wife. I tried to stop them and when they jumped on her I hit them with an axe. When I woke up I saw my family drowning in blood. Then they lit fires and our village burned."

Maryam stood weeping. The Greeks and Mattityahu also stifled tears but surprise came when Yeshua opened his mouth and spoke.

"If you are blind, how did you see this? This horror you speak of?" he asked.

"I saw it. I was not blind before. And when I saw it, I wanted to dig out my eyes. Instead, I cried and cried and when I stopped crying, I was blind. Curse this world and curse the one who created it!" And the man shed what seemed like buckets of salty water from his empty sockets.

Yeshua motioned to Mattityahu, who kneeled quickly as if expecting a secret message but Yeshua held no hidden miracles.

"Find clean water and bring it here!"

The Taxman ran as if pursued by furies to fetch clean water. The villagers sat around crying or moaning, and Yeshua had no help when asking for the clean well, for it was well known that one of the Sicarii methods of striking fear into the population was poisoning the water supply by throwing in the rotting carcass of a dead donkey. The tactic worked. Entire villages would be wiped out while the liberators simply stood aside and listened to the news, spitting out grape seeds while their victims died of dysentery. The villagers relied on their stores of drinking water and did not dare risk drinking from springs.

Carcass or no carcass, Mattityahu found clean water and rushed back to Yeshua who was busy comforting the blind man.

"Here, Yeshua. Water!"

Yeshua grabbed the cup, and holding the man's skeletal fingers told him, "Now wash your face and your eyes."

"What for?" The blind man protested but Yeshua was persistent.

"Do it. Wash!"

Slowly, with trembling hands, the man began to wash while Yeshua held his head and guided him.

"Wash..." Yeshua kept saying. "Wash and you will see again. Sometimes it is easier not to see. I know this. But be strong, man. God gave you light and sight. Protect the sight, protect those two little globs of jelly. Use them. Use them so you can tell the others what you saw! So they can pass it along and keep it in memory, for that is all we have. Otherwise you're dust!" And when the man kept missing the mark, Yeshua would yell at him: "Wash, damn it!"

"Yeshua!" Mattityahu protested. "He is blind, be gentler!"

Yeshua raged back. "He can see! He just doesn't want to!" And turning back to the man, he now spoke more gently.

"You are not blind! You are in shock but you are not blind. I see that your eyes are not opaque. See me! See the world! Do not become blind like the others!"

The film was lifted from the man's eyes. *"All I saw were devils, devils around me crawling out of the wells, setting fires... jumping out in front and sticking out tongues. What do I see now? A young man bringing me water. Kindness still remains somewhere..."* It was then that things came into focus and the man thought he was in the presence of a sorcerer.

"How did you? How did you do that?"

"You were never blind!"

"I was, I tell you! And you have healed me!"

"I did not. I only wished for you to open your eyes and not be afraid of what you saw," said Yeshua. "God knows that there is no shortage of pain in this world. Why he keeps silent, I don't know. Perhaps he does see the truth but chooses to wait nonetheless. I wonder what he waits for? If it's for the Messiah, then-"

"Yeshua, you cured the man!" Andreas yelled out, interrupting. "What did you do?"

"I did nothing, Andreas. He was not blind. He simply didn't wish to see any more. If you had seen what he saw and were as weak as him, you too would have wished for your eyes to be closed forever, but God still wants him to see."

"Then why does God allow this, Yeshua?" Petras became inflamed.

"It isn't God, Petras." Yeshua responded with confidence. "It is us. WE allow this to happen. The people do."

They left the formerly blind man and continued to walk along like phantoms among phantoms, each wondering who is the subject of the dream and who the dreamer. The exit was not as tidy as they had hoped, for news of Yeshua's "cure" of the "blind" man spread like wildfire. Before the ragged group managed to make their way out of the village that still smoldered with fire and misery, a soldier ran up to Yeshua and pleaded, "Healer! Healer! They say you are a healer! Please! Please help us!"

Almost dragging Yeshua down into the dust, grabbing desperately onto the sleeve of his rags, the man was persistent until Yeshua stopped and bracing off the man's arms from his filthy clothes, turned to speak in anger with a power and authority he never realized he possessed until just recently but which he now fully embraced. He looked at the soldier, one whose duty was to protect the people of this ill-fated village and recalled that his own father was Roman. Would that man have shown such obsequious behavior, he wondered.

"How do you want me to help you?"

"My servant… He is dying, sir. Can you help? Is there any way you can help?"

Staring directly into the soldier's eyes, as the man groveled, Yeshua felt anger and his blood started to boil. Conflicting emotions ran through his veins—how he wished he had met his biological father conflicted with scenarios about how he would have confronted him.

"Would my father beg for forgiveness? Would he beg for help the same way that his man who is most likely nothing more than a scumbag soldier begs? Would he feign it or genuinely ask for assistance for his servant? What would my father do? Would he hold me and protect me? Would he care about me the way this man cares for his servant? Is a dog more important than a bastard like me? Why should I care about him and his plight? Am I only wondering this because I am part Roman? Is that why? When I can just tell him to go to hell?"

"You were supposed to have been here protecting these people! Where were you? Locked in your house?" he berated the soldier.

And then as quickly as the thoughts about the Roman sperm donor came, they left, and ran to memories of Yosif.

Yeshua's father's selfishness returned to the brain. *"He cared naught for me. It was all about him…He never spoke to me. Never told me the truth… Maybe he couldn't. Maybe he didn't know the truth. But how couldn't he? He knew! He knew! Such a weak man! But I understand… I must pity him. I must pity him. But I will not pity this fucking Roman!"*

The soldier continued to plead. "There were too many! There were too many for me and I had no backup! None! It was certain death for me! Healer! Please, help my servant! It was just said that you had performed a miracle! I am fine, but I do not want my man to die. I do love him! I treat him as family. Is there nothing you can do?"

Yeshua was cold. There were too many other demons tickling him and he turned to his followers and said what he could to keep it all going.

"Come, let us leave this place of misery and death. There is nothing we can do for these people." And the disciples started to walk away. He turned to the soldier and shouted back. "I am not a healer. Do no evil and have faith, soldier. It is all we have. Your servant will live…"

They carried on wandering, just like so many others, seeking meals with discreet charm, trying to find meaning in the world in between their searches for supper. Just when his followers thought they'd had enough, something would burst out of Yeshua's mouth that would make them stay and ponder.

But there were certain "others" who were quite deft and clever who had very different plans.

THE ENEMY OF MY ENEMY

"One who is afraid of death is surely a coward," Bar-Abbas mused while looking over the congregation as they gathered around him waiting for the next instructions. The brain and the eyes in the periscope of his spinal column slowly surveyed the believers and after giving them some time for the blood pressure to rise, he spoke.

"Tomorrow we will go to Bethany. The market is sure to be filled with people now, after the end of the holiday, and many will see us when we kill the Roman dog. Let us draw lots to see who will have the privilege of carrying out this noble deed and whose martyrdom will bring the children of Israel closer to removing the Great Satan—Rome—out of our land forever."

As one of the militants brought out the bundle of reeds, Bar-Abbas was surprised that no one volunteered first. *"No one wants to die for their land...cowards. All cowards..."*

It was a man named Yehuda who drew the short straw and when he did, he immediately tasted blood. Not the blood that Bar-Abbas had hoped he would thirst for but the blood that shot up into his nose from his own pockets of plasma when he realized that tomorrow would be his last day on earth. Still, he tried to restrain his fear despite the uncontrollable shaking. Bar-Abbas smiled.

"Congratulations, Yehuda. Well done. You will be a great martyr and your rewards in paradise will be incalculable. We shall all sleep now. Tomorrow we march at dawn."

The insurgents stood up and started to wander back toward

their tents. Yehuda slowly raised himself, resigned to his fate but Bar-Abbas interrupted his plans to think back upon his life—on this, his last night on earth.

"Not you, Yehuda. Come, we need to talk. And you too, Nahum. Both of you!"

Bar-Abbas nodded his head for Yehuda to sit next to him and Nahum, a strategist in the art of terror, picked up a stick and began to draw a map of the town in the sand while Bar-Abbas spoke.

"Here, after we pass the city gates, the road leads straight to the marketplace. We want to do it in the morning, for the morning rush as everyone will be hurrying to buy fresh meat. We'll show them fresh meat." He smiled. "Wouldn't it be fun to send a cart into the market filled with some Roman corpses and paint a sign on its side 'Free Fresh Meat'? Eh? What do you think, Nahum?"

Nahum smiled but as the tactician it wasn't his obligation to comment on the romanticism of brutality. He stuck to his instructions as he scribbled in the sand and illustrated to Yehuda precisely the spot where he would carry out his assignment and subsequently be martyred, that is, killed by the police. Nahum said nothing while Bar-Abbas, taking on the role of supreme commander, spoke.

"Here, you will pick the right moment and stab a Roman. Any fucking Roman. Stab him in his stinking gut! Get it?"

"I get it."

"Not many are chosen for this honor."

Bar-Abbas was confident in Yehuda despite noticing the trembling hands. Just to make sure, he repeated.

"Yehuda! Not many are chosen for this honor!"

Yehuda could no longer tell if any of his limbs were shaking. He felt like a paper puppet in the wind, and a puppet he was. Vacant. Bar-Abbas had to prod his cattle again.

"Yehuda?"

"I am honored," he stuttered. "I am honored to carry out this operation."

Bar-Abbas went up to the man and kissed him deeply.

"You will do a fine job. A fine job. Now it is time for us to sleep."

Yehuda walked over to the other end of the cave and tried to meditate on his life but his life was nothing to him. Now, like that dying mare still trying to reach for one final taste of a blade of green grass as Yeshua recently reflected, he kept his eyes open and wondered: *What was my life if it shall end tomorrow?*

Staring at the stars through the tent's mouth, he paid no heed to the pair of sandaled feet that stopped in front of him, nor did he move his eyes away from the night sky when his fellow Sicarii spit out: "What's the matter, Yehuda? Afraid to die or something?"

Yehuda didn't answer. He continued to lay in silence, looking up at the majestic indifference of the heavens above him.

In the morning, the heat was unbearable. Nothing but hot and yellow and yet even without a bullwhip—the whip was his lips—Bar-Abbas moved the herd forward, onward. Yehuda dragged his legs along as best as one could when chosen for execution by proxy, as glorious as that execution might be. Destined for the honor of a sacrificial lamb, he tried to keep pace while Bar-Abbas seethed. Yehuda was the one most uncomfortable with the heat and the trek, and when someone yelled out "Look, sir! There is a grove of fig trees just to the left! Can't we please stay and rest a bit and have something to eat?" was when Bar-Abbas finally stopped and let the others break.

Bar-Abbas went over to the tree, and with his machete tried to crack open one of the tiny fruits. The fig was dry. Such a big weapon for such a small fruit, but neither the blade nor the screams could make the fruit produce more juice or flesh. Bar-Abbas screamed at the sky and began to demolish the tree.

"Damn you! God damn you! If *you* can't feed us, the children of Israel, you whore, then you won't feed any other nation!" And Bar-Abbas butchered the tree in the same way he would instruct his followers to butcher unbelievers. It did nothing to the fauna. All he was able to do was leave scars in the trunk. The fig tree was used to the pain of living where it did, in the desert.

He ordered the others to set up camp and wait another night.

As the sun goes down and hastens to the place where it rises, men sleep and dream and each man dreams differently. In another corner of the land, Yeshua dreamt that he finally met his father, a strong, hardy blonde who lifted the boy up in his Aryan Roman arms and bounced him as he showed him around the German encampments, as if he were Il Duce showing his son-in-law, Ciano, progress on the construction of the Via Dei Fori Imperiali.

Only the dreamer of the day was devoid of dreams. And that dreamer awoke to the sounds that confirmed his beliefs—that venom works wonders.

"Bar-Abbas! Look! A miracle occurred!" One of his followers came running. "The tree which you cursed yesterday has now withered and bears fruit no longer!"

Bar-Abbas smiled.

The morning remained brutal. Just a short time into their march on Bethany, the heat became overpowering, nauseating, exhausting. It was the type of day when the dew evaporated immediately and one knew that the next dozen hours would be spent in stifling agony. Among the Sicarii who wearily stumbled toward Bethany, even those who had never seen the Mediterranean Sea and could not even imagine it, began to form startling and bizarre visions of an infinite body of water.

Yehuda dragged but carried on. It was his passion for his people, for their independence, his resentment of the "occupiers" that made him leave his family to join the Sicarii years back. It was only now that the reality truly hit him—that he would have to give up his life for his beliefs. Taking another's life was something he was used to, but his own hide was still important to him. He was not ready to die.

Bethany was a typically destitute town which was made particularly miserable recently due to the amount of police raids on its citizens. The Romans were aware that there was a network of safe houses for the Sicarii within her walls and they periodically tried to purge it of the problematic elements but to no avail. The result was blood on both sides.

Yehuda and the others hadn't ventured into a town in broad daylight in quite some time. When they wished to inflict misery on the residents, they did it under cover of night, hiding in corners among shadows. Though they entered town as a group, all knew that the minute they passed through the checkpoint they would need to disperse in different directions. With a nod and a wink, they were told where to find the houses of supporters. These households had blood on their hands only by proxy, and of this they absolved themselves, through their Kol Nidre.

Yehuda and Bar-Abbas were the couple who stayed together on their walk. Bar-Abbas, like Mother Death, gently leading Yehuda to his fate, arm in arm; Yehuda trembling in anticipation of having to close his eyes forever. He could not conceive of nothingness and placed his bets on paradise and a new Garden of Eden. Passing the beggars and wretches heaving with misery, his eyes bulged and he tried to focus on the reason he joined the murderers—to fight the injustice and inequality caused by the occupation, but now it was for his own life that he feared the most.

"Oh Lord, let me be a beggar, let me writhe on the ground and beg for a scrap, let me shit my pants from dysentery, let me lose limbs but don't take away my life… I will even live sightless if need be, but what happens to you there? There? What happens? I will denounce

him! I will run to the police! Please tell me, God, what can I do to stay alive?!"

Suddenly he was snapped out of his miserable reverie as Bar-Abbas noticed a particular wretch and decided to stop. A Greek woman, sitting in the dirt with a beggar's cup, stroking her daughter's head was begging in the most pitiful fashion. The child was sick, malnourished, and looked as if she was on the short list for the next world. Still the mother pleaded desperately. "Anything you can help, kind people..." in between verses of a maudlin song.

Bar-Abbas stopped and stared. A hint of a smile formed on his pencil lips.

The woman stopped singing and met his gaze, defiant at first, and then lowering her eyes, spoke in heavily accented Aramaic.

"Kind people, anything you can spare, kind people... Anything will help. My daughter, she is sick, starving! Just look at her!"

"You are Greek, I see?" said Bar-Abbas with the haughty insolence of someone who is confident in his utmost power.

"I am, sir," the woman replied in a soft voice, coy and almost *soliciting.*

Bar-Abbas looked over at her wheezing child.

"Your daughter doesn't look so good. This *is* your daughter, isn't it?"

"Yes, sir. Yes, kind sir."

Bar-Abbas smirked and then with a wide sweep of his arm began to lecture a woman holding a dying child.

"Well, if that is your child, look around you! These are my children! All of them!"

His arm swept across the whole town. "And my children are the children of Israel! Our land! This land is ours! Not yours!! And they are my children because it is I who is the King of the Jews! And therefore it is to take from children and throw to the dogs!"

The Greek woman prostrated herself at Bar-Abbas' feet and

whether pure or disingenuous she writhed and when he was within arm's reach, she grabbed onto his tunic and begged with desperation that started to grow deeper and darker.

"Please sir! May these wretches who cling together remind you of your good fortune! And sir, these dogs, us Greek dogs, will humbly take any crumbs from you, whatever falls from your table!"

She darted her eyes around to make certain that no one was watching and clutched his clothes as if to try and drag him down to hear her whisper. Bar-Abbas didn't budge. Looking up with only the whites of her eyes showing she made one last desperate attempt, again in a whisper:

"Sir! Her father was a Jew, sir! Please…"

Bar-Abbas tossed a few coins onto the ground and holding Yehuda under his arm, walked away as the woman scrambled in the dust for the few Denaria he threw her.

She pounced on the coins as if they were meat and bread.

Yeshua and the sacrificial lamb carried on and at the entrance to market square they stopped. Bar-Abbas grabbed Yehuda's hand and drew him closer.

"Friend, do what you are here to do!"

He kissed Yehuda and smiled, glowingly.

"Strike terror into the enemy of the Lord and the enemy of our land and our people. God is great!"

Yehuda's teeth chattered and he felt moisture running down his legs but managed to stutter "God is great" in response as Bar-Abbas walked away, leaving him to his fate. He stumbled forward, entering the market, greeted by a typical scene of loud haggling between thrifty buyers and impatient merchants. He knew he had to stab the first soldier within his sights. And so his eyes landed on the victim. He was no ogre. A young man, tall and skinny, standing awkwardly in his ill-fitting, too-large uniform looked hardly like an occupier. With his gaunt frame and fair hair he looked too frail to even be a soldier. There he stood, leaning on his Hasta Lancea for support rather than deadly force and talking amicably with a Jewish merchant. It even looked like they were sharing jokes. Yehuda took out his sicarius, dropped it on the ground…

…and ran like hell.

THE LOST SHEEP

Yeshua had become more skilled at oration but was still met with taunts and jeers. What was so special about a young man speaking to small tribes of distrustful clans about the power of love and decency when the holy law books were so ingrained in the people and provided the only stability they had?

In the middle of the square he tried to draw large startling figures for those who were nearly blind, mostly by their own choosing, and shouted to those who refused to hear.

"Where is the kindness that you would want bestowed upon yourselves? Where? Where is the kingdom that the priests and sages speak of? If it's in heaven, well the birds can already fly there now! If they tell you it's in the sea, then the fish and the whales are there way before you! God's kingdom is within your hearts! Can't you see how simple it all is? Love, do not hate. Love your neighbors, the Romans, the Greeks, the Armenians, the Parthians, the Egyptians! Be kind, not cruel! Don't just quote from strange old books to justify your own flaws! This too shall pass, and you too shall perish from the earth but when your mortal shell leaves you, the spirit will always remain! The Lord created the earth, why make it hell when it can be paradise instead? Abandon your violence and practice peace! If you follow this, the kingdom will arise right here in Judea, right in front of your eyes! And if you don't follow it, then you will continue to live in poverty and will be poverty incarnate! God is not Caesar! Why should you fear him?"

It was all too simple and contradictory for the crowd that gathered around him. Their catechism was ironclad. "Nonsense!" They yelled, "He's spouting nonsense!" or "Who taught you all this rubbish anyway?"

"No one taught me!" Yeshua would yell back. "I saw that the ignorance of fools is shameful and bloody!"

"It is you who is shameful for speaking heresy!" the Pharisees would shout.

The crowd would stir and Yeshua would become more aggressive, trying to break hammers with his head until his anger got the better of him, and then he could no longer contain himself and so he would shout back.

"Wherever I go it is you people who wish to silence me most! You 'priestly classes'! You Pharisees! You blind men are like a dog in a manger! A rock that lies at the mouth of a stream. You don't drink the water yourself but you don't let the water flow to the plants—the plants who need it most and who thirst for it. And the stream is right here in front of you people!"

"Stop speaking like a Greek! Some philosopher he thinks he is, this one!" They would taunt him, and rage would flow through Yeshua's veins and he would discredit his own teachings about love and peace.

"You know what?" He would turn to them and stare directly at the smarmy crowd and explode. "You are not even like the rock in the water. You are like the drainpipe of a toilet! Plastered outside, sure, but filthy inside and filled with shit. Just like graves that are decorated above when all they do is house the bones of the dead!"

And he would walk away in disgust, or Maryam would grab him and lead him away before he had a seizure.

It was on just such a day in Yeshua's ministry, just after one such exchange in a town not far from Bethany that Maryam had to intervene and so she dragged Yeshua away, away from the crowd that was almost ready to lynch him and his group. Dodging the hail of garbage the townsfolk threw at them as they retreated, they sat next to a well at the edge of the town as if by the river of Babylon, and chewed bread and apples in silence until they saw an animal close by, struggling to stand upright. When the animal couldn't stand up straight, it would collapse again, but though failing to stand, continued to crawl. They did not move but observed the beast as it came closer. It was an unusual animal and soon they saw it was not a beast at all, but a man, a leper who had lost his mobility to affliction.

Yeshua stood and started walking toward the man-beast but Maryam grabbed his shirt. He pulled away from her violently, enthralled and engulfed in compassion for this sorry sight.

The Leper began to mouth words. His teeth and tongue were still intact but the disease had taken its toll and he was reduced to an odd, crooked shape that was not conducive to locomotion. His mouth still managed to form words and so he implored.

"Anything you can spare, kind people! Some small change or some food! Throw it on the ground for me so I don't touch you."

"Come closer and try to stand!" Yeshua told him. "Come. You will eat with us."

And he put his hand under the Leper's armpit to help him trundle half-simian/half-human over to the group where they had laid out their fruit and bread. Maryam gasped and tried to pull him away.

"Yeshua! Don't touch him! You will get his pest!"

"They would say that about me..." Yeshua smiled and continued to help the man. Just as the poor devil was about to reach the cornucopia, a rotting melon hit Yeshua in the back of the head. He dropped the Leper and spun around. Behind him stood a gaggle of townspeople and priests laughing at how the pot shot left the preacher covered in the seeds and flesh of an overripe gourd. After the requisite laughter, the priest motioned for the crowd to quiet down, and though he enjoyed inflicting the humiliation he needed to assert his own authority and so he bellowed with all the proper rhetoric befitting a religious official.

"Unclean! Look at this man! He has defiled his own body and mankind itself for touching the unclean!"

The blood shot up into Yeshua's head and he felt the taste in his nostrils. "What is wrong with you people?" he roared back. "What nastiness you spread among your own kind! Is that why you need laws? To keep you and your own herds in check? Is it because you're too damn stupid to stop doing evil? Six hundred and thirteen commandments?! You need it spelled out for you like that? How about one commandment? Do not be cruel for it is a sin!"

During his speeches, his declamations, his outbursts of fury, sometimes a different imp would jump right up into Yeshua's breast and instead of whispering or cackling like the other little demons this one would blatantly scream at him. *"You bastard! Number one, you really are a bastard but number two, you're a figurative bastard as well. You've forgotten all about how you've talked to your mother, haven't you? And here you are, telling other people how to behave, how to live, how to be decent? The things you said to your mother, and then abandoning her? Yeah, sure she's got your brothers, but you left nonetheless and she could use all the help she can get right now, and you tell these people what to do? Why don't you look at your own sins? Huh? How about that? Bastard! Bastard! Bastard!"*

Yeshua tried to shoo these imps away. They would usually be swatted rather easily but a replacement would be sent in return. What could Yeshua do to redeem himself? He himself struggled to believe in what he was saying.

A villager held a rock in his hand and was about to raise it and hurl it at the Leper but Yeshua noticed him and shouted "You! Don't you dare! Don't you dare hurt this man who has suffered so much!"

To Yeshua's surprise, the man let the rock fall to the ground and looked down while Yeshua continued.

"If you or I only knew what his suffering feels like! You sin against God with your cruelty. Your hearts are made of stone."

"*Tap-tap...*" went another imp, but Yeshua continued.

"Depart and repent! And may the true King of the Universe, not the vicious, petty little godling all jealous, the one you worship, have mercy on all your souls."

The crowd began to disperse and walked away from Yeshua and the disciples. Most murmured and grumbled variations on *"The man is crazy... The man is possessed... The man is a lunatic..."* but the one who held the stone that he wished to throw kept turning his head and looking back at these odd strangers.

Yeshua did not look back as he returned to their "table"—a blanket covered in fruit and ants. Maryam held his hand. At this point she could predict just when Yeshua might have a fit and she knew it wasn't going to happen now but still, he needed comfort. Yet there were things nettling her—the obvious ones were *"What are we doing? What exactly are we doing?"* She kept repeating those lines in her head over and over. What was the point of talking to brutal people perpetuating their own legacy of brutality and egging on the newest mutation of intolerance?

She spoke softly so as not to upset him or make him feel as if she were abandoning him or criticizing what he did, though at this point, it was not only her but the others who felt rootless and confused.

"We should go to Jerusalem, Yeshua," she whispered. "The people here, they are rural desert people, set in their ways. Their hearts are cold."

"They are blind..." he spoke softly while trying to squeeze juice out of a pomegranate. "And when the whole world is blind they won't notice that the whole world is burning. Are they truly like this? Everywhere? Is it truly in their nature to talk trash and do evil?"

Petras spit out a fruit stone and mumbled despairingly, "They're like that everywhere, Yeshua…. The people are the same the world over." Just as he was about to speak further, Maryam heard a rustling in the bushes behind them—which she felt was a man and not an animal.

"Shh! Quiet, all of you!"

She asserted her authority. Over time, Maryam came to be respected as Yeshua's wife and though she rarely spoke out as such, but when she did, the followers listened.

The rustling returned and all eyes fixed on a stand of olive trees immediately behind them. One cannot hide well behind a bunch of scrawny branches, not even to defecate. There is no privacy, no shame. The culprit was a man who was trying to make his way into town and he stopped when he saw Yeshua and the disciples pelted with rotten fruit. He crouched in a poorly chosen place to hide and was thus quickly noticed.

"Who's there? Stand up! Stand!" Maryam commanded and the man raised himself up. A mid-height, dark and muscular, hairy Jew, nothing exceptional. He spoke meekly as he raised his arms and hands.

"My name is Yehuda. I'm sorry. I don't mean harm…"

"Why were you spying on us?" Maryam was incensed.

"I wasn't… I was just… I didn't want them to see me."

"Who? Who are you hiding from? Why were you spying on us—we who have nothing to hide?"

Yeshua stood up and motioned to Maryam to stop her badgering.

"Come here, Yehuda," he said. "You have nothing to fear from us. What do you want, and what is it you seek?"

Yehuda walked forward meekly. At first he glanced at the Leper who, unfazed, continued to eat whatever his barely functioning finger would let him pick up from the blanket of Yeshua's generosity.

The rest of the group stopped chewing but Yeshua reached out to the man and smiled.

"You're looking at our food. Come. Come and sit down. I see you are hungry, and no one should go hungry." With Yeshua's disarming smile, Yehuda sat down and bit into an apple as if it was his last meal on earth. His hunger was great enough that it surpassed his disgust for the Leper sitting next to him who patiently continued to chew and smile.

Maryam stared at the stranger as he shoveled food into his mouth, eyes darting around nervously. His pock-marked face showed fear and gratitude, but there was another emotion hidden within that peered out from the surface, as if the pitiful look was actually a ruse, and Maryam became intrigued. She sensed there was a secret within this stranger that was itching to be divulged.

She had always found fascination in men of all different kinds, an amateur psychologist of sorts. The problem for her was that this amateur psychology often mixed with infatuation and that was just how she ended up with Theudas. Now she was even questioning her involvement with Yeshua, but that was a different feeling. She wanted to know this strange man and her gentle prying came off as both sensitive and flirtatious. As she watched him greedily feeding himself she again recounted those thoughts in her head which she found fascinating, odd and contradictory. *We have laws in the books about chastity and purity, but babies are made through fucking. We have ritual baths and we try to purify ourselves but our bodies are made up of blood and shit.* In conjunction with her interest about how other people think, despite her mistakes, she wanted to know more about what drives a person to do what he does, to be who he is, and so she let Yehuda finish his apple and then leaned over and asked, withholding as much provocation as she could. "You're on the run, aren't you?"

Yehuda almost choked, but he looked over at the inquisitive

woman, nodded and reached over for another piece of fruit which he proceeded to munch like Chaplin's Tramp. She saw he was hungry and let the man eat and even put her hand on his shoulder, patted him and smiled, but she wanted to know more. Yeshua sat next to her. He felt no jealousy but he was slightly irritated by her curiosity. Apart from her, the others were simply others. He had no desire to delve into each of these peoples' personal issues. He himself knew that what he spoke of was abstract and maybe that was the problem he faced. Maybe if he would do one act, one singular act to wake the people up… but he would not resort to violence—that would go against everything he preached… so he stayed silent, chewing on stale bread while inwardly boiling as he looked at Maryam. He thought she was making advances at this stranger. In fact, she even stroked his hair. What was she going to do next? Pop his pimples?

Maryam did indeed stroke Yehuda's greasy locks and as he was into his second apple and there was no further need to reassure him, she dropped her hand and composed herself.

"Who are you on the run from?" She was dying to find out everything she could about this man.

The minute she said those words, out of the blue came a flashback of her life as a child, and Yeshua too, for some reason, had a brief injection of a picture of his father darting into the brain. Their visions were so close but how would they know what the other thought? They did not make eye contact. Maryam stared at the fugitive instead. Yehuda put down the remnant of the fruit and spoke softly, deliberately, as if practiced, though still with a mouthful of apple flesh.

"Sicarii…"

Yeshua was unfazed but Maryam insisted, moving closer.

"What did they do to you?"

Yehuda spit out a seed and looking around to determine his

safety mumbled "I was one of them" and immediately, what looked like a million eyed monster fixed its gaze on him. He kept his cool and continued.

"I ran from them. I am… I couldn't, I did not…" The tongue stumbled and stuttered. "I ran away.... I was with them but I ran away. I couldn't do it. I couldn't-" Yehuda choked and stifled tears. "I am innocent! Please believe me! I am innocent!" These were not crocodile tears. Yehuda narrowly escaped death just the other day and his sobs came out of a genuine gratitude for life itself.

"Come Yehuda, eat." Yeshua smiled slowly. "Eat, have some bread, eat another apple if you want. We pick them from the trees when the farmers aren't looking."

Despite a moment's hesitation and darting his eyes back and forth, he dug his teeth back into the fruit and answered with a mouthful of pale yellow flesh, spitting out "I ran frwmwom thwem…"

Thus Yeshua smiled, for he too, like Maryam, found excitement in new converts and so began to prod him further.

"You asked us if we are Jews. Who is a Jew, Yehuda? There are no Jews, no Romans, no Greeks… There are only people, do you understand?"

Yehuda nodded as he kept on eating but recognizing that Yeshua was a leader of sorts, he dropped his fruit, swallowed what he had squirreled in his cheeks and stared dumbly at Yeshua. He was used to leaders since childhood and knew he had to obey them.

It was then that Maryam expressed her newfound morbid curiosity as she leaned over to Yehuda and asked "Who did you kill?"

The bile rose up and Yehuda lifted his eyes and again saw a million-eyed monster to which he replied.

"I have never killed! Never! I never did! They tried to make me do it but I couldn't! They told me to kill a soldier but I couldn't do it. That was why I ran away!"

Yeshua spit out an olive stone and turned to the man.

"Does it not say in the books 'You will not kill' ?"

"I am sorry, sir… We believed…. We believed…Do you not believe in his coming? That of the prophecy, that of the Messiah?"

Under other circumstances, standing on a fish barrel, fighting against genes and biology, daring the heavens to strike him down with a seizure, Yeshua would have planted himself firmly twixt two overturned vessels— shoot me, shoot fish in a barrel—and he would have screamed up to the heavens if he had a little bit more strength. Now he was weary, so wearily he spoke to Yehuda.

"Again the Messiah. You'll waste an entire life waiting for him. Why not seek to find what is in your own soul? Why do you need someone else to do it for you?"

Yehuda stopped chewing on the next fruit he cautiously helped himself to and dropped his head. He knew not to tell them about the people he had murdered in the name of his faith. Free will had granted him a reprieve from the martyrdom the other Sicarii aspired to. "Will God forgive me, sir? I only sinned in my mind…"

Yeshua smiled. He was not savvy enough to see through Yehuda's lies.

"Your heart is weary, isn't it? It is weary from the awful burden, the sin you were just about to commit, the one you told us of. And what a sin! Imagine if you took that life, Yehuda! The dead man would haunt you forever and your transgression would be a millstone around your neck until the end of your days. Each night your victim would climb into bed with you, embrace you and then you'd start to get a suffocating feeling as his ghost squeezed and choked your neck… You would forever be betrothed to the one you robbed of life, and his nails would justifiably dig into your heart and make it bleed forever."

Yehuda replied with his eyes on the bread and fruit instead of his hosts.

"I am sorry, sir. I do repent. The others, they disobey the laws and their punishment in the next world must be awful. They call on us and tell us we will be martyrs but does the Lord call for martyrdom?"

"He does not." Yeshua smiled for a second and then became more stern. "Don't repent because you fear God! It is not as simple as kneeling before your master! If you so loathe being a slave to Rome, why would you choose to be a slave to heaven instead? Come. God is not Bar-Abbas. You have given up your past."

"But who are you? Jews or what? Which god do you pray to? Just tell me who you are!" he pleaded, exasperated. The questions still burned.

Yeshua smiled again and replied gently.

"There is only one God, Yehuda. He is the Emperor of all the worlds, on earth and in heaven. He is not the emperor of Rome and not the god of Judea. There is no God of Israel. There is he, the one who will shelter us when we pass. In the meantime, we have the gift of life to thank him for and for that we should praise him and while here, we should indeed chastise those who do not value life, the divine miracle of life itself, for they are the ones who are the sinners! If people would only remember this, how much pain and blood would be spared! Do people not live lives that are bittersweet? Do people not suffer alongside their pleasures? Is that God's fault or ours? If he created misery, then is that the god you wish to somehow appease? That is not the god I believe in. I believe God gave us brains and hands and hearts to make this world heaven and we have been steadily turning it into hell."

"But what about the Jews, sir? The Jewish nation? The future of it, the-"

Yeshua worried that he might bark. Instead he bit his tongue and spoke with compassion.

"The world, Yehuda. Think of the world. Not just of the Jews."

And then Yehuda broke free of humility and stared directly into Yeshua's eyes.

Yehuda relented, turning away and muttering, after a pause "I will" and "I will try" and as he stuffed his face with another fruit, stripping the flesh to the stone in what appeared to be nanoseconds, he muttered to himself "God is great..." to which Yeshua, acknowledging the original meaning of the phrase that had been usurped by the terrorists, nodded in agreement.

BREAKING BRICKS AND HANDS

Pilate, blinded by the sun, hobbled along, inspecting the construction site, in pain from his quotidian hangover. His gout, which had recently worsened, wasn't helping matters either. It made the simple act of walking painful and he cursed the gods. He could barely hear what the flunkies and factotums were saying as he hobbled. He did not care. All he wanted was to get it over with and leave. *"To hell with the gods, to hell with the Jews and the whole lot of them all, just let me fucking walk normally and give me back my goddamn foot!"* he cursed and swore inside.

The sound of the architects and officials talking about *"this, that, and the other"* formed into a shapeless cacophony of nothing and the only thing that prevented him from stopping and shouting out "Shut the fuck up!" was the pain he had to endure on this walk of inspection. He realized that he needed to be present, not so much to keep his job as to keep his job long enough to retire, so he endured his personal agony.

"I'm sorry, what?" He would keep asking the engineers and the bureaucrats as they told him their plans for the aqueduct. He kept wishing that they would just simply go away, his constant asking and re-asking the questions was intended as much to annoy them as to shirk responsibility and to avoid work—a petty jab here and there to make them repeat their drivel as he pretended he didn't understand. Eventually he came to realize that he had to man up and pay attention, and so he stopped and tried his best to listen.

And so came the repetitive, boring drones when all he could think of was a new and different pair of shoes to ease his discomfort.

"With all due respect, sir..."

"We really have no idea..."

"If the Emperor will come...."

"The Emperor might sail to Judea..."

"We don't have funds to..."

"The Aqueduct...."

"Emperor will be pleased...."

"We are not sure if he will attend but..."

"Aqueduct must be finished..."

"The Emperor's birthday..."

"Praise be to Jupiter..."

"We need more slaves...."

Pilate stopped and stomped his ailing foot, feeling immediate sharp shooting pain and grit his teeth before he appeared comical. *"Harpies! Sirens!"* he surveyed the vile bunch around him and then gathered up his strength and spoke imperiously.

"Do what you must. Do what is necessary. The aqueduct must be finished. The enemy must be destroyed." He did his best to improvise in order to quickly end the charade but then came the incessant questions of logistics and practicalities yet again.

Again came the same refrain.

"We need more manpower, sir. Without more hired workers or slaves, it will be months before the aqueduct reaches the city walls!"

Now Pilate had to stop and consider. Snapped out of his delirium, though just barely, he knew he had to follow orders.

"And with hired help? Or more slaves purchased?"

"We can finish the project in weeks but we need more manpower, and we have no money. We will bankrupt Judea! We are already behind for what we owe for the stone!"

It was then that Pilate decided to make an executive decision.

"Then bankrupt this blighted land that the Jews love so much!" he shouted, and silence fell like a curtain over the other players whose entomic chatter was just adding to Pilate's petty sufferings.

One dared to speak up.

"Sir, we have already increased taxation! If we increase taxation further, we will only risk more unrest!"

With that, Pilate turned lucid and angry.

"We have unrest here every fucking day! Don't you see that it isn't about the Emperor?" He now tried to remember what the pitch for the aqueduct's construction was from Lucius and continued as best as he could, though he couldn't care less. It meant little to him now personally, but he repeated the pitch.

"Don't you see that construction projects like this one, bringing fresh water to their stinking city may help win over some of those pesky homicidal elements among these people? They will see that we are doing them good and helping them, and it will be worth it in the long run! *This* is what this project is about. Not the Emperor!"

"I understand, Sir..." A bureaucrat protested. "But we cannot afford this extra expense for hired workers or the purchase of more slaves! Where will the money come from? This land has nothing and we cannot afford to borrow from Syria..."

Pilate smiled as he put the bureaucrat, a petty accountant aptly named Servius, in his place with a brazen but pragmatic suggestion.

"Servius!" Pilate called out, twisting his toes and somehow trying to relieve the pain of the spasm shooting up from his metatarsal ligament. "Judea may be broke but the Jews are filthy with money. Use the Temple Treasury."

More tumult came from the delegation.

"Governor..." Junius tried to speak as humbly as possible. "Don't you think it would be a ... a dangerous provocation?"

"Servius..." Pilate smiled with annoyance and vinegar. "Who is the Governor of Judea?"

"You are, Sir."

"Tell the Chief of Police that the architects can take whatever they need from the Jewish temple—gold, whatever, anything of value and use it to buy more slaves so we can finish the aqueduct in time."

Pilate wanted nothing more than to get this problem solved as quickly as possible and he walked away, accompanied by his bodyguards. His work was done. Behind him, he heard how the accountant shouted, asserting his own authority in turn, passed down from Pilate: "How many more men do you need? We need this aqueduct finished!"

A HORSEMAN BEARING A FIG TREE

The high desert sends cold through the night, covering the people in chills, sometimes coating the land in frost or even a dusting of snow. In Bethany, Bar-Abbas chewed on dates and sipped wine in the safety of a partisan's house, patiently waiting for screams and sounds of commotion to rise from the streets. Just at the moment when his restraint started to wane, a frantic Sicari ran in to announce that Yehuda abandoned his mission and deserted.

"He ran! Bar-Abbas, he ran! The bastard dropped his sicarius and ran!"

Bar-Abbas spit.

"He did what?"

"Ran! Ran like a traitor!"

Bar-Abbas tried to maintain a Napoleonic composure and spoke calmly but vehemently.

"I want him dead. Spread the word that there is a snake among us who values his own skin more than God and God's people, and just like with all serpents, it will be God's will to decide when and how his skin is indeed shed!"

Of course he was genuinely vexed, despite the braggadocio. If the murder/suicide did occur he could have stayed in Bethany for a few more days enjoying the figs and the dates and the adulations. In the obvious interest of saving face, he and his soldiers were forced to leave the stronghouse to pretend they were seeking out Yehuda and so they spent another cold night in the desert, teeth chattering, dreaming of a vague glorious future.

In the morning, Bar-Abbas awoke to the sound of horse's hooves and a messenger's yells. Crawling out of his tent to meet the man, while the others slept, he fumed, *"What a bunch of lazy bastards I have to deal with. How am I supposed to create a new world with this lot?"*

Even from far away, Bar-Abbas heard the desperation in the horseman's voice. "Yeshua! Yeshua!" he heard from afar, the rider addressing him by his given name. *"Impetuous!"* he thought at first, then realizing something was serious enough for the messenger to be so brazen in the way he addressed him, he let the man come closer and refrained from chastising him for his insolence. The rider dismounted and wringing hands, alternated between sobbing and raging.

"Terrible news, my lord! Terrible news! May God save the children of Israel!"

Bar-Abbas pushed him away while the man still wept. Not out of pity but out of a desire to know the news—he was quite used to histrionics and always treated them with suspicion—he threw him his goatskin flask and barked "Drink, then speak."

The horseman had only a small pull of water before he began, sitting on the ground and rhythmically rocking back and forth, beating his head with his hand and fists, weeping and wailing.

Bar-Abbas kicked him in the ribs.

"Speak. What is it? Well? Speak damn you!"

The kick helped stop the hysteria but it did not stop the rider from further groveling. From his worm's eye view, he spoke. "I carry word from Jerusalem, sir. Pilate is stealing from the Temple!"

The rage, the indignation shot up and immediately damaged the cardiovascular system. If Yeshua was there he would understand the symptoms, though he'd disagree with the cause and if such a thing was possible in theory, they would have embraced and kissed in empathy. The rider kept talking.

"We learned it from Yefet in Jerusalem, Sir. The aqueduct! The new aqueduct they're building! The heathens are using the temple treasury! We have to do something, sir! We need to! Can't we do anything? The holy treasure of Judea!"

"Shut up and stand up!" Bar-Abbas was calm and resolute.

The rider stood up and looked sheepishly at the man who most of his ilk had come to venerate as a near-Messiah. Bar-Abbas' words came smooth and slithery at first and gradually accelerated to megaphone volume.

"We will do something, my brother." He swapped the stick for a carrot. "Something we have been waiting to do. Something I knew we would have to do. And now is the time."

The tents opened up. The slaves to the "prophet" crawled out like a leper colony exiting their pitiful caves. One Sicari, Avram, who was awake throughout but did not dare exit, came and straightened his spine, though his soul was still simian and bent in many places. He had belief. It was the only thing he had. The slave approached the master and dared to speak.

"The cursed aqueduct. Their damn construction projects. They try to 'win us over' and as always, they commit an atrocity! How can the people not see it? See their hypocrisy? And they call *us* terrorists? When Caesar is the biggest terrorist in the world?"

"Quiet, Avram!" Bar-Abbas barked. "We know all that. Now it's time to fight. Do you know who Solon of Athens was, Avram?"

Avram was put in his place by his great leader and lowered his eyes. He knew that he spoke out of turn and that it was a mistake. Of course he knew nothing of Greek history and so, duly humbled, he resumed the timid position of his kin in this family of murder. He didn't have a chance to respond.

"Of course you don't," Bar-Abbas continued. "Let me educate you. Many years ago, when Athens and Sparta were at war, it was during the siege of Kirrha…. There was a man named Solon who put black hellebore into the aqueduct. It was wonderfully effective. You don't know what black hellebore is, do you?"

There was silence from the sheep, so Bar-Abbas continued.

"The residents of Kirrha lost the game as the black hellebore in their water caused every single one of them to shit their brains out! Not that they ever had any. It causes quite a fine case of diarrhea— at minimum. While they were squatting, the city was crushed… Black hellebore grows plentifully here in Judea…"

At this point the whole tent city was listening to the leader. The women, holding their infants who had a "play" dagger attached to their swaddling sheets were particularly enthralled. After a pause to let the most obedient ungulates posing as sapiens assemble around him, Bar-Abbas spoke with even greater conviction and improvised a plan.

"We will go into Jerusalem, and make sure that those who support their so-called construction projects will have only themselves to blame for their own sickness and death. Construction projects. They are not construction projects. The Romans are occupying a sovereign land. Very well. We will make sure this crime is not left unpunished. Their aqueduct will bring death to the citizens and they will see that all the occupiers do is bring death! Avram!"

"Yes, my lord!"

"We will gather as much black hellebore as we can. I will climb the walls of the aqueduct myself, and their fresh water will turn into poison. For that is what the Romans are—poison. They and all those who kneel and live under their thumb, they are also poison and they too shall perish, as will all those who do not fight for justice and all those who do not join our cause!"

"Yes, sir!"

"Then maybe those who fancy themselves civilized and Greek will see what the Romans are truly like. Perhaps a few rotting dogs or maybe the corpse of a leper in the water would help them get extra sick. We will see if we can throw in something special on top! Let's do it! Are you ready?"

The chorus was affirmative.

"We are ready!"

"Now say it."

And they said in unison, "God is great!"

Bar-Abbas smiled and was pleased but not pleased enough. His speech needed a coda but just as he was about to continue speaking, a henchman interrupted his maw as it was about to spew more bile and whispered. "Sir, what if you are caught? It is too dangerous! Jerusalem is a viper's nest of soldiers and spies and without you..."

"Shut up!" he barked. "I will do it myself. I want to. This is the direction that my life has been pointing to since I was born! It is my fate and our salvation! I have come to this earth to fulfill my destiny and I am to do what I am forced to do, for it is not for me but for the Lord to decide what it is that I must do, and if and when I must depart this earth. And as in the book of Jeremiah, the Lord Almighty, the God of Israel, says: 'I will make these people eat bitter food and drink poisoned water.' "

"But if you are captured, sir, what shall we do without you?"

"Then let me be captured. What matters but the freedom and glory of Israel? It will only help the cause. Yes, perhaps I will die. But it shall not be death but holy martyrdom. When the crowds see me sacrifice myself for Judea, when they see me beaten and speared, when they see me flayed and scourged, knocked to shit by those bastards, we will have a true uprising, a true revolution! Rome will leave Judea. And if I die, my death will not be in vain. It will eradicate the parasites out of the Holy Land. Now we march! To Jerusalem!"

The crowd hesitated, murmuring, and Bar-Abbas was genuinely confused and fearful that his speech didn't immediately send up a swell of fervor and support when he said "To Jerusalem!" Marching on Jerusalem was suicide for the lot, or so many dreaded, but as the most dedicated voices started to chant, the lonely oboes were picked up by bigger bassoons, expanding from a chamber quartet to a full orchestra. Or more appropriately, the penile shaft of a rapist swelling with blood at the prospect of his terrible pleasure, expanding with excitement, the tip of the micropenis salivating with the prospect of a pathetic, subhuman victory.

The ungulates began to break down their tents and even during their mundane labour still sounded out, "Glory to Judea!" and "God is great!"—all in unison like an army of cuckoo clocks.

God is great…

They dragged their rags behind their leader.

God is great…

THE BEAST

One moist morning during their travels, Yeshua's ministry—yes, it had become that by definition at this point—approached a hamlet situated in a thicket of tamarix. Yeshua immediately fell into a reverie, reflecting on the sorrow of things. It was the shrubs that reminded him of a song his mother used to sing, a dreadfully sad song that spoke about death and which featured the salt cedar shrub in the lyrics. It spoke of how sorrow roamed the land and how an unfortunate group of peasants met her as she wandered into their village in the form of a strange traveler who took his own life.

He was snapped out of his *"mono-no-aware"* when he realized the hamlet was completely empty, though not abandoned. If the men had gone hunting or fishing, the women and children should still be at home. Presently, they heard commotion and fierce yelling coming from the copse, as if the entire population was out trying to net a beast. *"But what manner of beast could be netted that was kosher?"* he wondered. *"Surely one wouldn't be able to net an antelope?"*

The beast emerged. It was a naked man pursued not by furies but by people, and dodging the lassoes, and the hands ready to tear him to pieces, the naked, hairy man-beast burst out of the grove, his ankles still in the remnants of his shackles. He lunged straight towards Yeshua, landing at his feet. The shackles were not iron but thick, tanned camel hide. For months since his initial captivity he had chewed on them each night and finally, this morning, he broke free.

The beast-man felt no shame to be so exposed and covered in filth. Behind him the hunters ran, shouting "Stop him! Stop the possessed one! The demons will leave him and enter us if we don't catch him! Hold him!"

In fear for his life or the threat of the perpetuation of his pathetic existence in captivity, the Beast grabbed onto Yeshua's ankle and could only implore with his eyes at first but then quickly started to beg. "Don't let them! Please, don't let them chain me up again! Don't let them torture me anymore!" And he held onto Yeshua's leg like a child. Yeshua felt the pain of the whole world inside this man.

When his torturers approached, bearing their nets, ropes and pitchforks Yeshua yelled, "Stop right there! Don't come any closer!" Crouching down to the Beast, he helped the man stand and motioned for Petras to cover him in some cloth.

The Head Priest spoke first, after a few moments of assessing the situation in silence.

"That's all right. You can hand him over to us now. We thank you for catching him but we will take over now."

"We did not 'catch' him," Yeshua spoke calmly but forcefully. "He ran to us for help. What do you want from this man? Why do you shackle him?"

"He is possessed by demons, this one! Evil spirits have taken hold of him and he is contagious! That's why we chain him! If we kill him, the demons will leave his body and might enter ours, but if we keep him chained, we are safe. Now come on, let us have him. Whoever you people are, this is no time for playing around."

Thunderclouds moved in at a gallop. Yeshua felt an immediate feeling of calm which was suddenly supplanted by worry. It was that feeling of calm that he would experience when a fit would come on for no reason, and it would often happen just before a thunder storm.

The Beast beat him to it. One moment he was standing up straight, huddling with Petras and suddenly, in the next second, he fell to the ground and began to twitch and writhe. And the rain began.

"You idiots! You see? I told you he was possessed!" the Priest shouted. "Now the demons may come out and get inside of all of you!" With that, the villagers ran for shelter. Yeshua was calm. This storm had not affected him.

Yeshua commanded Maryam, "Help him!" She knew what to do. Gently, she held the Beast's head and stuck a cloth in his mouth so he wouldn't bite off his tongue. They huddled under the shrub.

The Beast's fit passed as quickly as the thunder storm and he revived, shaken but calm and now only shivering from cold. The villagers also returned and began to make their way toward the victim of their torture. "Don't touch him!" the priest ordered. "Get away from him or the demons will come out and enter you! Why don't you listen?"

"You stay away from him and from us!" Yeshua yelled. "It looks as if the demons have already entered you—and way before you even saw this man! There are no demons other than those of your own making, you fool! The man is sick!"

The Beast continued to plead. "Don't let them chain me up again. Don't let them torture me."

"We won't..." Yeshua said gently, and stroked his head. (*"Why am I petting him like a dog? Am I insulting him? Will he think that I too think of him to be an animal?"*) but continued to reassure him. "We won't let them hurt you."

The Priest and the villagers kept approaching, kitten-footed from their fear of demons but still predatory. The Priest spread his arms out to discourage the others, still sticking to his belief in possession, but one of the more brazen men came forward and while cautious, took a more aggressive stand and spoke to Yeshua.

"How is this your business? Who are you, anyway? Are you the magician that goes around in these parts that we have heard about? The one who claims to heal the sick and yet they die right after he leaves?"

"Magician." Yeshua smiled spitefully. "You mean pulling tricks? Fooling people? I think there's more than just one magician in this land. And this man who you said was possessed is merely sick. He needs comfort, not chains."

The Priest stepped forward enraged, but out of fear still kept his distance and his words were braver than his actions.

"That is for us to decide, you! And yes, there IS one going around these lands, claiming to perform miracles, claiming he's a son of God. A sorcerer! If he comes to our village we will kill him on the spot!"

Yeshua stood up and spinning around to the others nodded and simply said "Let's go!"

They picked up their satchels and started to walk away. "What shall we do with him?" Maryam asked as she watched the Beast regain his humanity, her eyes darting around in search of anyone to answer her. She was again enthralled.

"He will come with us," Yeshua answered calmly. "They will murder him here if we leave him." And so the Beast huddled between Maryam and Petras and walked away from his captivity. Petras covered his nakedness.

The Priest, still not comprehending what had passed just now, but not daring to provoke further—for it appeared to him that Yeshua was indeed a sorcerer—howled out one last question: "Who are you, then?"

"My name is Yeshua, from Nazareth," he replied calmly.

"Then stay out of these parts, Yeshua from Nazareth! Insulting us! Insulting our laws! Insulting the Jewish nation! Don't you dare come back here, Yeshua from Nazareth!"

And the villagers joined in hurling at first insults and moments later, rocks and rotten fruit that the trough animals left to waste. As they were pelted, Yehuda, the former Sicari and newest convert could bear it no longer and as the blood shot up to his head, he dove for the biggest rock he could find, and just as he aimed it at the Priest, felt a hand grab his forearm.

"Drop it, Yehuda." Yeshua told him. "Come, let it go. Come."

They walked wearily, in silence. Finally, it was Mattityahu who spoke:"We will have better luck in the next town, Yeshua."

Yeshua walked on. He was in another place now, a jumble of confusion. *"Blind leading the blind. A ship of fools which sails to nowhere. We have come to discover the world but instead we have dug up a carcass."* Exiting the grove, they were back on a desert road.

STARDUST

Everyone was resting after setting up camp. In the silence of the night, lit by a campfire and by the stars and the moon, Yeshua brooded. People bothered him less than memories of his parents—the mysterious father he never knew, the mother who was weeping in the dark by herself back home. The followers knew to leave him alone and let him meditate, though they all had more questions than answers which they desperately wished to press on him…

It was Yehuda who decided to approach. He sat down next to Yeshua and watched him stir the embers, lost in thought.

"Yeshua…" he started, but Yeshua was silent and absorbed in the licking flames and Yehuda stammered, the sheep put off by the shepherd's silence.

"Yeshua, I love you. I love your preaching and I love you for accepting me and saving me from death… but we must change what we are doing. Don't you see?"

Yeshua kept looking at the fire and waited to respond.

In another corner, Maryam wondered in solitude *"What happens to you when you die? Will I ever experience the sea again? How sad it must be for someone who has lost his limbs never to have sprinted, for someone who died before their time never to have seen the blue sea…"* A jumble of emotions overwhelmed her and so she went fetal and hugged her legs. *"God!"* She laughed. *"All they talk about is God but who is he? Yeshua can't stop talking about God and heaven and all that but what I want from him now is to undress me again!"*

And she once more thought about having a baby.

In the adjacent tents, the fears and doubts of the disciples ranged wildly.

"What will happen to me when I die?" was one that was shared by all, but then came variations on theme.

Maryam still thought about children, wondering *"What kind of a family could we possibly have? What kind of father could he be? How will we eat? How will we raise children?"*

In another tent, Mattityahu, the former tax collector who joined the ministry on a whim and left his comfortable life behind was entertaining thoughts which were turning bitter—in the direction of bitter pollen and resentment when he recalled how Yeshua spoke recently about the rich, and declared that it would be easier for a camel to pass through the eye of a needle than for a wealthy man to enter the kingdom, and that the poor shall inherit the earth. Mattityahu was familiar with the rich and the poor. When he worked as a civil servant he was far from well off but he was comfortable enough and he thought back on his life experiences. Passing by gated villas, which he could only see from a distance, he wondered. *"What does a man with so much money do with it?"* and *"Why does he even need it?"* and the answer would pop right up: *"Because it's great to be rich!"* At that moment bitterness would pop into his head and resentment against Yeshua. *"Camel, needle, dung... The poor shall inherit the earth? Truly they will, when they are dead and buried, they'll have all the earth their bones can feast on while maggots strip their flesh. What rubbish to preach, Yeshua. Just because you will never be rich gives you the right to spread such rubbish? You only say it to make yourself feel better because you will always be poor and you know it, but if given the chance to own a mansion and slaves and have all the meat and wine and fruit you could wish for, I daresay you wouldn't refuse."* And Mattityahu stifled his rage and meditated on the constellations, distracting himself from what he now thought was a sorry, wrong decision it was to join the mendicants.

In the other corner, Yehuda continued.

"Yeshua, don't you see? The Messiah is who we need and who we wait for, all of us, all of us Jews. It is the Messiah who will come to give us back our land and bring in the promised age, but in order for him to come, we must make war against the Romans. Is it not said—'Obey the law and give your lives for the law, and give your lives for the covenant of your fathers?' "

Yeshua had other thoughts going through his brain. Most of them were about the mother he abandoned. The second was doubt. The third was simply "What to do next?" He had stage fright, he knew that when he spoke, he spoke in earnest, knew that he was saying something few would venture to speak out loud, much less in public. And at the same time he also knew that he spoke a lot of fluff in nebulous terms, and when confronted with strong convictions like those of Yehuda's he resorted to the same vagueness just to make the man stop talking. He responded calmly and innocuously.

"People need to change their ways, Yehuda. Then there can be peace and then will come your promised age. Not before. Love the world and cease to be wicked. Forgive and move on. My message is so simple—so simple and yet no one can get it through their heads…"

"I think more can be done, Yeshua., Yehuda began, now plotting, pretending to think out loud. "More can be done. Much more."

Yeshua did not look up but kept stirring the embers. He wondered if it had rained in Nazareth lately, and if it did, whether his father would have appreciated it, since he always complained about the weather. Then he remembered that his father was in the ground, and that he wasn't even actually his father, and now there was this gnat, Yehuda, hovering and buzzing around him. He became annoyed with himself and with his company.

"If you wish to join Bar-Abbas again, be my guest. We welcomed you here." He struggled to say something to defend himself and the failure of his ministry. He wished he could defend their wandering and explain the concepts they flirted with but which they themselves struggled to grasp. For the Almighty is unknown and unknowable, and all the more so when your stomach is growling. Reality begets more pressing concerns.

Yehuda had no choice but to stay with the group. He was sure there was a bounty on his head, and cached within this tattered bunch he felt safer than if he were alone. He bent to Yeshua and feigned apology. "I'm sorry, Yeshua. I just don't understand what you plan to do on these travels. Good night."

"Good night, Yehuda." Yeshua mumbled.

Yehuda looked back before crawling into his tent, wishing for the leader to say something but Yeshua remained silent, staring at the remains of the fire. *"When this whole world is burning..."* was the phrase which kept ringing through his head.

In the tent, Maryam tossed and turned and could not force herself to sleep without Yeshua. She crawled outside and saw that Yeshua was alone so she walked over and sat down next to him and rested her hand on his knee gently as he continued to stare at the dying fire.

After several minutes of silence he spoke, stuttering…

"Why am I doing this, Maryam? Why do I do this? I don't even know what it is I'm doing!"

Maryam did not quite know how to respond. There was an uncomfortable pause until she started to improvise—something she was quite skilled at.

"Yeshua…" she started. "You are helping people. You teach the people to avoid evil." In her mind and heart she wondered what this man really could accomplish, how many people will really listen to him and most importantly, *"What am I doing with him?"* Yet she continued. "You help the people. You make them open their eyes.

Your path is not easy" "*And it is not easy for me to do this, we are hungry...*" "And you teach the people to avoid evil!" "*And when will we make some money?*" "*And God will provide? How will God provide?*"

"Yeshua," she turned confessional. "I never wanted to do this, you know. You know we found each other by accident."

"I never wanted to do this either." he replied without turning his eyes. Maryam tried to strike the most delicate of balances—to raise Yeshua's confidence while simultaneously admitting her own fears.

"You have no choice now," she told him. "A dozen people have joined you and come to believe in you! They're struggling out of the darkness and you have reached out to them and so they follow you, but you need to give them an idea of what they can do, I mean practically, we wander and-"

"We wander. We search for truth. What is truth? A dozen people, while thousands still eat from a pig trough, wallowing in hate and war. All I teach is for them to be human and to have compassion."

Maryam stood up. Yeshua's response was unsatisfactory and she knew he could sense her frustration as he repeated the same abstractions which by now had started to sound like a rehearsed alibi.

"I'm going to sleep now." She walked away and crawled back inside their tent.

Yeshua stayed and said nothing, still watching the night.

There was drama unfolding in another tent—the one which belonged to one of Yeshua's newer followers: Shimon, who left his life behind just recently and took his young wife Yael with him. Shimon became enthralled with Yeshua the minute he saw him preach, and despite protests from Yael he dragged her along to join the ministry. Tonight, Shimon considered that he may have made a mistake, for he thirsted to understand something he found terrifying and now no longer knew if Yeshua had any answers.

Yael was half-asleep but conscious—conscious enough to sob, and it was her sobs which woke Shimon just at the same moment that he himself was forced awake from a disturbing dream. The vision was starkly bleak—he was in the same place, the same tent, but Yael wasn't there, and he awoke in fright. He felt her thigh and knew she was present but that brief second engaged in dispelling a nightmare, the one that happens upon awakening was not enough. He had to feel and squeeze and make sure this was real, that Yael was real and that they were alive. And then Shimon began to weep as he squeezed his woman and sobbed in her neck and in her armpit, waxing metaphysical while his wife only wanted to sleep some more. He gently moved her arm away from him and stayed for another few moments watching in wonder and adoration as she slept, snored, and sweated in the heat of the tent. Shimon rested his head on her shoulder and held her tightly. He did not want to wake her but when the idea that she too was temporary kept coming back, it was overwhelming. He could not control himself and so, he whispered.

"Yael... Yael, I love you."

She held on to his arm and he held her tightly for as long as he could until he felt stifled and the embracing arm slithered away from her ribs. He sneaked out from the tent while she snored and went out into the cool night. He only wished to be alone at this point, to sit and think, and when eyeing just such a solitary place he saw Yeshua, sitting at the fire by himself, poking around with a stick, solitary. He thought that surely, if anyone, this man would understand him.

Presently, he wanted to return to the sweaty warmth of the tent and squeeze Yael again. He was afraid of both the inside and the outside. But Yeshua was here and he decided to approach him.

Yeshua kept looking at the dying flames and when Shimon sat

next to him, he said nothing.

"Yeshua..." Shimon spoke as gently as he could. "I am afraid. I am afraid of no longer existing. I love my wife. I want to hold her forever. Yeshua! I am afraid of no longer seeing the sun! I know I won't know it if I don't exist.... It wouldn't bother me because I would no longer be here—or anywhere—but it scares me, Yeshua. I will tell you, it terrifies me! One minute you're here and the next, the candle is snuffed, but what happens next? Can't you tell me, Yeshua? Can't you tell us? What does it mean to not exist? Do we die forever? And if we do, then do the dead somehow awaken?"

Yeshua struggled for an answer but he had learned what to say, whether he believed it or not, and came up with the requisite response.

"Do not fear, Shimon." he spoke gently without raising his eyes. "What is death? There is no such thing. Some see it differently but they are wrong. Death does not exist." And pausing as Shimon listened, wide-eyed, he continued.

"If you are part of the earth, how can you be destroyed? Look at that tree! The tree bears fruit, the fruit rots to make earth.... Out of the mother and home to the mother. You are part of the earth. There is no death."

"But Yeshua..." Shimon began to weep. "Is it not cruel that I will miss Yael, or that Yael will miss me?"

"Listen to me" said Yeshua half-convinced, "Everything will exist forever..."

"But we rot, Yeshua! You and I are rotting as we speak! What joy is there in this body if it literally rots? You've seen and touched the lepers. Does this decay help the earth? Are we just fertilizer for the plants? We are born screaming in terror and then we walk among each other like blind men and just as we begin to learn something, the world is cruelly snatched from us! All the beauty here... I see what you mean. But how shall I rejoice if my corpse only nourishes the soil? And will that tree that sprouts from my dead flesh be able to know and feel and think? And if Yael's corpse gives birth to a tree as well, and we sprout from the ground together reborn, how would the two of us embrace again?"

They lapsed into a moment of silence, interrupted by the sound of a nocturnal bird sounding out a strange and haunting mating call. Yeshua's eyes panned across and saw two moths, those maudlin little bits of life that only live for a day drawn to the light from the fire but careful not to singe their wings in this, their final exalted stage of living. And what did the insects do? Spray stardust and tinsel? Far from such fabulous wishful thinking, the moths landed on a piece of animal shit and began to feast. *Just like us...*" Shimon smiled bitterly and continued to explain his struggle to Yeshua.

"The beauty, Yeshua. The awful, terrible beauty of it all! Awful because it's here to taunt us. It's all given to us for a blink of an eye and then God cruelly takes it all away from us!"

Yeshua continued to stare into the fire and spoke in a low voice. He understood what Shimon was saying but if he said out loud that he agreed, he would risk losing the family he had created around him.

"If you think like that you will hate the world. Just as you hate those who live in their gilded cages. Just as you will hate the woman you know you could never wholly own... There is something else out there, Shimon"

"Yeshua, I know! If we didn't think there was, we'd all be dead of grief or by our own hands. There is something else besides this temporary shelter, this tent of a life. There must be! We didn't just invent it to keep a razor away from our own throats, did we? Yeshua? We didn't, right?"

"We didn't... There is..."

"But Yeshua, how do you know it?"

Yeshua struggled for the answer, and staring at the embers he pictured himself as a homunculus who when asked such a question would have simply leapt into the flames to avoid answering, but he managed to get it out.

"How can there not be, Shimon?"

Still avoiding eye contact with the doubting believer and looking up at the stars, he repeated, "How can there not be?"

Shimon returned to his tent in weary silence.

It was then that Yeshua met with an apparition. One that resembled a man, a wise man perhaps, who smiled softly at Yeshua.

He was startled, but before he could ask, this apparition, a sage dressed in exotic Eastern garb, spoke first.

"Everything exists in the brain." said the ghost. "God created you, and hence you may only exist in His imagination. And when you die it will be up to him to determine whether you are still alive or not. Immortality is a fickle thing, sir. Have you ever slept, then woke but felt as if you were still asleep and in the realm you were just in? That might be what you are seeing. You are not sure who is dreaming, you yourself, or someone who dreamed you up! But wait, it's not so frightening. Or is it? Imagine if the one who dreamt you awakened. Then you wouldn't exist anymore, isn't that so? Nothing wrong with not existing, unless it bothers you. But imagine if it was you who woke up and saw that this was your reality. I suppose you would be horrified…? Is that not also so? Is it not the same as knowing you never existed?"

Yeshua felt his neck incline and his brain hit the inside of his skull and he screamed and bleated. Maryam heard him, and just a few seconds into his agony, she rushed out of the tent, lifted his head and kept him from convulsing further. She helped him back to the tent and rocked him to sleep like an infant.

Yeshua slept in the safety of Maryam's arms.

THE FALL OF MAN

In the morning, on they walked, kicking up dust and sand as usual, minds gravitating toward shared thoughts about food, water, heat, where they were heading, how they wished they never left their homes, and occasionally a reflection or two about God.

Yehuda had grown more solemn in the past several days and his initial gratitude slowly began to be supplanted by frustration. Trying to assess which of the other disciples would be most receptive to him, his eyes darted around like that of a prey animal, when in fact he had always been a predator. It was a case of strength through weakness. He saw that Petras was weary and lagging in his step, so he slowed down until they were walking at the same pace. Once in place he spoke, as if just making small talk, but he had other motives. Fleeing the Sicarii saved his skin, but the beliefs still ran through his veins and he was frustrated with how ineffectual and pointless Yeshua's wanderings were. He'd had his fill of kindness. It was time to do something, to militarize….

Yehuda waited to find the right moment as well as to find the right ice breaker, something to provoke but to do it somewhat mildly. And then he found it. He spoke in just above a whisper to Petras the Greek.

"He lets the woman be too close to him. Have you noticed? There shouldn't be any women here anyway. They need to be kept separate."

Petras kept walking. He too, was weary and doubted the whole affair but he had no interest in Yehuda's complaint and responded dispassionately. "She's his wife, Yehuda. What are you saying? Separate the women? We don't even separate beasts, all of us live together here. What do you propose? Stop talking rubbish."

"She touches other men's hands!" Yehuda tried to make the argument more valid. "And she leaves her head uncovered! It is not right! It is who we are. It is our land and our tradition! We bow before the Lord and ask for mercy, for he is the most merciful and most magnificent!

Petras did not reply. As a Greek it was not in his tradition and even the Jewish customs were rarely observed by the wanderers. They kept walking in tandem, Yehuda trying to think of another way to turn this mission into something more effective toward the goal of expelling the "settlers."

At the front of the procession walked Yeshua and Maryam. When they tripped and stumbled they would cut their feet against an occasional thorn, but there was one pricklier thorn in their group that was starting to irk Maryam. She spoke softly, almost in a whisper, as she held Yeshua's hand and bent over closer. Her earlier fascination was now turning into fear.

"Yehuda is still a killer at heart, Yeshua. He still talks of the Messiah day in and day out, and of a Holy War against Rome and other nonsense. It's nonsense, isn't it? Isn't that what you have always said? To never say holy and war together?" And pausing for a moment, waiting for Yeshua's response, she quickly added: "Can we get rid of him?"

Yeshua smiled.

"No. We can't let him go. Don't you see? If I can get through to someone like him, then I will be able to reach anyone!"

"And if you cannot?"

"Then I will have failed. I just told you that I feel as if I have already. This whole thing started with the fish barrel. I have no idea what I am doing."

"But look how many have chosen to believe in you! You just need a plan! What do you want to achieve?"

"I wish for the world to change. For people to live their lives a different way."

"You are already seeing it! You haven't failed because of one soul, but if such a soul carries the pest, might it not be wise to remove the diseased plant from the garden you have so carefully planted and which you so cherish?"

"If I drop him, I will have failed."

"And if you don't?"

"I have failed already."

"You haven't!" she blurted out and then quickly dropped her eyes and changed the subject before Yeshua became morose. After a moment of silence she returned to practicalities. "I am getting hungry and we have nothing in our bags but crumbs, Yeshua. Where is the next town? Do we even know?"

He turned impassive.

"We will find something soon. We are leaving this patch of desert, you can see the green leaves up ahead."

"There is nothing left to eat," she despaired. "I am tired of being hungry and so are the others, I am sure. If Caesar speaks of bread and circuses, he probably knows what he's talking about."

Yeshua was provoked and her words stuck in his craw.

"Well, you know what? It was your idea for us to become beggars and tramps. I wanted to work. In case you don't remember, I told you I wanted to work on a Roman farm, I've wanted nothing less and nothing more than a simple life, and that one stupid episode where I yelled at a bunch of scum, the scum that will always be there and the scum that always rises to the top, that was when you decided just then and there, that I had something unique. We could have laid low and earned some money…"

"Stop blaming it on me!" she scolded him. "It is indeed what you need to do, you didn't choose your life! Your life chose you!"

The entire band was weary now and their sandals dragged even slower than before. They pressed on for an hour and then, just as Yeshua had promised, green showed up on the horizon, though the horizon, as is well known, is unreachable. A slight smile of vanity and self-satisfaction emerged on Yeshua's lips and for a second he wanted to pat himself on the back for this trickery or clairvoyance. *("I told you there was vegetation up ahead!")*

An apple orchard lay up ahead. As his footsteps slowed so did those of the others. He was the one leading them after all. He turned to Maryam and smiled proudly.

"You see? What did I tell you? Apples! Food! God will provide and God does provide! Come on!"

Maryam was not so much doubting Yeshua as she doubted again the entire mission. *"How naïve…"* she thought. *"Does he think he works miracles or something?"*

"Apples! Come on, people, let's gather some for dinner!" Yeshua beckoned and so they went over to the trees and started to pick the fruit. Yehuda immediately saw an opportunity. On their travels, all had lost track of time and dates and he knew this was the moment for him to prove himself most pious of all, even though he also had no idea what day it was. He ran toward Yeshua and implored, while making sure his voice was loud enough for the others to hear.

"Yeshua! Yeshua! What are you doing? Stop this!"

Yeshua chuckled. "We're picking apples for dinner, Yehuda. What does it look like we're doing?" And Maryam, busy with the picking, also turned around and smiled, smiling somewhere between blushing and pride, like a peasant girl noticed by the lord of the manor.

"What day is today, Yeshua?" Yehuda shouted, and this time the others, busy among the rows, slowed down with their work and picked up their ears to hear. "Well, Yeshua? What day is today? It is the Sabbath! The Sabbath! What are you doing? What are you people doing?! It is against the law, the law of God!"

Shimon, who had begun to doubt everything just last night, dropped the apples and his sack and approached the leader.

"He is right, Yeshua. It is against the law. It is forbidden to work on the Sabbath. And if that isn't bad enough, you are stealing!"

A tumult stirred, much like the ones Yeshua experienced among the Pharisees and the Sadducees and those he called the blind people, but this was the first time he witnessed mutiny coming from his own flock. Now was the time for action, to speak, to save whatever minor achievement Yeshua had made so far. So he spoke, starting gently but escalating according to his perception of the mood and how it would be received.

"Yehuda! And you, Shimon! You both know your history, your books. Your holy books." Yeshua disarmed them through his smile and a nod to their alleged erudition. "Do you two not remember how even our King David, when he and the others were hungry, how they went into the temple and ate consecrated bread? Consecrated! And those priests in the temple, are their sins not greater? Priests, who lay down laws, when only God can tell you his laws and the laws are quite simple. Be kind and do no evil is the only law you need. You will listen to them? Will you believe in divinity, in the mysteries or in the laws of the priests? Or perhaps you'd prefer to listen to those who call themselves 'holy men'? The men who have blood on their hands? The blood not just of beasts but of the men they condemn? Sacrifices. All to appease God. That's not the god we believe in, Yehuda. My god is a god of mercy, not a god who invented death."

Yehuda was duly challenged and now he could respond with an authority of his own, the authority of an adversary, or of a democratic opposition.

"You transgress against the laws of God, Yeshua! We are Jews, after all, are we not? Aren't we, Yeshua?"

It was a powerful thing to reach into the pocket of national identity and Shimon, who so despairingly voiced his fears to Yeshua just the other day, chimed in.

"He's right, Yeshua! We are Jews. Well, except for those two." He motioned at Andreas and Petras but continued on. "We cannot throw away our faith just like that. It is who we are. The others, well, they're not like us and you know it. We are not heathens. We are not Romans, we are-"

And Mattityahu the Taxman joined in, interrupting him.

"He is right, this man! Verily, he's right! And you, Yeshua, maybe you've lost track of time, but Pesach comes soon! We should go to Jerusalem and visit the temple!"

A wave of appreciation came around in the form of a low murmur, whispered as a group mouthing variations on words such as "He's right... The man is right...." It was Yeshua's moment to improvise a way to hold on to power but he felt crippled as more grievances came from the disciples.

"It's true, Yeshua! You transgress against the law of God!" said Yehuda, asserting theological supremacy. Yeshua's mouth was dry and his brain boiled but remembering the fish barrel he gathered up the strength to speak and the strength to yell, and yell he did. "The temple! Where you offer sacrifices? Did you not listen to a word I said?"

Yehuda's serpent tongue lashed out again with immediacy for he knew that Yeshua stood little chance of defeating him in a catechism when it came to the religion they were both born into. Yehuda had learned well from his teacher, Bar-Abbas.

"No, Yeshua! You are wrong!"

His confidence again sent a wave through the crowd which took full notice of the fact that there now appeared to be two leaders and prayed they wouldn't have to choose between them.

"The Temple! The Temple where we celebrate freedom from slavery! How we were slaves once, and how we were freed from the Egyptian yoke, just how we are slaves again to the Romans now but shall be free again!"

"I know what you say, Yehuda..." Yeshua spoke calmly. "And yet you will never be free with your ears plugged up with rubbish, and if you listen to rubbish, your people will always be slaves. Yes, your people, my people, all people. Slaves to your God! That is not the God I have come to tell you about! If a sword is all you understand then you tempt me to brandish a sword to make you understand peace!"

Yeshua turned around in disgust and started to walk away. Maryam dropped the apples from her makeshift apron and rushed after her husband.

"Yeshua! Yeshua! Wait!"

Yeshua ignored her and walked further. He did not run. He wanted for Maryam to catch up to him, and when she did and grabbed his sleeve, he turned around in anger and screamed.

"What?"

She stopped and smiled.

"Yeshua, don't be so angry."

With the woman's hand, he wilted.

"I don't know what I'm doing, Maryam..."

She smiled softly, gently, almost maternal.

"Let's go to Jerusalem, Yeshua!"

Tears welled up in his eyes and his voice cracked.

"To do what?" he choked. "Jerusalem, the Temple, those self-righteous priests. The stories we hear about that war zone. Dozens of people die there every day. Women are raped every minute. I don't want us going there with you. What will we do there?"

"You can't change people overnight. You are trying, and doing well with these and they are learning, be patient with them."

"The way they are patient with me?"

"Yeshua, they are. It's just Yehuda who is rash, but the others, they are decent and kind. They are gentle people. They should be allowed to go to the Temple for the holiday. And what a holiday it is for people, what joy it is to enjoy a holiday! Allow them some joy, Yeshua. What a gift you can give them. We are all weary and we have all seen too much pain and misery lately. Besides, we can spread the word more there. The people will be more accepting than these coarse desert folk. And we will receive more alms and we won't be as hungry. Let's try it. Can we?"

Yeshua, his eyes rested studiously on the ground, thought it over and then lifted them up and turned to Maryam and admitted defeat."Very well. We will go to Jerusalem for Pesach."

Maryam embraced him and kissed him passionately. Pushing him away, with a smile on her lips, she went out to the others, through the apple orchard, and almost as a preacher and leader in her own right, with full voice proclaimed: "We are going to Jerusalem for Pesach!"

THE DEATH

Un bel dì, vedremo
levarsi un fil di fumo
dall'estremo confin del mare.
E poi la nave appare.
Poi la nave bianca
entra nel porto,
romba il suo saluto.
Vedi? È venuto!
Io non gli scendo incontro. Io no.
Mi metto là sul ciglio del colle e aspetto,
e aspetto gran tempo e non mi pesa,
la lunga attesa.
E uscito dalla folla cittadina
un uomo, un picciol punto
s'avvia per la collina.
Chi sarà? chi sarà?
E come sarà giunto
che dirà? che dirà?

Luigi Illica / Giuseppe Giacosa

UN BEL DI

In Caesaria, the sun and sea were smiling and so was Pilate. It wasn't the memories of Rome and Ostia, the ones that gave him reminders of a happy childhood. He could have those every day if he wanted to. The waters of the Mediterranean were the same throughout Mediterranea, and each moment looking out onto the warm blue sea gave him the same yearning for the past and the same nostalgia. Today it was different. Today he felt as if he had earned a reward for his civil service, though he had little pride in his work and actually played no part in today's events, but as the top ranking official, credit was given to him automatically nonetheless.

In the morning, it was reported to him that the police found a terrorist armed with a bushel of black hellebore asleep on the final end of the construction site of the aqueduct, at the last few meters before the waterway was to be sealed and ready to be flooded.

According to the report, the insurgent was acting alone, and when prodded by the policeman's spear he offered no resistance, smiled and gave himself up freely. He was currently detained in the dungeon below the Roman fortress in the center of Jerusalem.

Pilate knew that the Emperor wasn't coming to attend the grand opening of the aqueduct as he told the Syrian governor. Nonetheless it was still his duty to attend and preside, without Caesar, over the inauguration, to show Roman magnanimity at work. As the representative of the senate and the people of Rome, it was his obligation to be the master of ceremonies when fresh, cool water would finally quench the thirst of the people of Jerusalem.

The terrorist miscalculated. The flood gates were not due to be opened for another two days. Now, after his interception and additional security in place, there was no rush on Pilate's end. He let the slaves take their time as he took his, meditating on the sea while they prepared him for the journey.

Pilate always dreaded these trips. He despised that town and would have been perfectly content to never see it again. He had a fine setup in Caesaria—as dull as it was, it was an apartheid paradise for him—but duty called and he only wished to be finished with this duty as quickly as possible and return back to drinking and ruminating. The journey was unpleasant but he would soon enough be in the Jerusalem governor's palace and be attended to. He would not need to do any work in the evening, and in the morning, other than waiting for the aqueduct to be opened, his duties would mostly be devoted to simple matters, such as deciding who to execute and whose lives he should spare. Cakewalk. He was in the finest mood he had been in a while, for the tedious aqueduct was finally finished.

The journey was surprisingly swift and pleasant this time. He felt no dread upon entering the city, the dread he would always experience, the perennial feelings of misery and rotten fate battling it out.

He was brought to his quarters and after washing off the dust, high above the pathetic masses, he drank and reflected. It was still early and he had plenty of time to further attend to peacefully destroying his liver before crossing the line which would make for a sloppy profile the next day. And so he ruminated, high above the filth, trying to drink as slowly as he could manage.

After a cool bath, he sat on the balcony and engaged in his favourite pastime: thinking.

He recalled that when walking past the ruins of buildings he would experience his "Ozymandias Moments" when observing that only the foundations still remained, and he would drift off to his own ruins, the more personal ones.

His laments were not so much for the forgotten civilization, but for his own, that of his family, and that of his people. In his heart, he already knew that he would die here in Judea, never to return to Rome. And yet it was just the idea of impossibility—the finality of death, of never being able to return from exile, never to go back in time—that was what he struggled to make peace with and the futility of which only made him angrier.

"How things disappear... How to make things last? How things fall prey to time... How fire destroys things is understandable, it's how salt destroys things slowly and how people destroy themselves is what sets the mind reeling..."

He longed not only to return to the past but also to recreate it and to prevent the present from rotting. Sometimes there would be self-doubt and the acknowledgement of flaws in his argument—for whom exactly was it that he wished to preserve these things for? Certainly not for humanity—*après t-il la deluge* —then for whom? He had no children. It would have made sense if he was trying to preserve something as a legacy for his son. But there was no son. Why, then? Was it to keep his own memory alive for himself? Did he, fearing senility, try to create mnemonic cheat sheets so as not to look foolish in front of the public when he would start forgetting things? (He was already starting to forget, but that was due to the wine, he was not that old yet). It was compulsive. He did not try to make sense of it, he just observed and rambled.

When the sun set and Pilate returned to his chambers, he asked for parchment and a reed pen and started to work on some architectural plans, but they were not for future projects. Meticulously he tried to recreate the layout of every place he had lived in, from his mother's house in Rome (the most important for him to remember), to the Emperor's Palace, and even the placement of the wet and moldy tents during his army service in Germania. All through the night, until dawn broke upon the sea's horizon, he worked on this project, testing his memory and pickling, preserving what he could, frenetically racing against the wasting of his brain until the terror struck him—the parchment too would fade, and if time destroys marble and the pyramids, then what's left? A manuscript would fall apart and disappear oh so much quicker. What will remain? How to stay immortal? How do we fight against this traitress "time"? It was overwhelming. He drifted off to sleep, into memories of past times, drooling on his pillow, but awoke after a few hours of sweaty sleep and the folly continued. Summoning his secretary, he instructed him to find a complete collection of Thucydides, like the one his mother had in her house. He did not wish to read history, he only wanted to own the codex.

Familiar refrains began, in monotone: *"Is this real? How do I know my wine is red? What if I'm just a player in Jupiter's dream who will soon awake and at which point I will die. He will chuckle and turning to Juno, say, 'I had a dream about an idiot who was drinking green wine, thinking it was red'."*

Terror struck him again and it was as if the very foundation of the world buckled. Quickly, he turned his thoughts away from phenomenology and just as quickly hit a dead end. The problem of immortality is what he was struggling with. How does one conquer death? Can one conquer death by death? How does one become immortal?

These troubles and his first night at the Jerusalem residence were erased the next morning due to the quotidian alcoholic blackout. He came to in a luxurious chamber and felt a cocktail of shame and frustration. The shame was just a drop. The rest was frustrated annoyance. For a while now he had been aware that he was drinking too much, to excess, really. The frustration was from the simple fact that he couldn't remember things. The shame was from the self-realization that he had become vulgar and porcine. If he came across a beggar digging into a simple bowl of groats (*"Just to stay alive,"* he would think. *"And for what purpose?"*) he returned to gentle thoughts of suicide when he considered himself in comparison to this poor less-than-human who did indeed struggle to stay alive while he, the governor, could vomit up the flesh of most expensive and rare birds on as many mornings as he chose. Nonetheless, the recognition of his dipsomania was also fodder for yet more philosophical musings. The familiar reflections on memory and time would become accentuated. He treated his frequent blackouts clinically enough, without shame or guilt. He recalled how once he had ordered an execution and didn't remember it the next day. And yet, at the moment, he was not focused not on the unfortunate death of the innocents which he had caused, but on philosophical matters, a meditation on the fleeting nature of time, how we exist in just a temporary place, entombed between memories that fade away and become dimmer and dimmer, and an unknown future. And he despaired that there were no ways to stop it.

He briefly became concerned about his drinking again and recalled an unusual case. Two brigands were brought to court for allegedly murdering their other comrade and cannibalizing him. During interrogation, the man-eaters readily confessed to their gruesome crime and blamed it all on the fact that they were hungry—and drunk. Pilate had them sent to a colosseum in Syria. Although he believed they should have been put to death on the spot for the gruesome nature of their crime and their lack of remorse, he decided it would be best if the public knew that those in the ring were beyond savages and could hold their own against wild beasts for they themselves were beastly and less than human.

As they were led away, after the sentencing, Pilate questioned: *"How could one commit such a ghastly crime..."* and then quickly concluded *"Man is capable of anything, and doubly so when drunk."*

Pilate looked over at his wedding band, iron, the third finger leading directly from the nerve that ran straight to his heart. The heart still pumped and prevented the flesh from sagging too much, the arthritic fingers still filled with blood and cartilage—forget Claudia, we are talking about fingers—and thus another Ozymandias moment: *"What a joke!"*

Two thousand years before Herr Röntgen could see underneath the skin, Pilate saw the bones underneath his ring. The bones that turn to chalk and dust. All that glitters is gold.

"No, the only things that remain are those that are set in form." he thought. *"This ring will outlast me for thousands of years. And when Rome crumbles, as it surely will, our columns, forums and theaters will remain as reminders and breed dreams among those who will walk upon our tombs. And what will be inside the tombs? Nothing but dust. But maybe those who will so disdainfully traipse upon that dust—our dust—will recall what happened here once, who lived, who perished, who was of virtue, who was ignoble, though that too will be rewritten. We need to have it set in stone, chiseled in marble. Here lived a man. This is what he did. Not much of a point, but better than nothing. Or is it? There are legends, stories after all, that immortality can be quite boring. Those sarcophagi in Etruria, what do we care about them now? Here lies a nobleman. He's dead now. The tomb is nice. So what? And yet the world is based on memories. We create and continue only by learning from those who are dead."*

"Odd how we create the world...." he continued. *"We build and build but it isn't us who will survive. It is the boring lifeless chunks of marble that will last. The things we did, the things we created, the things we shaped. The slave outlives the master... Marble, pigment, stone... They have no brains and yet we give them life and they*

become immortal whereas we perish. So this is how it goes. We create things which persist in order to make us last longer. The Jews have it right. Their one God made men out of clay so they would build monuments to him, and with their prayers ensure his immortality. Quick thinking, God of the Jews! Without your worshippers you would be dead. A dead God, now that's a joke!"

"Clay, marble, pigment! Who gave who life? Dumb marble takes over the world, while noble human reeks of putrefaction!"

The rot of the body bothered him, the concept irked him but it is true that the damned don't cry and Pilate did not weep. He despaired in the marmoreal realms.

On some occasions, during his longer drinking bouts, when Pilate had a hard time differentiating between night and day, between dog and wolf, he would have a very specific recurring dream. He would picture himself on the balcony of a castle situated on the top of a cliff. He had a magnificent view of the land and the sea from his residences both in Caesaria and Jerusalem. He even had other palaces throughout the province that he was free to command whenever he wished, but when he slept he would picture an entirely fictional, almost unimaginable place.

The structure was so tall and the views were so spectacular, that it didn't quite seem to him how even he, of all people, could command the right to live in such a dwelling, as the ocean and the earth unfolded below him in infinity. That was when fear would set in and strike him right in the heart and he would panic. *"Why was I elevated so high? What have I done to have this given to me?"*

Vertigo would sink in. He would think he saw another realm, another continent on the horizon, an Atlantis, and then his mind's eye camera would dolly back and he would see himself with another pair of eyes—a bunch of ragged cloths over a skeleton, held up by sticks and crutches. He would awake in sweaty fear, but the view from the promontory and that feeling of infinity would haunt him for days, then dissipate, and then return again. Sometimes it would get worse when he would listen to music. Pilate was hardly possessed of melomania—he was fond enough of music but not especially keen on it. The slaves were there to entertain him with flutes and kytharas, and the singing of women and eunuch castratos was always something to listen to in the background upon the snap of a finger—a pastime to fight boredom. He would call them into his chambers to play the instruments and sing but it was all grossly underwhelming. Pilate desperately wanted to hear one specific melody which came to him only when he was sleeping and imagining himself in the castle on the precipice. He was never able to fully hum the tune in waking hours, only a vague bastardization that had little resemblance to what he listened to in slumber. Yet it was not Apollo strumming a golden lyre who was producing the music. It was rooted in memory – a song from decades past resonating through white and yellow Roman streets when he was a boy. There was an odd refrain to it, something that sounded like *"Vale"*—farewell. Starting from one lonely voice, a woman in the course of humdrum work perhaps, the sound would drift through the alleys, picked up by the beggars, by the washerwomen, by the noblemen's wives making a journey into the filth of the inner-city, and was joined by others, swelling into an echo: *Vale, vale, aeternum vale...*

On that fateful morning, the one which we all know all about, Pilate was absorbed in self-pity and self-absorption. Also, being petty in the face of the universe made him feel assertive, and this feeling was in itself an act of defiance against Sol Invictus. *"Take that, Jupiter! It's not all about you!"*

He was occupied with the usual recurring motifs. *"We will never be young again, we will never live through the times we so savor through the prism of memory... Never, never... All gone, all gone. And when I am gone, how shall I be remembered? And am I dreaming after all?"*

And then it happened. His self-admitted *gateaux avec larmes* reverie was interrupted by the reality of the day. Whatever that meant in his philosophical musings on the nature of memory and the nature of time, his duty called. It was time to get back to business and be professional.

There were two prisoners that he had to judge that day. One was arrested for allegedly inciting a riot, the other held for attempting to poison the aqueduct. Pilate found both of these cases boring in advance before even seeing the miscreants. He could have dismissed the burden of seeing the prisoners and simply written off their fates and sent them to their deaths, but in a struggle against boredom and keeping up appearances of a diligent official, he maintained protocol and asked about the provocateur.

"A traveling preacher, or teacher as he prefers to call himself," came the reply.

Pilate perked up ever so slightly. "A preacher? Well, what does he preach?"

The Bailiff knew little about Yeshua's preaching and was speechless for a minute until he collected himself and was able to state the facts. The man had caused a commotion in the temple, overturning the money changers' tables and inducing a brawl which could have escalated into a riot until the police intervened.

"This is something new..." Pilate thought. A Jew turning against Jew sounded queer to the governor at first and his curiosity was mildly aroused out of the slumber and boredom of administrative work until he remembered the reality. *"What am I thinking? It's Jew against Jew all the time. And yet, violence was always off-limits in the Temple..."*

He tried to focus and when the sloppy lenses in his brain finally found their focal point he decided on whom to see in which order. "Bring in the preacher first," he commanded. "I will see the terrorist later."

SHACKLES AND SONGS

Bar-Abbas awoke not from the blinding sun but from the spear that tickled his nose. He squinted as he looked up, barely making out the shapes of the soldiers standing above him. No suicidal attempts were made. He smiled and allowed himself to be restrained as he was led to the chariot and taken to his cell. In some way, he was actually content.

He was silent as he was transported to the city, merely humming along to the sounds of people on the outskirts of town, rising in the morning light… the washerwomen singing their alternately joyous and defeatful songs of toil, passing by the Roman monuments, already shabby and crumbling; past the fishmongers coming back from their early catch, past the workers, the soldiers, the peasants, the laborers, the children and wives, and singing with closed lips along with the plaintive sounds, he thought of how well he would have done if he hadn't fallen asleep and what a different future he could have created for all these people. And for himself.

He offered no resistance as he was led into the dungeon. He wanted to bark out loud that Roman technology wouldn't have done much to stop bloody diarrhea from the poison he so wished to have put into the water and that despite the sickening violence it was a necessity – a sacrifice for justice and freedom. Frustrated but proud of his restraint, for he knew that he could have been silenced quite easily, he wanted to save his venom and vitriol for those who could hear him. He knew he would meet judges and prosecutors when locked in his shackles and perhaps even the governor. Spared from martyrdom for the moment, he felt excitement at the possibility of meeting the oppressor face to face.

Bar-Abbas smiled when he saw the man separated from him by two sets of bars. His smile was casual, slightly taunting, yet charming nonetheless. He did have a perverse charm.

"I see we meet again" he addressed the other prisoner calmly. "You do remember me, don't you? I remember you. Your face. Your naïve face. What are you doing here? I thought you were quite a coward. You should have listened to me and joined us."

Yeshua had huddled in the corner of his cell for two nights. He would sometimes hear Maryam's voice coming from outside, as she and the other prison wives would line up underneath the windows and sing together. Bar-Abbas remembered Yeshua quite clearly, and as for the latter—who could forget Bar-Abbas after meeting him? Yeshua recalled their first dreadful encounter and turned his back to the murderer.

"I am not one of your butchers, Bar-Abbas. You see where your actions have brought you."

Bar-Abbas laughed.

"But they brought you here too, you fool! They brought you here with me! Why are you here, little lamb? Because you believed it was your destiny? But you were too weak to pursue it to its fullest. Am I right? And you stumbled right into this same dungeon as me without even accomplishing anything."

Yeshua spoke calmly from within his cage. "God will judge me for my sins, as he will judge all men. I spoke out against hypocrisy and sin. As for my arrest, it was a mistake."

Bar-Abbas chortled, self-satisfied. "Try proving it to the judges about a mistake. You truly are an idiot."

"Say what you will." Yeshua replied without turning his face to the adversary. "They will set me free for I've done nothing wrong."

Bar-Abbas laughed. "Fool, fool… only a fool would trust the universe… Oh if you weren't so stupid, Yeshua, and so stubborn, you could have made something out of yourself and joined our struggle. Your weak brains aside, we really are very much alike, you just refuse to admit it. I'm different in practical matters though. I know what I am doing. And I know what you have been doing. I've heard about your preaching in the countryside. There's even been talk of miracles. Healing the blind. Casting out demons! It's everywhere and I know it's rubbish! What do you have planned for your next trick? Conjuring bread? Turning water into wine?"

"I never claimed any such things…"

Bar-Abbas hissed through the iron gates and smiled.

"Of course you didn't, do you know why? Because you're dumb! Rumors spread quickly! Think of how many followers you would have had by now if you had gone along with all those fantasies and took responsibility for the wildest fancies! I can sense it from you, and I've heard what you've been up to since we met on that magnificent night when you saw how my children butchered the pig. From the things I kept hearing, I surmised that you thought you were destined for something great when in fact you never really had anything to make yourself unique, am I right? Is that not so? "

Yeshua admitted to his brain that he was confused and remembered that he never chose this path.

"I never wanted this…"

"You don't want to die for your people?" Bar-Abbas asked in half-mockery.

Yeshua remained facing the brick wall. He was afraid of looking at Bar-Abbas but continued to speak.

"Why should I lie or make up stories about things that never happened? All I did was try to reach out to people! I never wanted to do it in the first place, but the stones started rolling, I could not stop them…"

"You have done nothing for the people!" Bar-Abbas' hissing became louder and more venomous. "Nothing! And if you could have, you would have! I know you have a lot of anger inside of you, just like me, a proud, just and vengeful anger! You are too angry to be the man of peace you claim to be, and yet you're also a coward. An unfortunate combination that means failure from the beginning. I told you all this when I first met you. Just as I told you we would meet again." He mumbled some more obscenities and curled up on the floor muttering, "Idiot! Idiot..."

Yeshua did not look back at the man and continued to stare at the wall instead.

JUDGMENT DAY

Outside the walls of the prison, Maryam sang and tried to shout out to Yeshua, bursting out her heart and lungs. Surrounded by other wives, she wailed desperately when they wailed, and wept mournfully when they wept. She would join them in a joyful chorus about the coming of the Messiah when the others chose to lapse into cosmological daydreams and she would hold their hands, wipe her tears and her "sisters' " laments only to return in camaraderie to gnashing of teeth.

Inside the prison, Yeshua and Bar-Abbas paced in their cells, both awaiting judgment.

That one blue morning (tragedy generally tends to happen in the morning), Pilate was absorbed in what some would call self-pity, though it was more than that. Self-absorption for sure, with a bit of petty defiance against God's maddening indifference.

He was occupied by the same recurring motifs. *"We will never be young again, never live through past times again, we see all through the prism of memory, save in dreams… Never, never, and when I am gone how I shall be remembered? And will I be remembered? And am I even dreaming after all?"*

And then it happened. His self-admitted topping of marzipan with lachrymose frosting on a self-pity cake broke apart, interrupted by the strange reality of the day.

A messenger arrived from Caesaria bearing not any official correspondence but a letter from Claudia, the woman who, at this point, was his wife in name only, and who was utterly disinterested in her husband and his work. The letter consisted of only two cryptic sentences: "Have nothing to do with that man. I had an awful dream last night and I suffered so much because of him." It both perplexed and irritated Pilate. *"What man? Why now? Why is she suddenly concerned with what I do?"* He dismissed it as a quirky female superstition, doubtless rooted in idleness, and thought nothing further of his wife's warning.

"Get up! You, preacher! Let's go!"

As he was led down the hallway to Pilate's chambers, Yeshua felt an odd sense of calm. He hoped it was not a fit coming on and tried to distract himself. From outside the windows he heard a cacophony of shouts and jeers and he wondered if they came from his supporters. In fact it was a man being mocked for an egregious show of public drunkenness. The noises made him wonder where the others were, and Maryam in particular. He admitted that he selfishly did not think of her as much as he should have during this time of his incarceration.

For some reason, it was Yosif, his stepfather, who now popped up in his brain more than anyone else, and he began to wonder how he was doing and what manner of world he was in now. He felt shame that he did not grieve for him as much as he should have. *"Why is it that I feel no sadness?"* he wondered. *"Is it because he has gone to a better place than this world—or is it because death does not exist? How do we conquer death? What if I were to take my own life knowing full well that I will live forever, will I have defeated it?"*

Pilate watched as the guards brought forth a scraggly but handsome young man. The prisoner did not resist and obeyed the jailers and the bailiffs with utmost courtesy, which made those in authority frustrated that they could not exercise some petty power, at least to yank a chain or do some damn thing to torture the dog on their leash. Yeshua was more than cooperative. Inside his heart, he kept hearing the songs that he imagined Maryam sang outside the prison gates and that helped calm him somewhat.

There was more than a moment of silence as Pilate scrutinized the prisoner who, with his peaceful demeanor, lonely almond eyes, and a hint of a benign smile on the lips was in contrast to the usual criminals. The "preacher" came in as a blank slate. Yeshua was cautious. He knew not to speak before spoken to in a situation as such, though the fear and the anger were percolating. Pilate relished these moments of tension, the times when he knew he was completely in control.

An uncomfortable few moments passed while Pilate waited for something to break. The Governor's mind wandered to other scenes, back to Caesaria, Rome, Ostia... and then snapped back to the matter at hand. He realized he would be wasting time if he tried to make this one speak and shout first. It would not happen and thus he began.

"What is your name, prisoner?"

"Yeshua Bar-Yosif." The prisoner answered, relieved that dialogue had finally begun.

"Do you know why you are here, Yeshua Bar-Yosif?"

"I do, Sir."

"Then if you know, will you explain to me, Yeshua Bar-Yosif, why you are here in front of me and why you are in shackles?"

Yeshua knew he had to retell the events in the Temple but he didn't want it to be just a simple admission of guilt. He waited to answer as he concentrated on preparing his response but Pilate interrupted his train of thought.

"They tell me you are a preacher? A teacher, something like that, whatever..."

"Whatever you wish to call it," Yeshua replied humbly. "That is what your men called me. I don't know what I am."

"Fine."

Pilate was mildly intrigued and wished to hear more. The answer *"I don't know who I am"* opened up philosophical flood gates.

"None of us know who we are. We are known only by what others call us but that means nothing. You had ideas when you were told you were going to meet me, the governor, is that not so? But yet you did not know anything about me, really, and you still don't and probably never will. And despite the fact that you are present here for an interrogation, I will never *really* know you either."

Some of it was said in earnest, genuinely confessional, some of it was a rehearsed technique to psychologically disarm the prisoner. The latter part did its work, for Yeshua was indeed now disarmed. He did not expect to hear such words from the governor. Pilate continued.

"I had a similar experience once. The first time I came face to face with true authority. When I first met the Emperor..." He started to confess but paused, it was becoming too personal now. His mind rushed back to bygone times, to his youth, to his own disappointments, and then just as quickly dashed back to the present when he remembered that he had a job to do.

"Anyway, forget that. For simplicity's sake, let's just say that you are a preacher, and that is what I will call you from now on. Now, preacher, do tell me, what it is exactly that you preach?"

Yeshua had to compose himself and quickly dust away the doubts and confusion. The answer came quick. "I try to tell people to live their lives a different way and to be decent."

Pilate chuckled.

"And? Not much luck, I suppose?"

"Well...no... "

"I didn't think so. It's a tough business to try to change the hearts of men. I know it from my own experience. Especially with these people. Trust me, I know. Anyway, they have their own courts and their own Jewish laws and all that buggery. If you wish to change them it will be a hard road indeed. Why did you wish to go down that road?

"The people have become wicked and their hearts are black and deceitful." Yeshua spoke calmly and with conviction. "It doesn't have to be this way. Their laws and their courts are a sham. And so is their God, the one they claim for their own."

Pilate smiled. He liked this preacher and became more and more absorbed. He remembered that the Jews considered the Almighty the "God of Israel" and that they were the chosen folk.

"Well, I am sure their laws fulfill some type of moral purpose don't you think? Anyway, you're here because I see you caused some mischief at the Temple."

"I quarreled with the money lender but I did not raise my hand against him and the dagger was not mine. You can find witnesses. I spoke harshly to him but that is no crime. I had come to the Temple for the holidays and when I saw this man and many others like him, doing business the way they were, I told him that it was a sin to bring money into faith. Then the others, they pulled me to the ground and started hitting me. I only spoke harshly to him. What I did was not a crime."

"No, of course not." Pilate was sympathetic. "Speaking loudly or quarreling is certainly not against the law. It's certainly 'cultural' in these parts. Why, you can hear that incessant yelling and babbling even from within these walls. So, preacher, tell me…" He fixed his gaze intently on the prisoner now that he had slightly disarmed him.

"Do you preach for the overthrow of Rome?"

"I have nothing against Rome, Sir." Yeshua surprised himself at how stoically he was able to respond. "My concern is people and their hearts. All people."

"You wish to change the world by changing human nature, is that it?"

"It is the simplest thing to be kind and decent but people have forgotten how."

Pilate laughed.

"Oh it's not so simple at all, preacher. Not simple at all. You are the one who is 'simple' if you really believe that. No offense but I'm older and far more experienced than you."

Yeshua continued as if in a trance, working out his ideas as he was saying them.

"All men sin but here they do it out of ignorance, abiding by strange old laws. They follow hypocrites, deceitful men, obscure ancient books. Their eyes are shut."

"And this is what you've chosen to do, then? To help people? To help them from their nature?"

"I did not choose it, Sir. My life chose me."

"Oh preacher, preacher. They will eat you alive before you yourself die for trying to help them. And when you expire, they will feast on your dead flesh and get drunk on your blood. How do you plan on changing them exactly?"

"Sir, the roots of plants and trees are hidden and if you expose them, the plant dies. The guts of a man are hidden as well. Has anyone seen a man with his insides showing who still lives? Once exposed, the man perishes. So it is with evil. It is the same. Show it for what it is and it too will perish. Show that death does not exist and you will have everlasting life. Death means the end to most of us, sir, does it not? Cessation? But when you walk upon the grass of the cemetery, the grass grows and flowers sprout up in the spring upon the bodies of the dead. And trees, young trees, begging to grow and form into hardy oaks and cypresses, so where is this so-called death? To believe in anything other is folly. There is no death. We will always be here and be here forever and together with each other."

Pilate shook his head in disbelief at the prisoner's naïveté.

"That's very poetic, preacher, but no, it's not quite the same.

The human realm is more like the kingdom of beasts than those harmless plants and trees you mention. Some men are sheep, some are lions. Others are birds who seek to soar into the heavens—poets or musicians perhaps—and yet others are scavengers who feed on rot and carrion. You wish to make all of them equal? They might listen to you and claim to believe the same thing but eventually they will return to their nature. And they will never be equal. Their nature, my child, I apologize, but you do seem so like a child, is a gift that the gods, or *your* God if you wish, gave them. You remind me of a crane that wishes to both soar into the sky and at the same time befriend the hyena. The hyena will listen to you, ape you, follow your exhortations and praise God with you in your Temple. But the minute you turn around, he will snap your gentle neck with his powerful jaw. He will bury your carcass so it putrefies and then dig you up and eat your rotted flesh with delight. He will spit you up, roll around in the vomit and then, howling at the moon, he will give thanks and praise God. Your God. The one you introduced him to. It is in their nature, preacher. If their priests can't teach them, what makes you think that you can?"

His argument was compelling. It took Yeshua a few seconds to answer.

"I try to have faith."

"Faith? What is faith?" Pilate delighted in this philosophical exchange. It had been many years that he was able to debate someone in earnest, just debate for its own sake. "There is only the rule of law that will keep people in check and that will keep mankind from reverting to mindless savagery. Your work will mean nothing. It will be wasted on them. Why don't you stick to your own laws, the ones of your nation? It seems to have worked for your people for at least a few thousand years. At least that's what I know. You *are* a Jew, aren't you?"

Yeshua struggled for the correct response. He did feel that he had a higher chance of success to be freed if he admitted his true paternity. He chose the middle ground and said "It is in my blood."

"Then if you are a Jew why don't you stick to what you know, and worship the same God as they do and leave it alone?"

"Sir..." Yeshua stammered. "There are no Jews or Romans or anyone else. There are only people. As for the God of the Jews, I cannot believe in a God that would flood the earth. A God that would spread diseases, plagues, pestilence. An ogre that kills livestock and blights crops. A God that allows for the rich to build palaces and to purchase gold trinkets while others literally starve to death. A God who wishes to test his servants and asks a father to sacrifice his son. No, that is not the God I believe in."

Pilate still found the conversation interesting but he was becoming frustrated.

"Well? What do you believe in, then?"

"I believe the simplest thing in the world is to live decently. I believe all people are capable of being decent. I believe that..."

Pilate smirked.

"Have you followed that example in your own life?"

Yeshua remembered his mother and said quietly "God will forgive..."

Pilate almost had him in checkmate.

"Oh, my poor boy. If only it were so simple. Live decently. As I said just now, but you probably weren't listening, the point is, to each his own. And let's be frank now, what exactly is decent? Those Jewish books helped your people survive through hard times. They served their purpose once and I will agree with you that it is all for show now and for hypocrisy. Or maybe for 'decency'? Hmm? And if God will forgive, then what's the point of being decent?"

He smiled and laid down another trump card.

"And what is decent? Does your God like something because it is decent? Or is it decent because your God likes it?"

"I try to believe in people, sir."

"That is not a belief." Pilate declared. He was still intrigued, but there was something in Yeshua's answers that was all too simple that it reeked of sophistry. "Frankly, it sounds to me like you don't know what you believe in exactly. How queer. For a minute I was feeling rather warm towards you in your naïveté. For all your peace and love routine you've actually got quite a chip on your shoulder don't you? Who do you think you are, you who has no need of gods? This is their faith, your faith, so why not just leave these people alone?"

"I do not need to offer sacrifices, sir. No burnt offerings. Is not life itself a sacrifice? Is not life itself a death sentence? Is not life pain and misery for so many around us? If this is God's will, why should I offer gifts to my tormentor? These gods, they-"

Pilate cut him off.

"And what do you suppose the people would do without gods? I do believe, provided they don't overstep their boundaries, peaceful religion can come in rather handy. It helps to keep the masses in check and for the most part, Jews practice a religion of peace. If all of them practiced their faith in such a fashion we wouldn't have a problem with the current insurrection!"

"Peace will come when they open their hearts." Yeshua replied. "Until that day comes, they will continue to turn to their wrathful God and continue their inhuman viciousness. And if the Sicarii and Bar-Abbas become more popular then Romans too will be praying to Yahweh in dozens of years, huddling together in fear. They will impose their laws on you and even Rome will accept and practice the ancient and intolerant Jewish faith soon enough."

Pilate had enough and decided to end the interrogation.

"I see. Well as you know, it is precisely my job to stop the insurrection and you, preacher, aren't the one who should be telling me how to do my job. Anyway..." He smiled amicably. "I find no fault with you. This has been an interesting talk and I appreciate you sharing your philosophy with me. In fact… I enjoyed this discussion quite a bit and in return I will dismiss the charges. Since you do not seem to be part of the militants, you should be free to go and tend to your flock… and to your hyenas. Good luck, preacher."

Pilate stood up and summoned the bailiff.

"Take this one back and hold him for an hour while I see the terrorist."

The guards took Yeshua back to the cell and held his arms more gently this time. Returning through the same corridor, Yeshua caught a brief glimpse of blue from out of one of the windows and smiled, knowing he would be free soon and back in Maryam's arms.

Pilate's mood was somewhat elevated by his engaging conversation with the preacher. Though he became frustrated toward the end, he longed for intellectual banter and he wished to hold on to this pleasant, satisfying wave of content. In advance he decided that the exchange with the terrorist would be short. *"All the idiot will reply will be some babble about God's chosen people and a Holy War and all that trash…"* All the rubbish he had heard before from these sheep. He wanted it to be done and finished as quickly as possible.

The terrorist, Bar-Abbas, was brought in. *"This one is calm as well…"* Pilate thought. *"Surely there's something up his sleeve."*

Bar-Abbas had just a curl of a smile on his lips, something that Pilate noticed immediately and that petty insolence and act of defiance was something which would always infuriate him when interrogating fanatics. He looked up from the scroll which contained the hastily written notes about the prisoner's charges. He knew the type and his blood always boiled when dealing with this sort and he began to taunt and mock immediately.

"Behold the man!" he smiled. "Is this really you? The one who calls himself the King of the Jews? That is what you have been calling yourself, is it not? Mass murdering filth. Well, it finally caught up to you, didn't it?"

"Mass murderer? That would be you and your Emperor, not me."

A guard rushed up and knocked the prisoner across the mouth.

"Shut it!" the guard barked, but Pilate motioned for him to stop.

"That's all right, leave him alone. His time on earth is almost over."

"It doesn't matter," Bar-Abbas spoke with immediate and insincere, rehearsed pomp. "There is a greater world that awaits and this world shall burn while you occupiers are still here in the Holy Land. I am going to be a great martyr."

Pilate had little patience for Bar-Abbas' drivel which he had heard from countless enemy combatant prisoners before but he allowed the man to speak, almost to see how far his own patience could be tried.

"Yes, that you will be. And that would be unfortunate for us, right?"

"Very unfortunate," Bar-Abbas replied, still defiant while nursing his swollen lips.

"Yes, well, regardless, I can't very well have you running around Judea alive spreading your 'mischief.' Martyr or not, you've caused quite a bit of trouble for some time now and it doesn't look like you're going to stop."

"Right again. I won't stop, not while I live."

"And you are the one who calls himself King of the Jews, are you not?"

"You said it, not I."

Pilate laughed. "The King of the Jews is Herod, you poor fool. He will be the King of Judea until he dies and currently he is in quite good health. Not only is he the King of the Jews, he is also wholly owned by us, the Romans, the rulers of this land. You're no king. You're a pesky little insect who is about to be squashed by my thumb. Since you really think you are a king, we will fashion a crown for you to wear. You can be king for a day and wear it on your way to your crucifixion. You've seen crucifixions before, I am sure. You really don't fear death?"

Bar-Abbas smirked in an artful spasm of doublethink. "There is nothing to fear from death. My reward will be so much greater. I will achieve more in death, much more than in life. Your days are numbered. You will see how many will join our cause to liberate our land from your illegal occupation! I will become immortal!"

Pilate was all but ready to send him back to the cell but with the word "immortal" he stopped and remembered… *"Funny. Did I not just speak to the preacher about immortality? Maybe not… Maybe we didn't get to that…"*

"Come closer," he motioned. Bar-Abbas dragged himself and his chains a few feet closer to the governor.

"Tell me the truth. You don't really believe in all of this heaven business, do you?" Pilate asked in earnest.

Bar-Abbas looked up and smiled. He knew that Pilate understood.

"I didn't think you did. And yet you send these poor bastards of yours into the unknown without any certitude of what awaits while you promise them this 'heaven.' That they will land in a lake of milk and honey. If this is what you promise them, why don't you kill yourself instead? You'll get there sooner and leave the rest of us in peace."

"I thought you were smart, 'Governor.' " Bar-Abbas giggled like an imp—just like the imps who latched on to Yosif and Yeshua.

"Stop laughing! I asked you a question!" Pilate roared.

Bar-Abbas stopped his chuckles which were meant for effect anyway—to aggravate the governor—and which they indeed accomplished. He spoke almost confessionally while maintaining utmost insolence.

"You stupid Roman. I know the afterlife frustrates you because your people don't really believe in it. Am I right? Well, guess what? We don't believe in it either. You know why? Because there is no afterlife, Governor. This is it. But there is immortality! Immortality is for gods, you Italians know it. Among us Jews, even Moses knew it. Why? Because it is only when it is etched in stone that one will become immortal. You're concerned about it I can tell. Well, listen up. *Memory* is immortality, you so-called learned man. When I am gone, whether by your hand or mine, or by your executioners, what will ensure my immortality? Unless I accomplish something incredible, my memory as passed down from my children to my grandchildren, possibly my great-grandchildren will only last for a couple of generations. But if I come with a sword and accomplish great deeds and great atrocities, I will be remembered forever. What will ensure my immortality? My fucking memory, you jackass! You and I know quite well that there is no world other than this, that we die and perish unless… unless we preserve our memory. How many millions of bones do we walk upon each day? It is a fact of life that we all die and become fertilizer... unless we become immortal! The world is a graveyard and we walk on the bones and ashes of our ancestors while the cynical flowers sprout up. But are not flowers beautiful? There is beauty in death. But even greater beauty in staying alive after you die. As for my soldiers, they are too stupid to know what they do. I dispatch them to their end for my own reasons and for my own purposes. I am muich smarter than them, or you, and I know exactly how they will serve me. Verily, they will remember me as the King of the Jews, and pass it down to generations, and I—my memory—will live on for infinity. *That is immortality,* Governor. No, I won't be around to witness it, but I will go and turn to dust and ash in contentment and peace. No sitting on a cloud, sir, no reanimating corpses. Immortality is sacrifice and blood and doing whatever is necessary to make certain that your name will remain here for eternity! In books. In scrolls! In stone and in the memory of people! That is eternity! And that brings peace to those who die. Yes, I will die but I will die knowing that my memory will exist for hundreds, perhaps thousands of years! Get it? It is your choice whether you wish to be remembered or wish to turn into compost. Do you get it, you greasy Latin idiot?"

"That's enough." Pilate was oddly detached from the provocations and though Bar-Abbas knew just where to hit Pilate's nerve, the governor was a soldier by profession and could handle the arrows. Pilate remained calm and uttered the standard proclamation. "By the power given to me by the people and the senate of Rome, I sentence you to be crucified first thing in the morning. Enjoy your last night on earth. Or don't. You body will be thrown into the trash and I will make sure that you will most certainly *not* be remembered."

He turned to the guards.

"Take him away! I want him executed tomorrow. Put him in another cell away from that preacher."

As they dragged him away, Bar-Abbas managed to yell out, "God is great!"

Pilate had many things to digest and he needed a respite so he dismissed the guards in order to be alone. He prided himself on his shrewd intuition in both political and human affairs and now he was being put to the test. He knew that there needed to be a creative solution, not only to ingratiate himself to the Emperor but it was also a matter of his own self-worth. The words of both the preacher and the terrorist collided in his brain as he sought out just what solution to take. The terrorist started to feel less important to him. His lot was a dime a dozen and with Pilate's near absolute authority, he had the means at his disposal to continue the annihilation of such insurgents and mountebanks until they were erased from history, even if it meant razing towns, executing innocents by the hundreds... His authority was granted to him by the Emperor himself. The insolence of the terrorist maddened him but now he was faced with a choice. A choice for himself, a choice for the Empire, a choice for history. And he also returned to the simple but inherent and perennial desire of men—to do one's job.

He went out onto to the balcony. *"That sun will always be there… And below me, the conflicts will always be there, the vipers nest, the filth of humanity… He's a cynical bastard but he's right, and just as they will tear each other apart for a crust, I need to keep my crust. We'll see what this whole immortality business is all about when we come to it. Right now it is my job and my future, and this piece of excrement just gave me a monumental idea… Afterlife, no afterlife, memory, no memory, I want to remember the sea, I want to go back to the sea. Vale, vale aeternum…"* Yet he knew what he needed to do. It was almost as if someone else, (*"A god perhaps?"* he thought for a second), had commanded him to do it. There was no choice. It had to be done, as repulsive as the concept was. The idea was perverse but brilliant.

He walked back into the chamber and asked for a scribe to take dictation. Slowly, deliberately, he began to speak. Authoritatively, in the manner befitting the rank of governor…

"In the name of Jupiter Victor, Jupiter Terminus, etc. etc. etc., you know the rest… the standard greeting…"

"Yes, Sir… The standard." the old scribe mumbled while trying to keep the reed pen in pace with the words.

"Your servant, Pontius Pilate, Governor of Judea, greets you with a report on the situation concerning the Jewish insurgency. It will please you to hear that we have put down numerous uprisings in areas that were strongholds of Sicarii and their supporters. In these operations we've been ruthless and have shown no mercy. The situation is quiet and peaceful in these towns and in most of our land here once again. In addition, Your Imperial Majesty will be pleased to know that we have captured a man named Yeshua Bar-Abbas who proclaims himself King of the Jews and who was the leader of many such uprisings for several years. I pray to Jupiter that you know my decisions and all that I do are in the best interests of you, your Majesty, and the Senate and the people of Rome... Despite the progress we've made in putting down the insurgency, Bar-Abbas has become quite popular among a large segment of the Jewish population. After initially sentencing Bar-Abbas to death by crucifixion, I have decided to rescind my decision and have chosen to free him instead."

Pilate had to pause, grinding his teeth, grinding his synapses. (*"Am I really about to do this?"*) He powered through, dictating the rest of the fateful document that would change history forever.

"The problem, your Majesty, is that Bar-Abbas is one of those maddening cases where he is actually too dangerous to be executed. His death will be considered a martyrdom and will incite further rioting and uprisings. Of this I am certain. I am undermanned here unless provided with additional armies from Syria to protect our interests. Even then, however, his public execution would undoubtedly lead to a large-scale revolt. If we let him go, he will leave and hide out in his caves. We will keep him under surveillance, and wherever we claim he is will give us unlimited authority to put down any revolts that may be stirring and crush them before they have a chance. Just as he cynically proclaimed to me that he will be more useful to his people and cause in death than in life, he may in turn be more useful to us alive than dead. He will be a constant reminder of the Jewish militant threat, and a very valuable demon. We can, in fact, continue to extend the empire beyond our current borders, into wherever Jews live under the pretext that Bar-Abbas is hiding in those lands. For this purpose, I have decided to spare his life. To prevent unnecessary bloodshed of Roman and Jewish civilians and to think further of our strategy. Complete strategy. What can you do with an enemy who wishes to die? We have to think of other means and use their own fanatic zealotry against them and to our advantage. Under the pretext of Bar-Abbas, we can seek out, conquer and subdue further lands ad infinitum. Nec Plus Ultra? No, *Plus Ultra*, my emperor, *Plus Ultra*! Odd as it may sound I firmly believe that in war we will find peace."

He had to stop to let the scribe catch up as he, in turn, tried to catch up with his own thoughts. *"This is wrong..."* he started thinking, *"This is so wrong..."* But the soldier and tactician in him repeated various philosophies about war which reassured him and so he continued dictating... "There is widespread support for Bar-Abbas throughout the land and in Jerusalem itself, in particular, which makes the situation especially precarious. Kill him tomorrow and half the city will be in flames the next day."

"In the meantime, this morning I was presented with the case of a certain itinerant preacher who was arrested in the great temple for causing a minor disturbance. Ironically, this preacher is also named Yeshua. I spoke with him at great length about his teachings and found that his ideas—which call for the abolition of all systemized religion—pose as much of a threat as the brazen violence of Bar-Abbas."

"This may seem unusual but I recognized an even bigger challenge. There is a threat that he will become too popular. He has enough charisma for his cult to grow bigger and it could further challenge stability in the region. Disdainful of the Jewish faith he was born into, he allows anyone to join his new artificial religion. If his cult should grow, its scope would be cataclysmic for we would now no longer be fighting a national insurgency but indeed a universal phenomenon which would threaten our way of life. I have now reversed my execution order, and sentenced the other Yeshua, the preacher Yeshua Bar-Yosif, to be put to death tomorrow morning. May the gods bless your rule over Imperium Romanum and may I be proven right in my initiative which I do for you and for the security of our state. Your servant, Pontius Pilate. Governor of Judea."

The scribe still tried to keep up with the words. He was lagging but Pilate was finished. It was done. He went over to a wash basin and rinsed his hands, muttering "Rotten. The Jews are rotten, the world is rotten… I am rotten. It's all rotten."

He motioned for a slave to fetch him a hand towel.

NEARER MY GOD TO THEE

Yeshua fell asleep on the floor after he was led back into his cell. He was exhausted and the meeting with the governor took much concentration and composure. The promise of freedom and relief at hand after the stress brought on an immediate and overwhelming fatigue. He glanced up at the sliver of sky and smiled. The enclosure was tiny and dark but there was a tiny opening in the wall to allow in some air and a bit of light.

Yeshua drifted off to sleep very quickly and the sleep took him to a nightmare world. He dreamt he was walking, struggling to hold up and drag a tree to which he would be nailed. A soldier whipped him and he howled in pain, but the pain was nothing compared to the sight he saw when he completed the ascent to the top of the mountain — the corpses still rotting on the trees, and the mountains of skulls and bones underneath.

He awoke with a scream.

There is a Reaper, whose name is Death,
  And, with his sickle keen,
He reaps the bearded grain at a breath,
  And the flowers that grow between...

Yeshua touched his palms against the cold floor. *"Alive... I am alive!"* he laughed, recognizing it was all a dream and that he had his breath and his heart was beating and it was indeed just a dream and that he would soon be released.

It was just at the moment that the guards came in.

"Yeshua Bar-Yosif?"

"Yes!" he smiled, expecting his freedom.

"In the name of the Emperor and the Senate and the People of Rome, you are hereby condemned to death for sedition."

At the sound of those words, Yeshua felt as if he had already died. His heart stopped. Inside the vena cava, the same imp that tortured Yosif to death was rubbing his little tummy, tickling himself, on his back, all limbs up in the air, giggling with delight.

The Guard continued, emotionless. He had recited it often enough.

"Your scheduled time of execution is tomorrow at dusk. The place of execution is Golgotha. The method of execution is crucifixion. Your hands and feet will be nailed to wood in the shape of a cross. The tree will be elevated and you will remain upright until you expire. Hail Caesar!"

The guards walked away.

Yeshua began to shake violently. He wiped the sweat off his head and when he wiped his hand on his shirt and saw it was blood, he collapsed.

The journey up to Golgotha was routine and happened nearly every week, particularly during these times of troubles but the residents of Jerusalem still fancied watching it and never ceased to tire of the cruel and sordid show. It was most comical when one of the criminals would fall and the guards would start beating this encapsulation of misery as he writhed in pain. If he couldn't get up in time, the soldiers would give a nod to those lining up, armed with rotten vegetables, rotten eggs, and sometimes something a bit heavier to give the townsfolk a go at it. It was democracy to let the locals participate in the savagery. This was their land, at least originally, and their customs and traditions had to be respected.

An elderly Jewess, helping her nearly blind husband to a local healer to attend to his toothache, stopped and tried to distract her spouse away from the discomfort of his malady. She guided his gunky eyes towards the cruelty and said in gentle words, the way one distracts a crying child. "Look! Dovid! They are leading the criminals up to Golgotha!" Dovid yanked himself away and barked "Who gives a fuck?! Can't you see how much pain I'm in? Come on, let's keep going!"

The blood loss and the pain from the rocks thrown at him made Yeshua's vision kaleidoscopic and at one point almost blissful, the only true survival mechanism against agony... Like the Chinese criminal with his arms, legs and genitals slowly sliced off to prolong the agony, his mouth stuffed with opium leaves, reaching up to the heavens to smile and achieve transcendence—but Yeshua wasn't there just yet...Vision fading, he still managed to see some outlines, odd shapes, as his hands and feet were nailed to the wood and the cross was raised. To his left and his right, two other criminals writhed in agony.

"So it ends..." he thought. *"And what if there is nothing more?"*

The crowd laughed, drooled, and continued to pelt the condemned men with rocks which were supplied to them by guards, soldiers, and friendly volunteers.

Delirium had not yet fully set in. Yeshua thought he was speaking to the figures at the foot of the crucifixion, but he was only talking to himself.

"My God. What a horrible thing life is... short, brutal, filled with endless pain... and yet how beautiful it all is... and how terribly sad... my God, how sad..."

A moment of lucidity came in when he saw the sky through the crimson canopy above his eyelids and he laughed the laugh of a madman; the laugh of a man who had enough of a joke played on him, someone wrongfully locked up in a mental institution who knows best just how sane he is.

"Who are you anyway, God? Why do you let this happen? My God, my father… my God…"

And then straining with every breath left, he finally let out what he had always suppressed.

"My God! You have abandoned me, God! You cursed me and the others here! No, you didn't even do that! You didn't even care! Life itself is a sentence of death and you created life! You have abandoned me. You have abandoned all! Who are you? Why are you silent, you, who I called my father! You! Why? Why, my God, my God, why have you abandoned me?"

What was left of the flesh and the brain from one of the writhing half-people to Yeshua's side made an attempt to speak — a thief, nailed to the adjacent cross, turned to him with loathing and whatever was left of his strength.

"Just shut up!" was all the writhing slab of meat managed to spit out.

Yeshua felt a tiny burst of adrenaline. He felt he needed to say something so as not to be classed with the pointless fate as these other wretches and so managed to talk back.

"Why should I shut up? We are dying here! Talk, scream, shout! It's our last chance to say something!"

The thief barked back, "I said shut up! Shut up and let's all hurry up and fucking die already! You're making it worse!"

There was another criminal on a cross to Yeshua's side who chimed in.

"He is indeed. He talks to God as if it's *his own god* and no one else's. The balls!"

This wretch, now blind, his eyes gouged out by birds, repeated his grievances.

"Shut up and let us all die already! The sooner, the better!"

"That's right…" said the thief who still saw a bit of the sky out of his vile jelly. "I got news for you, milksop. There *is* no God! Hell, if there was a god, why doesn't he take us down? If he's real, why does he continue to watch over all this shit and not do a damn thing about it?"

"I don't know..." Yeshua mumbled. "I don't know… water… so thirsty, I am so thirsty…"

"You think you're thirsty? You've only just started dying," the blind thief chortled. His sightless head by instinct still twirled around although he was in a sea of black and red. "Hey, soldier!" he called into the darkness. "This one says he's 'thirsty.' Want to help him out?"

The crucifixion guards were the lowest of the low in the army, picked out from the basest classes and not much higher on the social scale than the criminals they executed. They spoke a common language, and the guard understood immediately and laughed.

He knew what the blind criminal meant when he said Yeshua was thirsty. The Romans were quite keen on cleanliness and the guards who were stationed at the execution site had to shit once in a while like any human. The guard picked up the ass-wiping sponge on a stick and tried to shove it in Yeshua's mouth as the people laughed. Yeshua turned his face away and tried as best as he could to refuse this sad torment, resisting each time the filthy brush approached, the way a dog or service animal turns to the wall when a bowl of food is placed by the same hands that beat the animal mercilessly. The soldier was goaded to try and stick it into Yeshua's face again and again but it didn't work for much longer and the cretin in uniform gave up.

Yeshua refused the torture both with dignity and with bitter sadness. The storm which was brewing over the city made its way over to the hill and it began to rain. The eyeless thief chortled again. While appreciative of the water, he still wished to stick it to someone, anyone.

"Ha!" The thief tried to lick some of the rain off his face, tried to grab some rain water by curling his tongue and grimacing. Now he began to feel peace for he started to turn numb and realized he would be dead very soon. He spoke to Yeshua in a mixture of sarcasm and a bittersweet compassion that he had never expressed during his life before and uttered with genuine sadness: "Looks like you got your water after all…"

Yeshua's sight was fading… When the rain came, he saw silhouettes of people running for cover. He thought he saw Maryam, or a shadow of her, wrapping her shawl around her head, hurrying away…

He understood it was over. He had nothing to say to the few people below who remained nor did he have the strength. He knew that God would hear him whether he said it aloud or not, but in his last breath he managed to mouth it, inaudible to all but himself:

"Forgive me, Mother…"

THE GHOST

NEXT YEAR IN JERUSALEM

As her sandals cut a tear-stained, mournful trail through the dust, Maryam sang. It was an old Greek song she learned many years ago, one she used to sing in your youth, sobbing her eyes out over a boy who chose another. Now this was no longer about losing a marriage prospect or losing a false true love. Now it was about the almighty power of death.

> *There is a Reaper, whose name is Death,*
>   *And, with his sickle keen...*

And when she came to the line she always found so powerful, she stopped and had to sit down to weep, repeating that line in the song over and over: *"How I wish to the Lord, I'd never been born..."*

"How simple it is to sing it!" she contemplated over the monotony of her footsteps once she started back on her journey. *"But what does it mean to not ever have been born? If I hadn't been born would I have still existed in some way? And when I die, what will remain of me except my bones which, buried in the earth, will one day be nothing but the dust my shoes are covered in? But Yeshua would say that-"*

A wave of nausea rose up in her gut. Yeshua said this and that and many other things, but he was dead. She tried to pray, to come back to Yahweh...

And I shall love the Lord with all my heart...

She looked back, looked back in anger indeed, when she recalled how everyone left after the execution, how everyone dispersed so quickly, many without saying a word to her, she who had lost her lover, her husband. One even had the ludicrous idea of sailing to India, to continue Yeshua's teachings—or so he told her. She knew that all they wished for was to be finally rid of this folly and to go home, and despite her grief, she was no exception. So she continued on.

The path forked and she turned to follow the cooler road that passed by the coastal settlements, avoiding the harsh interior. She would find kind people who would offer her bread and give her shelter at night. They would take pity on her when she would tell them she was a widow. She wouldn't tell them about the type of man her husband was. "He was a farmer…" she would say, and then would wonder, "If that was true, if he was just a farmer, would my grief be different?"

Almost home, Maryam passed through a small town and witnessed a peculiar sight. Peculiar perhaps because it was so familiar. Even before she saw the man, she heard through the din of the crowd, voices talking about him, about "the Egyptian." And she knew.

"The Egyptian is here!" "The Egyptian is speaking!" The people rushed to the center of the square to see this "Egyptian" and she followed along out of bitter curiosity.

This Egyptian was a small man, unimpressive to the eyes but his speaking voice was as loud and as powerful as his supposed convictions. They were the same words she had heard many times before.

"And I say to you, people, come, pick yourselves up and follow me!" the Egyptian was saying. "We shall go to the Mount of Olives and the walls of Jerusalem will fall at my command, for we shall take what is rightfully ours and rule over Judea! For I am the chosen one, the one who was prophesied about. The Messiah!"

The people were enthralled but Maryam spat in disgust. She

walked over to the fountain, washed her face and kept walking.

At dusk she saw her house and dragging herself through the final stretch of her homeward journey she came to the entrance and dropped down on her knees so hard that she was sure she had shattered a bone and broke out in a hailstorm of tears.

When the tough old oak door opened, Maryam grabbed her father's sandal without looking up. She wanted to dig her face into the ground. She couldn't see anything anyway as the tears had blinded her and in a breathless sob, she fainted from exhaustion. Her mother ran to her. There was no resentment as she gently carried her girl up to her old room and put her to bed. The prodigal daughter had come home.

When she awoke, Maryam was too ill and too tired to eat. She was barely able to finish a glass of fresh donkey milk so her parents put her back to bed. She fell asleep and immediately began to dream. Maryam dreamt she was at a banquet at the court of the Emperor of Rome, the King of the World and was telling him that her husband had miraculously returned to life after being nailed to the cross—a resurrection, a miracle. The Emperor laughed at her, though not sarcastically but almost with a concern or a pity, a gentle condescension.

"My dear Judean woman," he began and picked up a boiled egg from a silver plate. "A man has the same chance of rising from the dead as this egg in my hand has of miraculously turning red!"

Maryam, defiant, picked up an egg of her own, held it out in front of the Emperor, desperately waiting for the miracle to occur, waiting for the egg to turn red, struggling to believe, to prove him and everyone else wrong. The tears ran down her face as she fought with all her might to believe that with the power of faith the egg would change color. She woke up before any such miracle occurred when her sister Rahel, gently tugging at her sleeve, broke up hope at such a crucial point.

"Maryam. You've been sleeping for a day and a half. It is the Seder. Do you think you can come down and join us?"

She turned away from Rahel and began to sob in her pillow.

Rahel wasn't going to miss the Seder. The family was pious and so she left her sister to weep, turned to the wall. She went downstairs and listened to her father recite prayers.

"Blessed are you, Lord our God, King of the universe, who has sanctified us with his commandments, his desire to us, and has given us, in love and goodwill, his holy Sabbath as a heritage, in remembrance of the work of creation, the first of the holy festivals, commemorating the exodus from Egypt. For you have chosen us and sanctified us from among all the nations, and with love and good will give us your Holy Sabbath. Blessed are you Lord, who sanctifies the Sabbath. Amen."

"Amen," they replied, though there was no joy in their hearts as long as Maryam was sick.

They broke the bread and their father turned to Rahel with eyes lowered.

"Rahel. Put a plate together for Maryam and bring it upstairs. God will forgive her for missing the Seder, let us pray that she gets well."

Rahel found Maryam still turned to the wall as she brought in some matzah, bitter herbs and an egg.

"Come. You have to eat something. And you have to do it for our faith…"

Maryam turned around and sat up. Sheepishly she picked up the egg, which so unfortunately reminded her of the dream, and began to peel it.

"Now is your hour of grief." Her sister tried to speak as wisely as possible without offending her. "But time will wash it away. Soon I will see you happy again, and no one will take away your joy."

"Rahel…"

"Yes?"

"I wonder where he is now. If he is gone forever. Oh, my Yeshua—murdered, then carried broken and dumped into the ground…"

She tried to hold herself together but broke down in tears of grief. The sisters embraced and Rahel too started crying.

"The Lord will swallow up death forever…" she reassured her sister in between sobs. "He will wipe away the tears from all faces… and he will remove the disgrace of his people from all the earth."

Slowly, Maryam calmed down. She tried chewing on some bread but her throat was dry and she had trouble swallowing so she told Rahel she needed to go back to sleep. Rahel went downstairs just as their father was finishing the prayers. In silence, she stood and waited for him to conclude.

"Then came the Holy One, praised be He, and destroyed the Angel of Death… Eliyahu the prophet… Eliyahu the returning… may he soon come to us with the Messiah, son of David…"

When father finished praying, he slowly opened his eyes and saw Rahel standing, covered in tears.

"She will get better," she said and sat down.

Mother sighed. "May that day come quickly, the one when the Messiah will come."

"The King of the Universe sees and waits," father said, with the wisdom that a patriarch was supposed to express. "And we will wait for him too. For that time to come. Well, that's it. Next year in Jerusalem."

And the others replied as obliged by tradition.

"Next year in Jerusalem…"

THE STAR OF WORMWOOD

"And the third angel sounded, and there fell a great star from heaven, burning as it were a lamp, and it fell upon a third of the rivers, and upon the springs of water; And the name of the star is called Wormwood: and a third of the waters became Bitter; and many people had died of the waters, because they were made bitter."

(Revelation 8:10, 11)

On the day of Yeshua's execution, Jerusalem was swollen with worshippers who had come to town for the holiday, though the prospect of a public spectacle like a crucifixion also drew many to Golgotha for some light entertainment—to watch some criminals meet their grotesque fate. Cruelty and holy days were not mutually exclusive to the people.

Few had seen Bar-Abbas in real life, fewer still lived to tell about it. The Sicarii attacked at night if they wanted to massacre an entire settlement, and on the lone suicidal attacks, the attacker-cum-victim would appear as if he had acted on his own. A rumour circulated that the Romans, fed up with prophets who called themselves "Kings" of the Jews, fashioned a crown of thorny twigs and added the inscription Rēx Iūdaeōrum on a plaque on the rebel's cross, and many wept.

Yeshua's broken body was taken down in a few days and dumped into the garbage pit, sparing the sad brown earth additional sorrow.

Bar-Abbas made his way out of Jerusalem before Yeshua was put to death. He had cells that would protect him and he stayed out of sight for a few days, but when further rumors started spreading that he was ordered to be crucified but was spared, he knew what he had to do. He would no longer hide in the safety of a tent or cave while his underlings did his bidding. Now he was ready to do a little magic. He had always used death to his advantage. Now it was time for him to use Yeshua's death to give himself life everlasting.

Slowly, the dead Yeshua became a Hydra, acquiring more and more heads but stuck onto the lizard body of Bar-Abbas. The murders became miracles, the cruelty became divine. And while the atrocities continued unabated at first, in a while the hybrid's tactics began to change as he sought to destroy Rome from inside by winning more and more converts. The Romans would pay him less and less attention without realizing that the people were embracing the hybrid in far greater numbers than ever before. Bar-Abbas spread conflicting messages—sometimes about love and sometimes about the need for a sword, but it worked. The people were confused but enthralled, it was like nothing they had seen before, and Bar-Abbas' talent for magniloquence became more and more polished and pronounced.

On the third day after Yeshua's death, Pilate had what he, upon reflection, described to himself as "the heaviest dream" and "his heaviest of burdens." He found himself walking through the garden at the foot of the Mount of Olives with Yeshua. They held hands and walked together and spoke softly. Pilate could not fully recall the whole conversation. All he could remember was a gentle inner peace at being able to see Yeshua again and speak with him once more. He wondered if this was a dream at all, for it felt as if he were awake throughout it all. And as they walked on, he began to feel frustration in this half-waking state. *What is happening? How can this man be alive? Did I not sentence him to death? Or has he returned from the grave? But that's impossible. How can such a thing be? It is unheard of!"*

They walked on and when they approached the burial grounds, Pilate tugged on Yeshua's shirt and said, "Come, let me show you where you are buried… You are dead, Yeshua. I'm sorry. I am so sorry…" He knew that Yeshua had faced an ignoble end with his squirming crucifixion and his earthly remains dumped into the rubbish heap like a common criminal, yet Pilate tried to do whatever possible to let this specter leave him so he would finally awake.

Yeshua slowed down, his soft brown eyes watered just so slightly and his lips formed a bitter, bitter smile as he pulled away from Pilate, turned back on the path and walked away from him.

"I do not wish to see it…" he spoke back.

The dream stayed with him for days. He sought in vain to find the meaning of it and became listless and vacant. He wondered mostly about the part that confused and frightened him. Why did he wish to show Yeshua his grave, and lie to him again? Was it a misdirected attempt at atonement? Pilate died soon afterwards.

How time passes, faster than in the blink of an eye… and with each eyeblink, one image fades and a different one begins to form. Yeshua was gone but he was hardly forgotten, although it was still some time before the news of his immortality spread throughout the land. It did not spread like a Hamsin—that would come later—much later when streets would run with rivers of blood and mountains of corpses would be piled up. It spread slowly, spread throughout the land with light spring zephyrs and images of his death and resurrection; the details of his miracles and deeds pollinating the people of Judea and its near abroad. First, though, the people had to stop the religion of Yeshua (whatever it exactly was), to smother it in the cradle and instead create a religion *about* him.

One cold spring day, a ragged bunch of Yeshua's new worshipers arrived in a town along their travels to spread the good news, led by their captain, Bar-Abbas.

Bar-Abbas had ostensibly renounced violence. He would never admit it, of course, but there were more than a handful of things he had learned from the dead Yeshua, and even went so far as to use his first name instead of the surname Bar-Abbas he was known by before.

Wretched and famished, huddled together but still maintaining the "righteous anger" that had been all the rage throughout these lands since anyone could remember, they had a hard time deciding what to do when entering the town—whether to beg for bread or to threaten the unbelievers with torment and damnation if they didn't accept that the new Yeshua was the prophecy fulfilled.

In the end, with Bar-Abbas' approval, it was the stomach that won and they began the pedestrian process of filling their burning guts instead of the noble task of saving souls. The townspeople, always searching for a savior, were interested in this band of travelers, and so they exchanged bread and wine for divine palaver.

When they sat down in a tavern, and news began to spread about the mysterious visitors, with a man named Yeshua at their helm, the one who was rumored to have risen from the dead, a great commotion occurred. The trickle of curious villagers began to swell. Bar-Abbas, now known simply by his given name, Yeshua, tried to maintain his kingly demeanor and chewed on bread and apples without responding but the people kept coming. His followers tried to keep them at bay but to no avail. The tavern groaned as more and more pushed themselves inside. He knew he had to say something but he was not ready. Spitting out seeds, he turned to one of his flock and calmly asked, "What is the name of this town?"

His chief underling, Shaul, the only one who was fully aware that Bar-Abbas had become the resurrected Yeshua, touched and squeezed the new Yeshua's thigh, motioning for him to be prudent and to hold his words until he was fully aware of the situation whilst feeding him spin.

"You are tired, my leader, my Lord. Truly you must be tired. Do you not recognize it? It is Nazareth. Your birthplace, our Lord!"

One place name changed everything. The stomach no longer growled, the butter knife gave birth to a sword, and Cain sitting in his chariot again pulled on the levers that propelled history into motion. The din escalated.

"It is true!" he heard a man speak. "There was a man named Yeshua who was born here and people have said that he had died and then came back to life!"

Bar-Abbas now knew how to handle it and turned to Shaul and spoke both to him and to the crowd. He feigned an air of nostalgia.

"My birthplace... How much it has changed. How time passes... faster than in the blink of an eye..."

The villagers crowding around began to badger him with questions.

"Were you born a son of God?"

"Was it not here that you performed your first miracles?"

"Did you not animate a golem here and send it to kill Romans?"

"And where you read the Scriptures before you even knew how to read?"

Bar-Abbas smiled and improvised as best he could. He did not expect to find himself in Yeshua's birthplace, though he was pleased with the way things were going, despite him gelling into the persona of a man he had previously called "soft-brained". He had never been so pleased that Yeshua was dead. If that man lived, he thought, he would have formed quite a powerful adversary against him in the struggle for the allegiance of the people.

"It is he. It is he indeed!" the murmurs came. "The Son of God has come!"

As pleased as he was, it was mystery and confusion that had always worked best for him. He felt uncomfortable and so he stood up and presented a powerful plea bargain.

"Yes, all these things have happened here in the town of my birth and more! But I have renounced everything for God and it is time that we now-"

"Yeshua!" someone shouted out. "Your mother is alive! Did you not know this? I will go fetch her! What joy you will give her! We bow down and worship you! You have come! You are the Messiah!"

Before anyone could stop him, the man was out the door. Bar-Abbas knew that he had to make a quick exit and motioned "Let's go!" to his soldiers and they made their way out of the tavern, but by the time they gathered and exited, it was too late.

Out on the street, the townsfolk formed a crescent and dragged a scraggly old woman into its center—an old blind woman clad in black, looking much older than her actual years, supported by the young man who ran to bring the alleged mother to her alleged son.

"Maryam!" He exclaimed proudly. "Behold! Your son is here, see? He has risen from the dead!"

The crowd fell silent waiting for Maryam to speak. Her sight was gone, her body wrecked from work and despair. She smiled the bitterest of smiles.

"What is it you all want me to see? Why do you taunt me? See? You all know that I can't see. See! Ah! What a joy it would be to see the green grass in the valley and the work of the Lord once more. I haven't seen anything in years. Spots. All I see is spots. Nothing more."

Undaunted, the young man practically leaped with joy.

"Then hear! Hear, oh dear woman! Your son, Yeshua, is here!"

"Son?" she asked in semi-seriousness.

"Your son! Your son, Yeshua!"

"I don't have a son named Yeshua!"

"Of course you do! Of course you do, how could you have forgotten? Oh dear lady, he's here! He's here now! He stands right in front of you."

Maryam swooned and the youth helped her from fainting and led her a few meters down to sit on a rock. When she caught her breath, she spoke.

"I had a son named Yeshua, it is true. I denied him. He denied me. He left and I never saw him again. Why do you torture me? Who are you anyway? Son? Son? I had other sons. They are dead, too. Died when the Romans came and cleansed Nazareth from the Sicarii. We were not Sicarii. We are plain people, plain people. They were killed in the streets like dogs. My boy, Yeshua, the one you speak of, he's dead too. Died like a dog as well. He left me, left Nazareth. Then I heard he was arrested in Jerusalem and crucified. For what? I was told he was preaching but I don't even know what he preached. What could he preach? He didn't know the Scriptures. He could barely read. We couldn't afford to teach him so he worked. He was helping his father. But he was not a killer, not a terrorist, they should not have killed him. He was a good boy, a good boy. He came from me. He was a part of me. Dead, dead, they're all dead. Now it's just me here, just me, alone."

The youth was undaunted for he still believed.

"Oh Holy Mother, please listen to me!" He knelt before her and implored "Please listen, Holy Mother!"

She tried to shoo him away with her hands, not sure where he was standing, circling around in her black daytime. Not only condemned to darkness, but too exhausted still to get up from her rock she continued.

"Why do you torture me? Leave me alone! Leave this miserable old lady to finish off her days in peace without you baiting me. All I ask from God is to finally let me die."

"But we bring glorious news! Great news, mother!" The youth

was ecstatic. "Your son, Yeshua, who was crucified, was resurrected and came back to life! He came back from the dead and he is here with you now! Come! It was a miracle! A miracle occurred!"

And as he rushed over and tried to pick her up, was when she summoned the strength to raise herself on her own, and anger filled her heart.

"A miracle? Who said that? Who said it? You?" She groped and poked around in her sightless world, unrelenting, like an angry blind hen pecking around in darkness. "Who said miracle? Who said it?"

She struggled out of his helpful arms and darted empty eyes across the crowd. It was that word, that accursed word *"miracle"* which almost made her leave the earth right at that moment. Death was the mercy for which she prayed each night but it refused to come. Now strangely, hearing the disgusting word *"miracle"* gave her strength to a have a final, last word of defiance before she hobbled away.

"A miracle?" She raised her voice as much as she could, as if she wished God himself would hear her.

"There *are* no *miracles!*"

A silence descended on the crowd.

"My son is dead..."

She turned and stumbled home from dark to darkness.

All eyes switched to Bar-Abbas, Panoptes looking straight at him, waiting for his reaction, waiting for a word from him.

Bar-Abbas did not miss a beat. He did not even need to clear his throat before he began, proudly. He knew that in his arsenal of the right words and the right promises were weapons that would erase what had just transpired. He could have even erased Yeshua's mother if he wanted to.

"My children!" he smiled. "Do you think I have come to bring peace upon the world? I come not in peace but with a sword! And whoever denies me will also be denied the Kingdom of Heaven! My mother? She just told you she has no son! And I have no earthly mother and no earthly father! I will pull apart men from their fathers, and daughters and sons from mothers, and a newly married wife away from her husband! Men's foes will be those they find in their own house. Whoever values their family over me will die by our swords and whoever does not take up his cross and follow me is not worthy of me! For I have risen from the dead. I am the Messiah!"

"Hail Yeshua!" the crowd erupted.

They knelt. He continued.

"We have no need of mothers or fathers or families, old laws or new laws! We will make our own laws. We have *us* and you have *me*. My flesh and blood! I will guide us to salvation and to the destruction of the empire. With faith, anything is possible! We will do what is needed and the empire will crumble before us! That wine you drink is my blood. The bread you eat is my flesh. I sacrifice all for Israel and for my followers. And you, my children, are the future! Anyone can join us—Jew, Greek, even the Roman who repents."

The last phrase caused a murmur throughout the crowd but Bar-Abbas continued, undaunted.

"Yes, anyone! For in unity there is strength! Unstoppable strength! All can join me and be my brother or my sister, and together we will defeat the enemies! Imperium Romanum? Tripe! We will build our own empire! An empire that will last for two thousand years!"

The crowd cheered wildly.

Bar-Abbas walked back into the tavern where the owner had a drink ready for him. He downed the cup of wine in one gulp and murmured to himself, "God is great."

Outside, the crowd was busy and aflutter. All struck their fists into the air to proclaim God's greatness and the greatness of their mission, as laid down by his representatives on earth, but inside, Bar-Abbas recognized that the minute he mouthed those words, the words he spoke with such conviction, a lightning flash of a thought darted into his brain: "*Who is God?*" and for the first time in his life he felt horror.

He squinted as he looked up at the sun and saw a fat, smug, calico cat lazily licking its bloated face with red and yellow tongues of flame. A few stars began to flicker in the twilight. To no one's surprise, the universe smiled and said nothing.

EVANGELIUM

No one really knew what happened to Yeshua Bar-Yosif's followers. Some said that Thomas had sailed to India, others dispersed to Egypt or other places. Some tried to keep preaching in Yeshua's footsteps. Yehuda was rumoured to have hanged himself out of remorse, although other speculations began to surface—that he was hunted and eventually killed on Bar-Abbas' orders for the treason he committed back in Bethany.

Mattityahu the taxman, one of the most taciturn of the followers, returned to civil service in a different town. He was a skilled worker with job qualifications which were in demand: literacy and penmanship, and since his association with Yeshua wasn't much documented or pursued, he started a new life and found a comfortable living working as a scribe for a provincial administration. Mattityahu kept silent about his controversial past and never mentioned Yeshua or Bar-Abbas or what transpired during those years. And the years passed, lonely but without incident. He never married.

Sometimes it seemed as if it were only yesterday that he was walking along with his strange friend Yeshua, the one who helped to try to open up his eyelids to reach beyond the tax tables and beyond the scope of his narrow world. In the decades that passed after Yeshua's execution, time flew by faster and faster.

Mattityahu aged quicker than usual. The memories he kept to himself made the humours eat away at him. He wished to speak about it, to confess to someone and tell everything he had witnessed but there was no one to talk to. In time he was too frail to work anymore. The Roman mayor of the town was fond of him and appreciated his skills, so he put him on a pension and let the taxman work part time, for the way he wrote letters and words was impeccable both in Aramaic and Latin.

The mayor pitied Mattityahu and asked him to work only when it was absolutely essential, but the former taxman wanted to keep himself occupied. The eyes were going, and it would take him tenfold longer to write something than one of the new scribes with better sight. However, when the mayor needed to impress his higher-ups with a finely written scroll, he would ask him to do the job and Mattityahu was grateful for it, knowing that he could still be useful for something.

Mostly, however, he would sit in the shade and drink wine. He drank slowly, savoring the taste. It was his way of holding on to the last sense he had that wasn't rapidly fading. Just as he would suck on a cherry, squeezing out all the flavor until the stone was nearly polished before it was spit out, such was the way he would savour every drop of wine, cherishing every molecule of grape. He was old and very tired.

One day, in the town square, while sipping his wine, some local children began to poke fun at him as he dozed off on a bench, drowsy from the heat and the grape. Mattityahu was drooling and twitching in a bad dream and the kids found it hilarious. He awoke to the sound of their laughter and taunts. It was one child in particular who pulled his nose and woke him up, but he found no fault with the child nor with the others and expressed no annoyance. On the contrary, he smirked kindly and recalled bittersweet distant memories of when he too, was once young. And then an odd thing happened. He called the children back as they were about to run away from the potential threat of Mattityahu's walking stick which he would never consider brandishing. He asked them if they ever read the holy books, if they knew about Tamar and Absalom, his favorite story from the Book of Kings. He started to recite it, with his own embellishments, but before he could get anywhere through the beginning of Absalom's miserable legend, the children began to boo and hiss.

"We know that story, old fool! We have no use for the Book of Kings anymore! Haven't you heard? The Messiah has arrived! Yeshua, the one who is risen from the dead! He's going to kill all the Romans and set us Jews free!"

The words pierced Mattityahu's heart like a dagger. He got up and stumbled while the din of the young believers followed him down the road of caked mud.

When the sun set that night, Mattityahu lay awake in his bed looking at the night through the window but he did not dwell on the nature of the starry sky. His thoughts were elsewhere.

"I have to set the record straight. I have to write down what happened. Most of them can't read but there should be a record left behind before I die. What happened to Yeshua, the real Yeshua..."

And so, struggling to see but still holding onto his gift for writing, he lit a candle and began:

"There was a man named Yeshua born in Bethlehem in Judea in the days of Herod the King..."

And so he continued until daybreak, when he fell asleep in exhaustion. When he woke, it was night again.

"It's no good..." he decided as he looked over the results of his toil through his half-blind eyes. "I need to start over."

So he began once more. This time it was easier. He understood that people would not have any use for a book that did not give them hope. For all of the books of the Tanakh, all of which he knew well and loved dearly, despite their adventures filled with horrors and tragedies, like his beloved Absalom, they all gave the people hope.

"This is what gave our people life and preserved them. Now it is time to preserve all men," he decided. So he started anew.

"Thus begins the book of the generations of Yeshua the Christ, the son of David, the son of Abraham…"

He wrote incessantly, and what a story he wrote! What miracles, what love and what deception, what purity and what hatred, what abyss of pain and what hope for life everlasting. What a gift he gave to mankind when he completed the book.